OTHER NATIONS

Animals in Modern Literature

Tom Regan and Andrew Linzey
editors

BAYLOR UNIVERSITY PRESS

Cover Design by Nicole Weaver, Zeal Design Studio
Cover Image: Stacked books © iStockphoto.com/René Mansi

Library of Congress Cataloging-in-Publication Data

Other nations : animals in modern literature / Tom Regan and Andrew
Linzey, editors.
    p. cm.
  Includes bibliographical references.
  ISBN 978-1-60258-237-8 (pbk. : acid-free paper)
  1. Animals~Fiction. 2. Human-animal relationships~Fiction. 3. Short
stories. 4. Fiction~20th century. 5. Animals in literature. I. Regan,
Tom. II. Linzey, Andrew.
  PN6120.95.A7b O84 2010
  808.83'0108374~dc22
                                    2010000802

Printed in the United States of America on acid-free paper with a
minimum of 30% pcw recycled content.

To Marion Bolz—colleague, friend

—TR

To Chris Nellist—for her comradeship and support

—AL

"[Other animals] are not brethren; they are not underlings; they are other nations, caught with ourselves in the net of life and time, fellow prisoners of the splendor and travail of the earth."

—Henry Beston, *The Outermost House*

CONTENTS

ıılılıılıılıııIIIIIIIIIIIIII

IV Other Animals as Prey

V Other Animals as Tools

VI Other Animals as Food

VII Epilogue

Preface

ANIMALS, LITERATURE, AND THE VIRTUES

||||||||||||||||||||||||||

Andrew Linzey

I

WHY STUDY ANIMALS?

One answer is given by the novelist and philosopher Iris Murdoch. In a well-known passage in her philosophical work *The Sovereignty of Good*, she unexpectedly lapses into the first person:

> I am looking out of my window in an anxious and resentful state of mind, oblivious of my surroundings, brooding perhaps on some damage done to my prestige. Then suddenly I observe a hovering kestrel. In a moment everything is altered. The brooding self with its hurt vanity has disappeared. There is nothing now but kestrel. And when I return to thinking of the other matter it seems less important.[1]

---

[1] Iris Murdoch, *The Sovereignty of Good* (London: Routledge, 1970), 84. One of the endearing oddities of Murdoch's prose results from the fact that she never allowed her work to be edited. One consequence is that her work frequently defies conventional punctuation. I have of course kept to the original in deference to her wishes.

That capacity of animals to help us forget ourselves, if only for an instant, might seem sufficient reason to spend time observing them. "It is natural and proper," Murdoch argues, to "take a self-forgetful pleasure" in what she terms "the sheer alien pointless independent existence of animals, birds, stones and trees."[2] By observing their world, we can—if only for a moment—be relieved of our own interior miseries and leave self behind.

But, for Murdoch—who had the unusual distinction of being both a best-selling writer and an Oxford philosopher—that capacity is intimately related to moral goodness, what used to be termed (in another age) "the virtues." "It is so patently a good thing," she continues, "to take delight in flowers and animals that people who bring home potted plants and watch kestrels might even be surprised that these things have anything to do with virtue."[3] Indeed, they might. But, according to Murdoch, the arts, especially painting and literature, are the means by which we transcend ourselves: "Art transcends selfish and obsessive limitations of personality and can enlarge the sensibility of its consumer." Even more revealingly: "It is a kind of goodness by proxy."[4]

"Proxy" means, by definition, an action performed by one agent on behalf of another, which the latter cannot undertake for him or herself. The use of that term logically implies that animals can do for us what we cannot do for ourselves. It is no exaggeration, then, to say that nature in general, and animals in particular, have the capacity to *make us* good by inspiring in us a form of selfless altruism which we couldn't otherwise attain.

Murdoch puts it this way: taking delight in animals "exhibits to us the connection, in *human* beings, of clear realistic vision with compassion."[5] In other words, it is not just that we see (or are enabled to see) and that experience takes us out of ourselves. Rather, that quality of perception—that "delight"—should issue in a deeper feeling for the subjects seen. As she cryptically writes, "The realism of a great artist is

[2] Murdoch, *Sovereignty*, 85.
[3] Murdoch, *Sovereignty*, 85.
[4] Murdoch, *Sovereignty*, 87.
[5] Murdoch, *Sovereignty*, 87; emphasis in original.

not a photographic realism, it is essentially both pity and justice."[6] We do not just see—we are compelled, at one and the same time, *to feel* for what we see. And something as apparently simple as looking at animals should engender (if it is a true seeing) what she calls "pity and justice."

II
WHY STUDY ANIMALS IN LITERATURE?

"Great art is liberating," Murdoch declares in another context, "it enables us to see and take pleasure *in what is not ourselves.*"[7] Again, this "taking pleasure" does not mean simply self-edification or self-glorification. Rather, it is precisely the capacity for "pleasure"—for "delight"—that enables a more-than-selfish view of the world. Far from lending itself to even more human self-centeredness, it helps us to liberate ourselves into other sensibilities—to see beyond ourselves, to find value in the other.

The Jewish theologian Martin Buber provides a moving account of just that experience of transcendence. He recounts the following incident that illustrates the nature of what he terms the "I-Thou" encounter:

> When I was eleven years of age, spending the summer on my grandparents' estate, I used, as often as I could do it unobserved, to steal into the stable and gently stroke the neck of my darling, a broad dapple-grey horse. It was not a casual delight but a great, certainly friendly, but also deeply stirring happening . . . I must say that what I experienced in touch with the animal was the Other, the immense otherness of the Other, which, however, did not remain strange like the otherness of the ox or ram, but rather let me draw near and touch it.[8]

[6] Murdoch, *Sovereignty*, 87.

[7] Iris Murdoch, "Philosophy and Literature: Dialogue with Iris Murdoch," chapter 14 in *Men of Ideas: Some Creators of Contemporary Philosophy*, by Bryan Magee et al. (London: British Broadcasting Corporation, 1978), 272; emphasis added.

[8] Martin Buber, *Between Man and Man*, ed. and trans. Robert Gregor Smith (London: Collins, 1947), 41.

Buber uses the term "reflexion" to describe how in our relations with others we behave "monologically," that is, without any real meeting or encounter with the other, but simply as part of our "monological self."[9] In other words, in our encounter with others, including animals, we fail to encounter them, and in doing so, we also fail to encounter the Other, which all true encounters mediate or disclose.

The move from the "I-It" to the "I-Thou" relationship is, for Buber, an essentially religious, mystical experience. Encounter with "the other" discloses "the Other." But that does not mean that the underlying insight is limited only to religious believers. On the contrary, Murdoch (a pronounced unbeliever) says much the same, citing with approval the line: "Not how the world is, but that it is, is mystical."[10]

The moral significance of this transcendence is that it releases us from a purely instrumentalist view of animals, that is, from the idea that animals are just here for us, and that their meaning or purpose can be adequately described in terms of their utility. This is the best way of interpreting what might otherwise appear to be Murdoch's odd remark about the "the sheer alien pointless independent existence of animals."[11] They are "alien" in that they do not obviously conform to *our* patterns of life. Their existence is "pointless" because it does not serve *our* measurements or *our* utility—they exist way beyond our calculation of utilities and benefits. The world is *not* made for us.

Instrumentalism reduces animals to the level of things, indeed, animals become things to us, things to use, things to manipulate. But it is not only animals that are reduced in this process; our relations with animals are also impoverished. Yet, once the essential "otherness" of other creatures is grasped, we are free to celebrate and take delight in their independent—to us—"pointless" existence."

[9] Buber, *Between Man and Man*, translator's note, p. 249; also cited and discussed in Andrew Linzey and Dan Cohn-Sherbok, *After Noah: Animals and the Liberation of Theology* (London: Mowbray, 1997), 11.

[10] Murdoch, *Sovereignty*, 85. The line appears in quotation marks but is unattributed.

[11] Murdoch, *Sovereignty*, 85.

To do this involves transcendence, certainly, but also the exercise of the imagination. Murdoch is explicit that only that faculty can save us. "Most of the time," she comments, "we fail to see the big wide world at all because we are blinded by obsession, anxiety, envy, resentment, fear." We become prisoners to ourselves. "We make a small personal world in which we remain enclosed."[12]

And what is the imagination? Murdoch is clear that imagination is the opposite of fantasy. Rather, imagination is a means of grasping truth. Another Oxford don, Rachel Trickett, offers this analysis of the relationship between believing and imagining. "The act of consenting or believing, like any act of the will," she writes, "involves that quality of imagination which can entertain and hold in the mind the completeness of a complex truth with all its many facets." "It is this quality," she continues, "that is delighted by good literature, responding to the extraordinary capacity of the writer to complete and make a whole pattern out of a fragmented human experience."[13] The "complex truth" to be encountered—in our context—is the meaning of other creaturely lives, who exist independently of our own wants and desires.

For while we know more about how other creatures live and function—arguably more than ever—we still do not know their inner lives. In fact, we know (in one sense) as little about animals as we do about other human beings. So much writing about animals—influenced by years of instrumentalist thinking—assumes that we know their purpose as little more than as means to our ends. But Henry Beston is surely right that the meaning and worth of animals cannot simply be judged by how they stand in relation to us:

> We patronize them [animals] for their incompleteness, for their
> tragic fate of having taken form so far below ourselves. And therein

---

[12] Murdoch, "Philosophy and Literature," 272.

[13] Rachel Trickett, "Imagination and Belief," in *God Incarnate: Story and Belief*, ed. A. E. Harvey (London: SPCK, 1981), 38, quoted in Brian L. Horne, "Seeing with a Different Eye: Religion and Literature," in *Heaven and Earth: Essex Essays in Theology and Ethics*, ed. Andrew Linzey and Peter J. Wexler (Worthing, Sussex, UK: Churchman, 1986), 121–22. I am grateful to Horne for his perceptive essay.

we err, and greatly err. For the animal shall not be measured by man. In a world older and more complete than ours they moved finished and complete, gifted with extensions of the senses we have lost or never attained, living by voices we shall never hear.

They are "other nations," as he famously concludes:

We need another and wiser and perhaps more mystical concept of animals . . . They are not brethren; they are our underlings; they are other nations, caught with ourselves in the net of life and time, fellow prisoners of the splendor and travail of the earth.[14]

The moral significance of the capacity for imagination, then, is that it helps us hold together the "complex truth" about animals. They are not simply "things" out there; they are not "mini humans," or even our "brothers" (understood in a humanly defined way); their very "otherness" should give us pause and excite our imagination. Of course we know that animals are in some ways highly similar—and in one way especially, namely their capacity for suffering—but we do them an injustice if we simply rush from instrumentalism to claiming that we know everything about them because they are "like us." In fact, it is their very *un*likeness—and our corresponding unknowing—that should inspire, at least in part, an attitude of reverential respect.

Imagination may seem a pretty airy-fairy kind of faculty, rather removed from contemporary debates about how we should relate to animals. But in fact, its absence can lead to dire results. One small illustration may help. Out of my study window in Oxford, I spent many hours looking out on a small Victorian garden with bushes and trees. One feature of the garden was its high, overgrown trellises that were ideal for nesting birds. The birds fed regularly at my bird table, and it was a delight to watch parent birds feeding their fledglings every year. It provided me with a regular source of experiences similar to the

---

[14] Henry Beston, *The Outermost House: A Year of Life on the Great Beach of Cape Cod* (Harmondsworth: Penguin, 1928), 25. I am grateful to Brian Klug for this reference. Also cited and discussed in Linzey and Cohn-Sherbok, *After Noah*, 131 and 137.

"kestrel observing" of which Murdoch wrote—moments that help raise life above the daily drudge. In time, the house and garden were sold, and a new owner set about a different regime. The trees were felled, the bushes removed, and the wonderful places for bird nests were all destroyed. I looked on in horror. Within the space of a weekend, a small ecosystem that had supported a multitude of life was reduced to cement—for a car park. The birds still come to my bird table, but there are fewer of them, and some species I have never seen again.

Of course, living with nature (even in our gardens) can provide us with problems and conflicts, and not all of them can be solved by leaving nature as it is. But perhaps the most tragic thing is that those who were engaged in this piece of ecological vandalism seemed to have little or no idea of what they were doing. They did not see the garden as shared territory, which with minor inconvenience they could have also preserved, at least in part, for other species. In fact, they did not see an issue at all. The birds did not exist on their moral radar. The local officials to whom I complained simply could not comprehend. In short: they had no *imagination* of other lives. No wonder Sylvia Plath once woefully remarked in her journal: "What I fear most, I think, is the death of the imagination."[15]

That I now hear from my window the sounds of cars rather than birdsong is doubtless of small account in the great scheme of things. But the "great scheme" of our lives is made up of hundreds of such incidents, which touch upon the lives of other creatures. During our lifetimes, we are individually responsible for the killing (directly or indirectly) of thousands, if not millions, of other-than-human lives. At the very least, we ought to have some imagination of these other lives and the consequences of our actions. There really is something worse than killing and destroying habitats, and that is killing and destroying *and feeling nothing.*

---

[15] Sylvia Plath, *The Journals of Sylvia Plath, 1950–1962*, ed. Karen V. Kukil (London: Faber & Faber, 2000), 210. She adds the following line, which resonates with Murdoch's own thought: "When the sky outside is merely pink, and the rooftops merely black: that photographic mind which paradoxically tells the truth, but the worthless truth, about the world."

III
WHAT CAN LITERATURE OFFER?

Over the last forty years, we have witnessed a revolution in attitudes towards animals. Questions about their status, how we should relate to them, and how we should treat them have emerged from the shadow of ethics to claim a position close to center stage. Of course, animals are a controversial subject, and increasingly so, but that in itself is a sign of how far we have come. Before, moral notions about how we should treat animals were often regarded as just that: "notions," like preferences about colors or opinions about extraterrestrials, often interesting in themselves but of little practical import. All that is now changing. The moral positions we adopt about animals are now seen to have practical relevance, and often of a direct, uncompromising kind. The world is now increasingly divided into vegetarians and omnivores, hunters and anti-hunters, trappers and anti-trappers, zoo supporters and zoo opposers, vivisectors and anti-vivisectors. In short: there is a major moral debate happening out there—one that is plainly analogous to previous (and current) debates about slavery, women, children, and gays.

This debate is increasingly seen in the classroom and lecture hall where animals now find a place alongside other issues like abortion, capital punishment, violence, and environmental concern in courses devoted to ethics, philosophy, and religion. There are now university and college courses in "Animal Studies," "Animals in Philosophy," "Animal Ethics," "Animal Law," "Animals in Religion," and even "Animal Theology." At the same time, we have seen the emergence of scores of high-quality texts designed to meet the needs of these university and high school courses.

For the most part, however, courses in literature have left animals to one side. This is a rather puzzling omission. Puzzling because writers of all genres have written extensively, perceptively, and almost always provocatively about our relations with animals—and often to significant moral effect. None have done so more forcefully than poets who have frequently anticipated and championed a more peaceful and less exploitative relationship with other creatures.

It is puzzling in another more important sense too. We have seen how Murdoch (and others) hold that literature enables those things that are essential to a full moral awareness: *seeing, feeling, and imagining*. Now, some may view these things as pretty insubstantial when it comes to making critical judgments and weighing conflicts. But, while they may not dictate the precise conclusions we may come to, they nevertheless form part of the essential bedrock without which our moral decision making is impoverished. We may recall the old saying that one should not judge anyone before one has walked two miles in their moccasins.

Some teachers of literature may look askance at the suggestion that the development of such sensibilities should have a place in their classrooms. The study of literature, they might say, should be devoted to acquiring familiarity with the various canons of literature, an analysis of these texts, and an awareness of the fruits of literary criticism. But the two views are not irreconcilable. There is no essential contradiction between the classical (and modern) methods of the study of literature and a thoroughgoing appreciation of the heightened awareness that literature can, at best, contribute to the development of moral sensibility.

Indeed, we should remind ourselves of Murdoch's view that, for all their dissimilarities, philosophy and literature are "both truth-seeking and truth-revealing activities."[16] In advancing the power of perception, the capacity for feeling and imagination, she even suggests that "art goes deeper than philosophy"[17] because it enables us to imagine other worlds: "to see and take pleasure in what is not ourselves." But these abilities are not, usually at least, something that we are born with. It takes work and study to understand, to grasp the truth of what is not ourselves.

More than a century before, John Ruskin put the matter even more emphatically: "The greatest thing a human soul ever does in this

---

[16] Murdoch, "Philosophy and Literature," 269.

[17] Murdoch, "Philosophy and Literature," 277. Murdoch also makes clear (in the same interview) that she thinks "literature is about the struggle between good and evil," 282.

world is to *see* something, and to tell what it *saw* in a plain way." He continues: "Hundreds of people can talk for one who can think, but thousands can think for one who can see. To see clearly is poetry, prophecy, and religion—all in one."[18] This facility of "seeing" differently and "taking pleasure in"—that is, delighting in the worth and value of the other separate from our own—is surely one of the great opportunities that literature offers its students.

What literature can do—as can probably no other discipline—is to reconnect us with the world of animals. No matter how much we may learn about animals from disciplines such as psychology and biology (for they have much to teach us), that knowledge cannot replace the insights that can come from the disciplined exercise of our imagination.

IV
What does the book offer?

Firstly, it is the world's first course text that employs the pedagogical power of literature, including fiction, to help illumine our moral relations with animals. To our knowledge, no one else has tried to do this. Our text is intended to serve new university and high school courses in "Animals in Literature." It therefore breaks new ground for both students and teachers.

Secondly, it offers an opportunity to study at first hand writers of great distinction (as well as some less well known) who have written on animals. To say that the writing is of the highest quality would not be an exaggeration. A glance at some of the names—Hemingway, Orwell, and Walker, to take only three examples—confirms that. But we also have worked hard to ensure that some lesser known, but also accomplished, writers have been included. Because the field is so huge, some limitation of period

---

[18] John Ruskin, quoted in Wolfgang Kemp, *The Desire of My Eyes: The Life and Work of John Ruskin*, trans. Jan van Heurck (New York: Farrar, Straus & Giroux, 1990); emphases in original. Irritatingly, the passage appears on the back jacket and is unsourced in the book. Not unrelatedly, Ruskin resigned from his Slade Chair in Fine Art at Oxford in protest of the University's endowment of vivisection. His rejection of vivisection on moral grounds is made clear on pp. 80–81. My favorite Ruskin line is this: "There was always more in the world than men could see, walked they ever so slowly" (257).

has been necessary. We have focused almost exclusively on modern literature, especially fiction, and chosen (as far as possible) representative pieces that are accessible, even to newcomers to the field.

Thirdly, it focuses on issues of contemporary concern, specifically our common relations with animals—as companions, as prey, as tools, and as food. By organizing the pieces under these headings, we have ensured topicality and relevance. No student could possibly claim that the issues addressed are irrelevant to them as individuals. On the contrary, these uses of animals touch us all, and, directly or indirectly, we all bear some responsibility as individuals, consumers, and citizens. Thoughtful teaching should empower the student to relate these texts both to their own experiences and also to the increasingly voluble discussion of these questions in the contemporary media.

Fourthly, it provides equal space for divergent, even opposing, sensibilities. Although the editors believe that the time is ripe for radical changes in the way we see animals and treat them, we have worked hard to produce a text that is fair and representative of various viewpoints. We have simply laid out the material in a way that focuses the issues of contemporary concern and makes them accessible for those who come new to the field. Students can engage the texts extracted here and come to very different moral conclusions. But whatever the outcome, it is impossible for any conscientious student to come away from this engagement without at least a clearer, deeper appreciation of the issues than before.

Finally, it offers many insights into the capacity of the imagination to conceive of different relations with animals. Charles Morgan once remarked, "There is no such thing as failure except failure of the imagination."[19] Whatever view is taken of the rightness or wrongness of our use of animals, it seems obvious that our appreciation of them is inextricably related to our capacity to imagine other worlds. There needs to be a renewed kind of confidence in what has been called "felt-knowledge"

---

[19] Charles Morgan, quoted in Sydney Evans, *Prisoners of Hope*, ed. Brian L. Horne and Andrew Linzey (Cambridge, UK: Lutterworth, 1990), 81. Evans's impressive sermons draw heavily on the work of poets and artists.

about the world.[20] As early as 1965, Brigid Brophy protested the absence of imagination:

> Where animals are concerned humanity seems to have switched off its morals and aesthetics—indeed, its very imagination. Goodness knows, these things function erratically enough in our dealings with one another. But at least we recognize their faultiness . . . Only in relation to the next animal can civilized humans persuade themselves that they have absolute and arbitrary rights—that they may do anything whatever that they can get away with.[21]

Whether Brophy's protest is the right one can best be judged after a careful reading of this volume.

---

[20] I am grateful to Paul Fiddes for this idea. See his illuminating discussion of it in relation to divine passibility, *The Creative Suffering of God* (Oxford, UK: Clarendon, 1988), 152–57.

[21] Brigid Brophy, "The Rights of Animals," originally published in the *Sunday Times*, n.d. (1965), and anthologized in Andrew Linzey and Paul Barry Clarke, eds., *Animal Rights: A Historical Anthology* (New York: Columbia University Press, 2005), 157.

INTRODUCTION

||||||||||||||||||||||||

Tom Regan

Human beings seem always to have had a special fascination for other animals. The earliest paintings of our ancestors, those that adorn the caves at Lascaux, France and Altamira, Spain, depict stags, horses, wild cattle, and bison. What possible symbolism these paintings contain, what questions they were meant to answer or Stone Age aspirations to satisfy, are likely to remain forever obscure. What is clear, and what is significant, is that the first painters were drawn, not to the sun or the moon, not to the trees or the flowers, not even to the human form as their principal subject matter, but to other-than-human animals.

The magnetism other animals have exerted on human creativity hardly is confined to ancient painting. Much of the great sculpture from both the East and the West, and from the ancient down through the modern periods, involves representations of nonhuman animals. The same is no less true of the decorative arts and crafts, and, of course, of literature in general. There is not a great painter or sculptor, not a great decorative artist or craftsperson, not a great thinker or writer who has not somewhere along the line been drawn imaginatively into the world of other animals and, after having visited, returned with some work—a bowl, a shape, a story—to commemorate the journey.

1

The history of our relationships with other animals has not always been salutary for them. Today most people find the spectacle of the Roman circus all but incomprehensible. The scale of the destruction, with hundreds, sometimes thousands of wild animals slain to the delight of the spectators, with a carnival atmosphere serving as backdrop, might make us loathe to admit the rich capacity for depravity sometimes lurking in the human breast. And yet echoes of the Roman blood baths live on, in illegal dogfights and festive bullfights, for example.

There is a growing number of thinkers, however, in philosophy, theology, and legal theory, who are turning their attention to animal protection issues (animal rights, broadly conceived). Similar developments characterize much of contemporary painting and dance, film and theater, sculpture and poetry. The present collection reveals that recent fiction and other literary expressions display the same tendencies. Well before animal rights was recognized to be the important issue of social justice that it is, writers were seeking to plumb the depths of the human psyche, there to find how much cruelty, how much compassion, resides in each of us. Not surprisingly, not all these literary explorers have returned with the same message. Some offer words of hope; others, words of despair; still others report that all is well just as it is. The present anthology permits writers with something important to say, whatever its content, the opportunity to say it.

Because humans encounter and relate to other animals in different settings, we have grouped the readings accordingly. There are common themes, of course, whatever the setting of the encounter or the identities of the humans and animals involved. Nevertheless, it remains true that raising nonhuman animals for food differs in some obvious ways from chancing upon a snake while hiking. Our method of organization reflects these differences. The remainder of the introduction highlights a few of the many themes found in the several selections.

HUMANS ENCOUNTER OTHER ANIMALS

The first two stories, both about a man's unexpected encounter with a snake, establish the broad terms of the dialectic present in some of the other readings. In Stephen Crane's "The Snake," the central figure views a rattlesnake with "hatred and fear":

> In the man was all the wild strength of the terror of his ancestors, of his race, of his kind. A deadly repulsion had been handed from man to man through long dim centuries.

Crane's protagonist does not ask himself whether his hatred and fear are rational, or whether other emotions might or should replace the "deadly repulsion" to which Crane alludes. It is enough that he feels what he feels, enough that he experiences the urge to conquer and destroy what is alien, what is "other," a "natural" urge, one "handed from man to man through long dim centuries."

William Saroyan's main character is importantly different. The same initial reactions and feelings are present: "the instinctive fear of reptiles," "the [intention] to kill the snake," the fear of "touching it with his hands." But something happens. He speaks to the snake. He whistles. He even sings. In Italian! And then something else happens: "He was amazed at himself suddenly; it had occurred to him to let the snake flee, to let it glide away and be lost in the lowly worlds of its kind." But the impulse to permit the freedom of the "other" is quickly challenged:

> Why should he allow it to escape?
> He lifted a heavy boulder from the ground and thought: Now I shall bash your head with this rock and see you die.
> To destroy that evil grace, to mangle that sinful loveliness.

Thus do we find in the stories by Crane and Saroyan, in miniature as it were, the larger patterns of opposition identified by philosophers, theologians, anthropologists, social historians, and others. On the one hand stands the human person, alienated from nature in general and undomesticated animals in particular, in bondage to the hatred and fear of what is wild and untamed, knowing only the urge to subdue and destroy. On the other hand we find the human person struggling to reclaim a lost kinship with nature, nonhuman animals included, risking thoughts and deeds that others have foreclosed, and exploring the possibilities of peaceful coexistence and shared liberation with the denizens of (in Beston's searing imagery) those other nations with whom we share the earth. Which option, if either, is the truer and the better is among the unifying questions addressed by many of the writers whose work is collected here, whatever the identity of the animals involved and regardless of the context of human interaction with them.

OTHER ANIMALS ENCOUNTER HUMANS

Certainly this is true of the next three stories, where other animals are the adventurers (the "trespassers," as it were), entering, as they do, into the day-to-day space of human life. In A. E. Coppard's "Arabesque—The Mouse," it is a mouse who enters the cupboard (and thereby the life) of a solitary middle-aged man; in George Orwell's selection, it is an elephant who happens to invade a village in lower Burma; and in Robert McAlmon's "The Jack Rabbit Drive," the animals are the jack rabbits of the story's title, whose population, it is thought, must be culled by the residents of a rural community in South Dakota. Who will destroy? Who will protect? And, in either case, what will be thought? What felt? Coppard's, Orwell's, and McAlmon's stories offer answers to each of these questions, and different answers in each case.

Needless to say, these three stories, like the opening two by Crane and Saroyan, mean more than they say. A snake, for example, is more than a kind of reptile. In its mysterious and (for many) fearful visage we find the fabled myths of our ancestors (recall the serpent's role in tempting Eve in the garden of Eden), as well as the powerful fears Freud and his followers found slithering along the dark corridors of the unconscious. To fail to grasp and explore the symbolism in Crane's and Saroyan's stories—and the same observation applies to other stories collected here—is to see only the smooth surface of fiction, not its churning depths.

And yet snakes are what they are, and not another thing. And because of what they are, or, rather, because of what we perceive them to be, snakes can have the symbolism they do, whether in a controlled work of fiction or in the raucous requirements of the unconscious. To understand an animal's symbolic possibilities, therefore, is not merely to gain access to literary or psychological meanings otherwise concealed; it also is to have one's mind opened to those cultural and other forces that have helped shape the human mind itself. Ironically, to understand a nonhuman animal's meaning in a story—a snake, a mouse, a jack rabbit—is to understand part of what it is to be human. In this way fiction is the parent of fact.

OTHER ANIMALS AS COMPANIONS

In addition to those normally brief occasions when humans enter the world of undomesticated animals, or when these animals enter the world of human affairs, some relations between humans and other animals are more enduring. Many nonhuman animals are chosen to be our companions ("pets"), the close bond formed by this association often lasting for years, the nonhuman animal becoming, in a very real sense, a member of the human family. The possibilities of humor and the need for compromise created by such a relationship are depicted in "Pilling the Cat," Cleveland Amory's account of his (and his cat's) travails on that fateful day when, for the first time, Polar Bear (the cat) is given a pill, or, to speak more accurately, when the attempt is made to give him one. Sometimes, Amory discovers, deceit and surprise are the better part of valor, even among friends.

Bobbie Ann Mason captures the love that binds many people to dogs in her sweetly sad tale, "Lying Doggo." Parents whose "first child" was other than a human being will find part of their own past in the married couple whose story Mason tells. Human life can be the poorer without a dog, a cat, or some other nonhuman animal with whom to share it, even if in the end the price of such friendship is real grief and a desperate sense of loss. The husband and wife in "Lying Doggo" are prepared to pay the price. And the reader knows that the dog's life is the better for having known them.

The same cannot be said of the parrot in Leigh Buchanan Bienen's "My Life as a West African Gray Parrot." In Bienen's hands, it is the parrot who is the narrator, the parrot who tells the story of the bonds of companionship cruelly broken by human neglect and callousness. Hear the parrot speak these opening lines:

> The dark, I am in the dark. They have put the green cloth over my cage. I am in the dark once again. I smell the acrid felt. I smell the green of transitions, the particles of dust in the warp of the fabric which reminds me of forests and terror. I am in the dark. I shall never fly again.

How has this once majestic creature found his way into a solitary world of darkness? Is it possible that the sweet breath of human compassion can turn sour? The West African gray parrot in Bienen's story has a particular tale to tell, and yet we cannot be far from the truth if we read it as one variation on the main theme of human domination. That power tends to corrupt is nowhere truer than in relationships between humans and other animals, when these relationships are based on our power, not their dignity. Unlike the main character in Saroyan's story, who entertains the possibility of "let[ting] the snake flee," the human characters in Bienen's story give no evidence of any inclination towards animal liberation. No sensitive person can read the parrot's autobiography (as it were) without hoping that what justice there is in the universe will not overlook his forlorn enslavement or the insensitivity of his masters.

OTHER ANIMALS AS PREY

Wild animals have more often been hunted and killed than captured and turned into companions for human beings. The next four selections explore alternative attitudes towards the theme of human-as-predator. The first one, by Ernest Hemingway, extols the pleasures of hunting. He writes:

Now it is pleasant to hunt something that you want very much over a long period of time, being out-witted, out-manœuvered, and failing at the end of each day, but having the hunt and knowing every time you are out that, sooner or later, your luck will change and that you will get the chance you are seeking.

Hemingway recounts one such hunt, during his first African safari, when he was joined by P. O. M. ("Poor Old Mama," Hemingway's wife), Pop (Philip Percival, a friend), and two trackers (M'Cola and Droop, sometimes referred to as Droopy). The prey: a male buffalo. The reward: a clean, fatal shot from four hundred yards. "It was wonderful when we heard him bellow," P. O. M. says. "It sounded awfully jolly to me," Pop volunteers. As for Hemingway himself, he observes that "you cannot live on a plane of the sort of elation I had felt in the reeds and having killed, even when it is only a buffalo, you feel a little quiet inside."

Kasyan, the old peasant in the selection by Ivan Turgenev, would not look kindly on Hemingway's elation. Kasyan believes that it is permissible to kill domesticated animals who are raised for food. But not wild animals; these should be "let to live on the earth until [their] natural end." The former, God has given to humans as food, but not the latter. In Kasyan's ethic it is a sin to take from nature what God has not given us. The narrator of Turgenev's selection is of a different view, one that resembles Hemingway's. When the narrator kills a wild bird, Kasyan remarks that he does so not for food but "for your own pleasure."

The narrator of Laurens van der Post's selection ("young David," as he is called) occupies something of a middle ground between Kasyan and Hemingway. Like Hemingway, he experiences "the excitement and the acceleration into a consummation of archaic joy [in] the process of stalking and hunting." But like Kasyan, David feels "an equal and opposite revulsion which nearly overwhelmed [him] when the hunt . . . was successful and one was faced with the acceptance of the fact that one had aided and abetted in an act of murder." If one hunts out of necessity, especially for food, then David finds the practice acceptable. But not otherwise, and certainly not in the case of the "murder" of whales, the animals hunted and killed in the selection by van der Post. Even so, young David stops short of condemnation of Thor Kaspersen, the captain of the whaling vessel *Larsen II*:

> Starting from a point where I was truly bewildered, dismayed and even mistrustful of the man, I soon discovered a far-ranging kind of fellow-feeling for him which uncovered unexpected depths of compassion and a sense of the importance of an understanding in the human spirit that is beyond censure and judgement.

How is it possible to find such redeeming qualities in a commercial whaler, a man who does what one is convinced is wrong? And how, if at all, would one's answer to that question differ from one's answers to similar questions asked about Turgenev's narrator, or of Hemingway, or of the Native American hunters depicted in Charles A. Eastman's "The Gray Chieftain"?

The two hunters, Wacootay and Grayfoot, are hunting for spoonhorn sheep among the remote inner cliffs of the Bad Lands, in what today is South Dakota. These animals were hunted not for their skins or meat but for their horns, which were used as spoons and ladles. To their surprise, the two hunters happen upon Haykinshkah, the patriarch of a clan of spoonhorns. Before the final encounter between the hunters and Haykinshkah, the gray chieftain of the title, Grayfoot praises the majestic sheep for his wisdom and courage. Like the other animals, who Grayfoot believes "are people as much as we are," Haykinshkah was created by "the Great Mystery . . . Although they do not speak our tongue, we often seem to understand their thought. It is not right to take the life of any of them unless necessity compels us to do so."

For Grayfoot and Wacootay, such necessity was found in the use of Haykinshkah's horns as spoons and ladles. It may seem an uncaring ethic that would permit the destruction of a majestic animal for such purposes, and yet neither Wacootay nor Grayfoot seems to be a cruel, callous person. "He is dead. My friend, the noblest of chiefs is dead!" Grayfoot exclaims at the story's conclusion, standing over his dead prey, "in great admiration and respect for the gray chieftain." Eastman's story thus forces his readers to consider whether and, if so, how it is possible for people to admire and respect the very animals they kill.

OTHER ANIMALS AS TOOLS

Because humans, especially when aided by technology, operate from a position of power, it is possible for us to treat other animals in almost any way we choose. Nowhere is this freedom more evident than in research in the life sciences. Here nonhuman animals are deliberately burned, starved, bled, socially deprived, blinded, rendered deaf, and denied sleep. Their brains are intentionally scrambled, their limbs severed, their internal organs crushed or exploded. They are methodically given heart attacks, peptic ulcers, epileptic seizures, and every form of cancer imaginable. They are forcibly made to smoke cigarettes, drink alcohol, and ingest heroin, cocaine, and other addictive drugs. They routinely are used in military research—in germ and chemical warfare experiments, for example, and in weapons development, including nuclear weapons. The list goes on. Suffice it to say that there are few ideas that could spark the scientific imagination in the life sciences that would not result in some other-than-human animals being forced to play an investigative role.

The usual justification given for using these animals as "models" or "tools" is threefold: first, the knowledge to be obtained is important; second, there is no other way to obtain it—unless we use humans instead; third, it is morally impermissible to use humans. Some philosophers, theologians, and other scholars have challenged this standard defense. The three selections in the present collection do not. Instead, they take us, each in its own way, behind the closed doors of laboratory science and suggest what that world might be like.

In "The Dead Body and the Living Brain," Oriana Fallaci opens those doors by describing cutting-edge explorations conducted by brain researcher Robert White at Case Western Reserve University in the 1960s. The subject of Professor White's explorations? Libby, a three-year-old rhesus monkey. The object of his research? To remove Libby's brain from her body while keeping the brain alive. As Fallaci observes, Professor White is the first man in the history of medicine to succeed in conducting this "difficult operation."

"The fingers of a surgeon," she writes, "are so enchanting, more than those of a jeweler or a pianist. There is always a moment when they seem to be the fingers of a priest celebrating a Mass. And because of this, perhaps, you didn't cry for Libby."

The procedure, which began at 10:00 a.m., ends at 9:00 p.m., when Libby's brain is allowed to die. Theoretically, her brain could have been kept alive for days, but the information Professor White was seeking already had been found. As for what Libby experienced once her brain had been severed from her body, no one can be sure. "I guess he [sic] is primarily a memory," one of Professor White's associates suggests, "a repository for information stored when he had his flesh."

Regardless of Libby's mental states, Professor White is certain of the importance of his research. In response to a question asked by Fallaci, he says, "I want to know what happens [in the brain] when [the brain] is smashed by a car accident, or when it's paralyzed by a stroke, or when it turns to insanity. I want to know why it works as it works, what it does when it dies, why everything is as it is inside it. This is the main purpose of my experiment."[1]

Whereas the perspective in the selection by Fallaci is that of the humans who use other animals in their research, the perspective in the next selection, by William Kotzwinkle, is that of the nonhuman animals they use. The narrator is Dr. Rat, a sagacious, determined rat who is able to communicate telepathically with the other animals in the laboratory in which he finds himself. He has been conditioned to be very pro-research: "A rat must give his all! That's our purpose, that's why we're here on earth!" And again: "Death is freedom, that's the slogan!"

[1] Oriana Fallaci, "The Dead Body and the Living Brain," *Look* 31, no. 24 (1967), 108.

But all is not well in Dr. Rat's laboratory. A dog is sending "intuition-pictures" that promise escape from the hell of the laboratory, and escape on a massive scale: all the animals are to be liberated, from all the laboratories. In the face of this revolution, Dr. Rat seeks to retain control: "Oh, you disgusting dog! Go back to the alleyway you came from and stop shaming the good citizens of this laboratory with your perverted view of life!" To his delight, Dr. Rat watches as a cocker spaniel is subjected to a burn experiment.

> The Learned Professor brings the flame right into the dog's nostril, shoots it right up there. Excellent, well-aimed. The cocker is being forced to *inhale the flame*. Now the assistant lights his own lighter and both nostrils are filled with fire, as the dog's mouth snaps open in a soundless howl.

Will the animals in this and other labs revolt and claim their freedom? Or will they subscribe to Dr. Rat's ethic of service to their human masters? Moreover, whatever these animals decide, might other animals choose differently? And, in either case, why? Part of the power of Kotzwinkle's imaginary tale will be found in how these questions are answered.

Only humans speak in M. Pabst Battin's "Terminal Procedure." This complex story features Boaz, a researcher, and Miaia, his assistant. Boaz is a neuropsychologist working in a large research institute. The goal of his study is to correlate events in the brain with a particular pattern of behavior. To induce the desired behavior, it is necessary to subject dogs to electric shock. This is the easy part of the research. Far more difficult is establishing the correlation between the induced behavior and canine brain activity. In the story, Boaz explains the procedure to Miaia:

> "The problem . . . is to determine just where the electrodes are. It's not easy to implant them precisely, and there's only one way to determine exactly where they are."
> "What's that?"

"By direct inspection of the neural region." He talks more quickly, enunciating the syllables almost too clearly, as if to conceal in scientific jargon something he does not quite want her to understand.

She sits still, saying nothing.

"The procedure is terminal," he says at last.

"I know that," she says flatly, and Boaz realizes that she is not going to cry, that her eyes are wide all the time.

With such shared knowledge of the ultimate outcome, and in view of Boaz's experience and standing in the scientific community, no one could expect that anything untoward would happen.

Yet happen it does, although both the "Why?" and the "Wherefore?" are questions answered by Battin in ambiguous clues rather than in precise declarations. What does seem clear is that, as Battin views the matter, research scientists need not be the sadistic monsters personified by Kotzwinkle's Learned Professor. Most, perhaps even all, of them say they really care about the animals entrusted to their hands. But how, then, can this professed care be reconciled with deliberately injuring and killing them?

OTHER ANIMALS AS FOOD

The closest daily contact most people in the Western world have with nonhuman animals consists in eating them. Food, we know, is very much a cultural phenomenon; had we been born and raised in, say, a small village in southern India, our diet likely would be as different as our beliefs about the sacredness of the cow. Nevertheless, most of us with lives rooted in Western culture regard our preference for flesh foods, or meat, as both natural and proper.

The scale of this preference is hardly inconsiderable. More than ten billion farmed animals annually are slaughtered just in the United States to satisfy this national gastronomic appetite. Because of the size of the demand (more than twenty-seven million animals must be slaughtered every day, in excess of one million every hour), modern farming methods have been devised. Called "close confinement" or "intensive rearing," the idea is to produce the largest number of marketable animals in the shortest possible time with the least possible investment. Widespread adoption of these methods has all but eliminated the small family farm.

The animals raised intensively (hogs, chickens, turkeys, and veal calves, for example) have limited opportunities for physical movement, lack the environment in which to establish a social organization (the proverbial "pecking order" among chickens, for example), and never see the sunlight or breathe fresh air. Some are raised in permanent semi-darkness, which tends to render them more docile, and many routinely suffer some form of physical mutilation, as when chickens are debeaked to reduce the rate of cannibalism. Among those philosophers, theologians, and other scholars in the humanities who have informed themselves about the practices that define factory farming, there is all but universal condemnation.

But questions concerning our proper relationship to the nonhuman animals people choose to eat go beyond the ethics of factory farming. Whatever rearing methods are employed, animals raised for food are killed. And this fact gives rise to a basic moral question: do we do anything wrong when we kill animals, not because eating them is necessary for our survival or good health, but because we enjoy how they taste? This is the question that, at different levels, and in different ways, the next five selections examine.

The first one—Isaac Bashevis Singer's "The Slaughterer"—tells the story of a ritual slaughterer, Yoineh Meir. By nature a softhearted man, Yoineh Meir is persuaded to accept his post because, as the rabbi of a neighboring town writes, "man may not be more compassionate than the Almighty, the Source of all compassion." As Singer's story unfolds, we observe Yoineh Meir wrestle with this profound assertion as he puts his faith in "the Source of all compassion" to the test. "An unfamiliar love welled up in Yoineh Meir," Singer writes, "for all that crawls and flies, breeds and swarms . . . How could one pray for life for the coming year, or for a favorable writ in Heaven, when one was robbing others of the breath of life?" The final pages reveal Yoineh Meir's answer.

Unlike the main character in Singer's story, whose own hands bring death to animals, Aloísio, the main character in João Ubaldo Ribeiro's "It Was a Different Day When They Killed the Pig," kills no animal himself; instead, in keeping with ancient customs, each year a few older boys have the privilege of being asked to watch as the sow is killed; this year, it is Aloísio's turn, an honor denied to his sister, Leonor, who cries when he tells her of the impending death of Noca, the red sow.

"Women are like that," his father says; for them, crying about the death of an animal is natural. But not for men; and not for Aloísio. Whatever else was ambiguous, this Aloísio knew: he "wanted very, very much to be a man, and he wanted nobody to be ever, ever able to say that he had not been a man even if only for an instant."

Aloísio's was a challenge not easily met, so overwhelmed was he by the horror of seeing the men "demolishing the sow Noca as though they were demolishing a house," so nauseated was he by the "many black and gray and white and red and limp and throbbing and slippery things inside a pig," many of them with "a hideous smell." Outwardly, Aloísio knew "he had behaved in the most correct way." His father said so himself. "Aloísio had behaved fine during the sow's dying. He is a man," he heard his father tell his mother. But inwardly, Aloísio felt ashamed. "He was still secretly bothered by what happened, but was confident that the next time it would not be like this." That, Aloísio implies, is what it means to "grow up." Which is why the ending of Ribeiro's story gives one pause: Did Aloísio lose more than he gained on that different day when they killed the pig? And, if so, what?

M. F. K. Fisher's attitude towards killing animals for food exhibits none of Yoineh Meir's anguish or Aloísio's ambivalence. For Fisher, one of the twentieth century's most admired and influential writers on "the art of eating," the problems associated with killing and eating animals are practical, not ethical. In the particular case of pigeons, the main subject of her selection, one problem concerns finding birds suitable for roasting; a second concerns finding men qualified to kill them. "In the country," she observes, "there are few farmers, any more, that have kept their dove-cotes clean and populous . . . and fewer hired men who will kill the pretty birds properly by smothering them."

Fisher's "How to Make a Pigeon Cry" was originally published in 1942, at the height of America's involvement in World War II and at a time when many people lived in grim economic circumstances. When she alludes to "the wolf [at] the door," she is referring to the day-to-day challenge these people faced in their struggle to put food on their table. She would publish a substantially expanded second edition in 1951; the additions are enclosed in brackets in this volume.

Fisher's selection is not limited to instructions on how to roast pigeon; also included are recipes for kasha, rabbit, pheasant, and, in her words, a "strange quotation" from a book published in 1660 that describes how to prepare a goose so that "[she] will be almost eaten before she is dead." "For centuries," she writes, "men have eaten the flesh of other creatures not only to nourish their own bodies but to give more strength to their weary spirits." A gourmand of undisputed stature, Fisher evidently believes that these are reasons enough for continuing to do so.

Even among those who eat meat, the flesh of some animals is taboo, not only when, as in the Old Testament prohibition against eating the flesh of "unclean" animals, the taboo has religious authority on its side, but also for reasons of a more personal nature. For example, most people, independent of anything any religion might say, find the idea of turning their cat, dog, or other companion animal into sandwiches or stews too repulsive for words; and yet many of these same people are not the least bit troubled when they dine on beef or chicken.

Certainly this is true of the small family (Lovey, the narrator, her younger sister, Calhoon, and their father) in Lois-Ann Yamanaka's "Wild Meat and the Bully Burgers." Meat is part of everyday life. Goat. Sheep. Turkey. Pig. Rabbit. Turtle. Frogs' legs. Rarely a day goes by that meat, in one form or another, is not part of the family's meals. While to Lovey some meats smell and taste better than others, no thought is given to what is being eaten: some part of the dead flesh of a once living, breathing creature.

Things change when the father and some of his friends bring home a baby calf, whom they plan to raise and slaughter before sharing the meat. The two girls befriend the doomed animal, visiting him often, bringing what comfort and companionship they can; it is Calhoon who names the calf Bully. "Don't name him. Don't you dare call him that," the father protests. "We going eat um and how you going eat if you name him?"

But the naming is a fact, leaving the father and his daughters to face the day when the meat on their plate is not from an anonymous cow who has met death at some unknown slaughterhouse but is the Bully burgers of the title. Will they be able to eat flesh from an animal who has been named? Or is meat from an animal with a name among the flesh that is taboo? In either case, what light does Yamanaka's story cast on the question, "Do we do anything wrong when animals are killed because we enjoy eating them?"

Alice Walker's implied answer to this question, as contained in "Am I Blue?" is that we do. "Blue" is the name of a white horse who grazes in a five acre pasture adjacent to a house rented by Walker and a friend. When she first meets him, Walker sees loneliness in Blue's eyes. That changes when another horse, a brown mare, takes up temporary residence; with Brown as his constant companion, Blue's mood changes: "There was a different look in his eyes. A look of independence, of self-possession, of inalienable *horse*ness." But that changes, too, when Brown, now pregnant, is taken away, leaving Blue alone again, his behavior like that of "a crazed person." For Walker, in fact, "Blue *was* . . . a crazed person," his look "so piercing, so full of grief, a look so *human*. . . ."

That Walker sees qualities in Blue that others see only in humans is not irrelevant to what she thinks she learns from her encounter with the white horse in the generous pasture. For Walker, Blue is a some-body, not a something, and his neglectful treatment at human hands is analogous to how some humans have exploited other humans, not because of a difference in species, but because of differences in race, or gender, or ethnicity. In the end, the lesson Blue teaches Walker is that injustice does not stop at the boundary of our species but extends to our treatment of nonhuman sentient life. When, at the conclusion of her essay, Walker tells her readers that she "spit[s] out" the steak she is eating, we are led to conclude that her days as a meat-eater are over.

Epilogue

The present volume ends with a chilling piece of science fiction by Desmond Stewart entitled "The Limits of Trooghaft." Planet earth has been conquered by the Troogs, faceless and largely gaseous creatures who are advanced far beyond human beings (homo insipiens, they call us). Before their conquest, the Troogs had been vegetarians; now they have developed a taste for "protein," as they call human flesh. In the Troog's hands, one group of humans, the largest caste, called "capons," are actually raised intensively in the manner of factory farms.

> Capons were naturally preferred when young, since their bones were supple; at this time they fetched, as "eat-alls," the highest price for the lowest weight. Those kept alive after childhood were lodged in small cages maintained at a steady 22 degrees [C]; the cage floors were composed of rolling bars through which the filth fell into a sluice. Capons were not permitted to see the sky or smell unfiltered air. Experience proved that a warm pink glow kept them docile and conduced to weight-gain. Females were in general preferred to males and the eradication of the tongue (sold as a separate delicacy) quietened the batteries.

Among those humans who survived the Troog invasion were the so-called quarry-men—wild, nomadic rebels who could be hunted only during specified seasons. It is the story of one such quarry-man's successful communication with an inquisitive Troog that Stewart tells.

In this imaginary world the Troogs subordinate human beings to those purposes which, in the real world, we humans subordinate other animals. The remorseful Troog wonders if this is wrong. We might wonder, too. For if we do no wrong in raising and slaughtering other animals for food, how is it possible that the Troogs act wrongly in doing the same things to human beings? That is the central question Stewart's story asks. The Troog featured in it offers one kind of answer.

In fact, Stewart's story asks more than one question. Other aspects of human relations with other animals, from the keeping of "pets" to hunting, become part of the fabric of Troog-human relations. "The Limits of Trooghaft," therefore, in addition to standing on its own, also obliges us to ask again those questions explored by other writers in this anthology, questions about the ethics of hunting game animals, others that inquire into the propriety of killing animals deemed to be pests, and still others that demand a justification for using animals as tools in the name of advancing scientific knowledge. For this reason, if for no other, Stewart's story seems the ideal one with which to conclude. When viewed against the backdrop of what has gone before, his ending is a new beginning.

I

HUMANS ENCOUNTER OTHER ANIMALS
ılıllıllılıllıllılıllıllılı

THE SNAKE
–Stephen Crane–

Where the path wended across the ridge, the bushes of huckleberry and sweet fern swarmed at it in two curling waves until it was a mere winding line traced through a tangle. There was no interference by clouds, and as the rays of the sun fell full upon the ridge, they called into voice innumerable insects which chanted the heat of the summer day in steady, throbbing, unending chorus.

A man and a dog came from the laurel thickets of the valley where the white brook brawled with the rocks. They followed the deep line of the path across the ridge. The dog—a large lemon-and-white setter—walked tranquilly meditative, at his master's heels.

Suddenly from some unknown and yet near place in advance there came a dry, shrill, whistling rattle that smote motion instantly from the limbs of the man and the dog. Like the fingers of a sudden death, this sound seemed to touch the man at the nape of the neck, at the top of the spine, and change him, as swift as thought, to a statute of listening horror, surprise, rage. The dog, too—the same icy hand was laid upon him, and he stood crouched and quivering, his jaw dropping, the froth of terror upon his lips, the light of hatred in his eyes.

Slowly the man moved his hands toward the bushes, but his glance did not turn from the place made sinister by the warning rattle. His fingers, unguided, sought for a stick of weight and strength. Presently they closed about one that seemed adequate, and holding this weapon poised before him, the man moved slowly forward, glaring. The dog, with his nervous nostrils fairly fluttering, moved warily, one foot at a time, after his master.

But when the man came upon the snake, his body underwent a shock as if from a revelation, as if after all he had been ambushed. With a blanched face, he sprang forward, and his breath came in strained gasps, his chest heaving as if he were in the performance of an extraordinary muscular trial. His arm with the stick made a spasmodic, defensive gesture.

The snake had apparently been crossing the path in some mystic travel when to his sense there came the knowledge of the coming of his foes. The dull vibration perhaps informed him, and he flung his body to face the danger. He had no knowledge of paths; he had no wit to tell him to slink noiselessly into the bushes. He knew that his implacable enemies were approaching; no doubt they were seeking him, hunting him. And so he cried his cry, an incredibly swift jangle of tiny bells, as burdened with pathos as the hammering upon quaint cymbals by the Chinese at war—for, indeed, it was usually his death music.

"Beware! Beware! Beware!"

The man and the snake confronted each other. In the man's eyes were hatred and fear. In the snake's were hatred and fear. These enemies maneuvered, each preparing to kill. It was to be a battle without mercy. Neither knew of mercy for such a situation. In the man was all the wild strength of the terror of his ancestors, of his race, of his kind. A deadly repulsion had been handed from man to man through long dim centuries. This was another detail of a war that had begun evidently when first there were men and snakes. Individuals who do not participate in this strife incur the investigations of scientists. Once there was a man and a snake who were friends, and at the end, the man lay dead with the marks of the snake's caress just over his East Indian heart. In the formation of devices, hideous and horrible, Nature reached her supreme point in the making of the snake, so that priests who really paint hell well fill it with snakes instead of fire. These curving forms, these scintillant colorings create at once, upon sight, more relentless animosities than do shake barbaric tribes. To be born a snake is to be thrust into a place aswarm with formidable foes. To gain an appreciation of it, view hell as pictured by priests who are really skillful.

As for this snake in the pathway, there was a double curve some inches back of its head, which, merely by the potency of its lines, made the man feel with tenfold eloquence the touch of the death-fingers at the nape of his neck. The reptile's head was waving slowly from side to side and its hot eyes flashed like little murder-lights. Always in the air was the dry, shrill whistling of the rattles.

"Beware! Beware! Beware!"

The man made a preliminary feint with his stick. Instantly the snake's heavy head and neck were bent back on the double curve and instantly the snake's body shot forward in a low, straight, hard spring. The man jumped with a convulsive chatter and swung his stick. The blind, sweeping blow fell upon the snake's head and hurled him so that steel-colored plates were for a moment uppermost. But he rallied swiftly, agilely, and again the head and neck bent back to the double curve, and the steaming, wide-open mouth made its desperate effort to reach its enemy. This attack, it could be seen, was despairing, but it was nevertheless impetuous, gallant, ferocious, of the same quality as the charge of the lone chief when the walls of white faces close upon him in the mountains. The stick swung unerringly again, and the snake, mutilated, torn, whirled himself into the last coil.

And now the man went sheer raving mad from the emotions of his forefathers and from his own. He came to close quarters. He gripped the stick with his two hands and made it speed like a flail. The snake, tumbling in the anguish of final despair, fought, bit, flung itself upon this stick which was taking its life.

At the end, the man clutched his stick and stood watching in silence. The dog came slowly, and with infinite caution stretched his nose forward, sniffing. The hair upon his neck and back moved and ruffled as if a sharp wind was blowing. The last muscular quivers of the snake were causing the rattles to still sound their treble cry, the shrill, ringing war chant and hymn of the grave of the thing that faces foes at once countless, implacable, and superior.

"Well, Rover," said the man, turning to the dog with a grin of victory, "we'll carry Mr. Snake home to show the girls."

His hands still trembled from the strain of the encounter, but he pried with his stick under the body of the snake and hoisted the limp thing upon it. He resumed his march along the path, and the dog walked, tranquilly meditative, at his master's heels.

SNAKE
–William Saroyan–

Walking through the park in May, he saw a small brown snake slipping away from him through grass and leaves, and he went after it with a long twig, feeling as he did so the instinctive fear of man for reptiles.

Ah, he thought, our symbol of evil, and he touched the snake with the twig, making it squirm. The snake lifted its head and struck at the twig, then shot away through the grass, hurrying fearfully, and he went after it.

It was very beautiful, and it was amazingly clever, but he intended to stay with it for a while and find out something about it.

The little brown snake led him deep into the park, so that he was hidden from view and alone with it. He had a guilty feeling that in pursuing the snake he was violating some rule of the park, and he prepared a remark for anyone who might discover him. I am a student of contemporary morality, he thought he would say, or, I am a sculptor and I am studying the structure of reptiles. At any rate, he would make some sort of reasonable explanation.

He would not say that he intended to kill the snake.

He moved beside the frightened reptile, leaping now and then to keep up with it, until the snake became exhausted and could not go on. Then he squatted on his heels to have a closer view of it, holding the snake before him by touching it with the twig. He admitted to himself that he was afraid to touch it with his hands. To touch a snake was to touch something secret in the mind of man, something one ought never to bring out into the light. That sleek gliding, and that awful silence, was once man, and now that man had come to this last form, here were snakes still moving over the earth as if no change had ever taken place.

The first male and female, biblical; and evolution. Adam and Eve, and the human embryo.

It was a lovely snake, clean and graceful and precise. The snake's fear frightened him and he became panic stricken thinking that perhaps all the snakes in the park would come quietly to the rescue of the little brown snake, and surround him with their malicious silence and the unbearable horror of their evil forms. It was a large park and there must be thousands of snakes in it. If all the snakes were to find out that he was with this little snake, they would easily be able to paralyse him.

He stood up and looked around. All was quiet. The silence was almost the biblical silence of *in the beginning*. He could hear a bird hopping from twig to twig in a low earthbush near by, but he was alone with the snake. He forgot that he was in a public park, in a large city. An airplane passed overhead, but he did not see or hear it. The silence was too emphatic and his vision was too emphatically focused on the snake before him.

In the garden with the snake, unnaked, in the beginning, in the year 1931.

He squatted on his heels again and began to commune with the snake. It made him laugh, inwardly and outwardly, to have the form of the snake so substantially before him, apart from his own being, flat on the surface of the earth instead of subtly a part of his own identity. It was really a tremendous thing. At first he was afraid to speak aloud, but as time went on he became less timid, and began to speak in English to it. It was very pleasant to speak to the snake.

All right, he said, here I am, after all these years, a young man living on the same earth, under the same sun, having the same passions.

And here you are before me, the same. The situation is the same. What do you intend to do? Escape? I will not let you escape. What have you in mind? How will you defend yourself? I intend to destroy you. As an obligation to man.

The snake twitched before him helplessly, unable to avoid the twig. It struck at the twig several times, and then became too tired to bother with it. He drew away the twig, and heard the snake say, Thank you.

He began to whistle to the snake, to see if the music would have any effect on its movements, if it would make the snake dance. You are my only love, he whistled; Schubert made into a New York musical comedy; *my only love, my only love*; but the snake would not dance. Something Italian perhaps, he thought, and began to sing *la donna è mobile*, intentionally mispronouncing the words in order to amuse himself. He tried a Brahms lullaby, but the music had no effect on the snake. It was tired. It was frightened. It wanted to get away.

He was amazed at himself suddenly; it had occurred to him to let the snake flee, to let it glide away and be lost in the lowly worlds of its kind. Why should he allow it to escape?

He lifted a heavy boulder from the ground and thought: Now I shall bash your head with this rock and see you die.

To destroy that evil grace, to mangle that sinful loveliness.

But it was very strange. He could not let the rock fall on the snake's head, and began suddenly to feel sorry for it. I am sorry, he said, dropping the boulder. I beg your pardon. I see now that I have only love for you.

And he wanted to touch the snake with his hands, to hold it and understand the truth of its touch. But it was difficult. The snake was frightened and each time he extended his hands to touch it, the snake turned on him and charged. I have only love for you, he said. Do not be afraid. I am not going to hurt you.

Then, swiftly, he lifted the snake from the earth, learned the true feel of it, and dropped it. There, he said. Now I know the truth. A snake is cold, but it is clean. It is not slimy, as I thought.

He smiled upon the little brown snake. You may go now, he said. The inquisition is over. You are yet alive. You have been in the presence of man, and you are yet alive. You may go now.

But the snake would not go away. It was exhausted with fear.

He felt deeply ashamed of what he had done, and angry with himself. Jesus, he thought, I have scared the little snake. It will never get over this. It will always remember me squatting over it.

For God's sake, he said to the snake, go away. Return to your kind. Tell them what you saw, you yourself, with your own eyes. Tell them what you felt. The sickly heat of the hand of man. Tell them of the presence you felt.

Suddenly the snake turned from him and spilled itself forward, away from him. Thank you, he said. And it made him laugh with joy to see the little snake throwing itself into the grass and leaves, thrusting itself away from man. Splendid, he said; hurry to them and say that you were in the presence of man and that you were not killed. Think of all the snakes that live and die without ever meeting man. Think of the distinction it will mean for you.

It seemed to him that the little snake's movements away from him were the essence of joyous laughter, and he felt greatly pleased. He found his way back to the path, and continued his walk.

In the evening, while she sat at the piano, playing softly, he said: A funny thing happened.

She went on playing. A funny thing? she asked.

Yes, he said. I was walking through the park and I saw a little brown snake.

She stopped playing and turned on the bench to look at him. A snake? she said. How ugly!

No, he said. It was beautiful.

What about it?

Oh, nothing, he said. I just caught it and wouldn't let it go for a while.

But why?

For no good reason at all, he said.

She walked across the room and sat beside him, looking at him strangely.

Tell me about the snake, she said.

It was lovely, he said. Not ugly at all. When I touched it, I felt its cleanliness.

I am so glad, she said. What else?

I wanted to kill the snake, he said. But I couldn't. It was too lovely.

I'm so glad, she said. But tell me everything.

That's all, he said.

But it isn't, she said. I know it isn't. Tell me everything.

It is very funny, he said. I was going to kill the snake, and not come here again.

Aren't you ashamed of yourself? she said.

Of course I am, he said.

What else? she said. What did you think, of me, when you had the snake before you?

You will be angry, he said.

Oh, nonsense. It is impossible for me to be angry with you. Tell me.

Well, he said, I thought you were lovely but evil.

Evil?

I told you you would be angry.

And then?

Then I touched the snake, he said. It wasn't easy, but I picked it up with my hands. What do you make of this? You've read a lot of books about such things. What does it mean, my picking up the snake?

She began to laugh softly, intelligently. Why, she laughed, it means, it simply means that you are an idiot. Why, it's splendid.

Is that according to Freud? he said.

Yes, she laughed. According to Freud.

Well, anyway, he said, it was very fine to let the snake go free.

Have you ever told me you loved me? she asked.

You ought to know, he said. I do not remember one or two things I have said to you.

No, she said. You have never told me.

She began to laugh again, feeling suddenly very happy about him. You have always talked of other things, she said. Irrelevant things. At the most amazing times. She laughed.

This snake, he said, was a little brown snake.

And that explains it, she said. You have never intruded.

What the hell are you talking about? he said.

I'm so glad you didn't kill the snake, she said.

She returned to the piano, and placed her hands softly upon the keys.

I whistled a few songs to the snake, he said. I whistled a fragment from Schubert's Unfinished Symphony. I would like to hear that. You know, the melody that was used in a musical comedy called *Blossom Time*. The part that goes, *you are my only love, my only love,* and so on.

She began to play softly, feeling his eyes on her hair, on her hands, her neck, her back, her arms, feeling him studying her as he had studied the snake.

II

OTHER ANIMALS ENCOUNTER HUMANS
ıııııııııııııııııııııııı

ARABESQUE—THE MOUSE
—A. E. Coppard—

In the main street amongst tall establishments of mart and worship
was a high narrow house pressed between a coffee factory and a boot-
maker's. It had four flights of long dim echoing stairs, and at the top,
in a room that was full of the smell of dried apples and mice, a man in
the middle age of life had sat reading Russian novels until he thought
he was mad. Late was the hour, the night outside black and freezing,
the pavements below empty and undistinguishable when he closed his
book and sat motionless in front of the glowing but flameless fire. He
felt he was very tired, yet he could not rest. He stared at a picture on
the wall until he wanted to cry; it was a colour-print by Utamaro of
a suckling child caressing its mother's breasts as she sits in front of a
blackbound mirror. Very chaste and decorative it was, in spite of its
curious anatomy. The man gazed, empty of sight though not of mind,
until the sighing of the gas-jet maddened him. He got up, put out
the light, and sat down again in the darkness trying to compose his
mind before the comfort of the fire. And he was just about to begin a

conversation with himself when a mouse crept from a hole in the skirting near the fireplace and scurried into the fender. The man had the crude dislike for such sly nocturnal things, but this mouse was so small and bright, its antics so pretty, that he drew his feet carefully from the fender and sat watching it almost with amusement. The mouse moved along the shadows of the fender, out upon the hearth, and sat before the glow, rubbing its head, ears, and tiny belly with its paws as if it were bathing itself with the warmth, until, sharp and sudden, the fire sank, an ember fell, and the mouse flashed into its hole.

The man reached forward to the mantel-piece and put his hand upon a pocket lamp. Turning on the beam, he opened the door of a cupboard beside the fireplace. Upon one of the shelves there was a small trap baited with cheese, a trap made with a wire spring, one of those that smashed down to break the back of ingenuous and unwary mice.

"Mean—so mean," he mused, "to appeal to the hunger of any living thing just in order to destroy it."

He picked up the empty trap as if to throw it in the fire.

"I suppose I had better leave it though—the place swarms with them." He still hesitated. "I hope that little beastie won't go and do anything foolish." He put the trap back quite carefully, closed the door of the cupboard, sat down again and extinguished the lamp.

Was there anyone else in the world so squeamish and foolish about such things! Even his mother, mother so bright and beautiful, even she had laughed at his childish horrors. He recalled how once in his childhood, not long after his sister Yosine was born, a friendly neighbour had sent him home with a bundle of dead larks tied by the feet "for supper." The pitiful inanimity of the birds had brought a gush of tears; he had run weeping home and into the kitchen, and there he had found the strange thing doing. It was dusk; his mother was kneeling before the fire. He dropped the larks.

"Mother!" he exclaimed softly.

She looked at his tearful face.

"What's the matter, Filip?" she asked, smiling too at his astonishment.

"Mother! What are you doing?"

Her bodice was open and she was squeezing her breasts; long thin streams of milk spurted into the fire with a plunging noise.

"Weaning your little sister," laughed Mother. She took his inquisitive face and pressed it against the delicate warmth of her bosom, and he forgot the dead birds behind him.

"Let me do it, Mother," he cried, and doing so he discovered the throb of the heart in his mother's breast. Wonderful it was for him to experience it, although she could not explain it to him.

"Why does it do that?"

"If it did not beat, little son, I should die and the Holy Father would take me from you."

"God?"

She nodded. He put his hand upon his own breast. "Oh, feel it, Mother!" he cried. Mother unbuttoned his little coat and felt the gentle *tick tick* with her warm palm.

"Beautiful!" she said.

"Is it a good one?"

She kissed his smiling lips. "It is good if it beats truly. Let it always beat truly, Filip; let it always beat truly."

There was the echo of a sigh in her voice, and he had divined some grief, for he was very wise. He kissed her bosom in his tiny ecstasy and whispered soothingly; "Little mother! little mother!" In such joys he forgot his horror of the dead larks; indeed he helped Mother to pluck them and spit them for supper.

It was a black day that succeeded, and full of tragedy for the child. A great bay horse with a tawny mane had knocked down his mother in the lane, and a heavy cart had passed over her, crushing both her hands. She was borne away moaning with anguish to the surgeon who cut off the two hands. She died in the night. For years the child's dreams were filled with the horror of the stumps of arms, bleeding unendingly. Yet he had never seen them, for he was sleeping when she died.

While this old woe was come vividly before him he again became aware of the mouse. His nerves stretched upon him in repulsion, but he soon relaxed to a tolerant interest, for it was really a most engaging little mouse. It moved with curious staccato scurries, stopping to rub its head or flicker with its ears; they seemed almost transparent ears. It spied a red cinder and skipped innocently up to it . . . sniffing . . . sniffing . . . until it jumped back scorched. It would crouch as a cat does, blinking in the warmth, or scamper madly as if dancing, and then roll upon its side rubbing its head with those pliant paws. The melancholy man watched it until it came at last to rest and squatted meditatively upon its haunches, hunched up, looking curiously wise, a pennyworth of philosophy; then once more the coals sank with a rattle and again the mouse was gone.

The man sat on before the fire and his mind filled again with unaccountable sadness. He had grown into manhood with a burning generosity of spirit and rifts of rebellion in him that proved too exacting for his fellows and seemed mere wantonness to men of casual rectitudes. "Justice and Sin," he would cry, "Property and Virtue—incompatibilities! There can be no sin in a world of justice, no property in a world of virtue!" With an engaging extravagance and a certain clear-eyed honesty of mind he had put his two and two together and seemed then to rejoice, as in some topsy-turvy dream, in having rendered unto Cæsar, as you might say, the things that were due to Napoleon! But this kind of thing could not pass unexpiated in a world of men having an infinite regard for Property and a pride in their traditions of Virtue and Justice. They could indeed forgive him his sins, but they could not forgive him his compassions. So he had to go seek for more melodious-minded men and fair unambiguous women. But rebuffs can deal more deadly blows than daggers; he became timid—a timidity not of fear but of pride—and grew with the years into misanthropy, susceptible to trivial griefs and despairs, a vessel of emotion that emptied as easily as it filled, until he came at last to know that his griefs were half deliberate, his despairs half unreal, and to live but for beauty—which is tranquility—to put her wooing hand upon him.

Now, while the mouse hunts in the cupboard, one fair recollection stirs in the man's mind—of Cassia and the harmony of their only meeting. Cassia who had such rich red hair, and eyes, yes, her eyes were full of starry inquiry like the eyes of mice. It was so long ago that

he had forgotten how he came to be in it, that unaccustomed orbit of
vain vivid things—a village festival, all oranges and houp-la. He could
not remember how he came to be there, but at night, in the court hall,
he had danced with Cassia—fair and unambiguous indeed!—who had
come like the wind from among the roses and swept into his heart.

"It is easy to guess," he had said to her, "what you like most in
the world."

She laughed, "To dance? Yes, and you . . . ?"

"To find a friend."

"I know, I know," she cried, caressing him with recognitions. "Ah,
at times I quite love my friends—until I begin to wonder how much
they hate me!"

He had loved at once that cool pale face, the abundance of her
hair as light as the autumn's clustered bronze, her lilac dress and all
the sweetness about her like a bush of lilies. How they had laughed at
the two old peasants whom they had overheard gabbling of trifles like
sickness and appetite!

"There's a lot of nature in a parsnip," said one, a fat person of the
kind that swells grossly when stung by a bee, "a lot of nature when it's
young, but when it's old it's like everything else."

"True it is."

"And I'm very fond of vegetables, yes, and I'm very fond of bread."

"Come out with me," whispered Cassia to Filip, and they walked
out in the blackness of midnight into what must have been a garden.

"Cool it is here," she said, "and quiet, but too dark even to see
your face—can you see mine?"

"The moon will not rise until after dawn," said he, "it will be white
in the sky when the starlings whistle in your chimney."

They walked silently and warily about until they felt the chill of
the air. A dull echo of the music came to them through the walls, then
stopped, and they heard the bark of a fox away in the woods.

"You are cold," he whispered, touching her bare neck with timid
fingers. "Quite, quite cold," drawing his hand tenderly over the curves
of her chin and face. "Let us go in," he said, moving with discretion
from the rapture he desired.

"We will come out again," said Cassia.

But within the room the ball was just at an end, the musicians were packing up their instruments and the dancers were flocking out and homewards, or to the buffet which was on a platform at one end of the room. The two old peasants were there, munching hugely.

"I tell you," said one of them, "there's nothing in the world for it but the grease of an owl's liver. That's it, that's it! Take some thing on your stomach now, just to offset the chill of the dawn!"

Filip and Cassia were beside them, but there were so many people crowding the platform that Filip had to jump down. He stood then looking up adoringly at Cassia, who had pulled a purple cloak about her.

"For Filip, Filip, Filip," she said, pushing the last bite of her sandwich into his mouth and pressing upon him her glass of Loupiac. Quickly he drank it with a great gesture, and flinging the glass to the wall, took Cassia into his arms, shouting: "I'll carry you home, the whole way home, yes, I'll carry you!"

"Put me down!" she cried, beating his head and pulling his ear, as they passed among the departing dancers. "Put me down, you wild thing!"

Dark, dark was the lane outside, and the night an obsidian net, into which he walked carrying the girl. But her arms were looped around him; she discovered paths for him, clinging more tightly as he staggered against a wall, stumbled upon a gulley, or when her sweet hair was caught in the boughs of a little lime tree.

"Do not loose me, Filip, will you? Do not loose me," Cassia said, putting her lips against his temple.

His brain seemed bursting, his heart rocked within him, but he adored the rich grace of her limbs against his breast. "Here it is," she murmured, and he carried her into a path that led to her home in a little lawned garden where the smell of ripe apples upon the branches and the heavy lustre of roses stole upon the air. Roses and apples! Roses and apples! He carried her right into the porch before she slid down and stood close to him with her hands still upon his shoulders. He could breathe happily at the release, standing silent and looking round at the sky sprayed with wondrous stars but without a moon.

"You are stronger than I thought you, stronger than you look; you are really very strong," she whispered, nodding her head to him. Opening the buttons of his coat, she put her palm against his breast.

"Oh, how your heart does beat! Does it beat truly—and for whom?"

He had seized her wrists in a little fury of love, crying: "Little mother, little mother!"

"What are you saying?" asked the girl; but before he could continue there came a footstep sounding behind the door, and the clack of a bolt. . . .

What was that? Was that really a bolt or was it . . . was it . . . the snap of the trap? The man sat up in his room intently listening, with nerves quivering again, waiting for the trap to kill the little philosopher. When he felt it was all over he reached guardedly in the darkness for the lantern, turned on the beam, and opened the door of the cupboard. Focussing the light upon the trap, he was amazed to see the mouse sitting on its haunches before it, uncaught. Its head was bowed, but its bead-like eyes were full of brightness, and it sat blinking, it did not flee.

"Shoosh!" said the man, but the mouse did not move. "Why doesn't it go? Shoosh!" he said again, and suddenly the reason of the mouse's strange behavior was made clear. The trap had not caught it completely, but it had broken off both its forefeet, and the thing crouched there holding out its two bleeding stumps humanly, too stricken to stir.

Horror flooded the man, and conquering his repugnance he plucked the mouse up quickly by the neck. Immediately the thing fastened its teeth in his finger; the touch was no more than the slight prick of a pin. The man's impulse then exhausted itself. What should he do with it? He put his hand behind him, he dared not look, but there was nothing to be done except kill it at once, quickly, quickly. Oh, how should he do it? He bent towards the fire as if to drop the mouse into its quenching glow; but he paused and shuddered, he would hear its cries, he would have to listen. Should he crush it with finger and thumb? A glance towards the window decided him. He opened the sash with one hand and flung the wounded mouse far into the dark street. Closing the window with a crash, he sank into a chair, limp with pity too deep for tears.

So he sat for two minutes, five minutes, ten minutes. Anxiety and shame filled him with heat. He opened the window again, and the freezing air poured in and cooled him. Seizing his lantern, he ran down the echoing stairs, into the dark empty street, searching long and vainly for the little philosopher until he had to desist and return to his room, shivering, frozen to his very bones.

When he had recovered some warmth he took the trap from its shelf. The two feet dropped into his hand; he cast them into the fire. Then he once more set the trap and put it back carefully into the cupboard.

SHOOTING AN ELEPHANT
–George Orwell–

In Moulmein, in Lower Burma, I was hated by large numbers of people—the only time in my life that I have been important enough for this to happen to me. I was sub-divisional police officer of the town, and in an aimless, petty kind of way anti-European feeling was very bitter. No one had the guts to raise a riot, but if a European woman went through the bazaars alone somebody would probably spit betel juice over her dress. As a police officer I was an obvious target and was baited whenever it seemed safe to do so. When a nimble Burman tripped me up on the football field and the referee (another Burman) looked the other way, the crowd yelled with hideous laughter. This happened more than once. In the end the sneering yellow faces of young men that met me everywhere, the insults hooted after me when I was at a safe distance, got badly on my nerves. The young Buddhist priests were the worst of all. There were several thousands of them in the town and none of them seemed to have anything to do except stand on street corners and jeer at Europeans.

All this was perplexing and upsetting. For at that time I had already made up my mind that imperialism was an evil thing and the sooner I chucked up my job and got out of it the better. Theoretically—and secretly, of course—I was all for the Burmese and all against their oppressors, the British. As for the job I was doing, I hated it more bitterly than I can perhaps make clear. In a job like that you see the dirty work of Empire at close quarters. The wretched prisoners huddling in the stinking cages of the lock-ups, the grey, cowed faces of the long-term convicts, the scarred buttocks of the men who had been flogged with bamboos—all these oppressed me with an intolerable sense of guilt. But I could get nothing into perspective. I was young and ill-educated and I had had to think out my problems in the utter silence that is imposed on every Englishman in the East. I did not even know that the British Empire is dying, still less did I know that it is a great deal better than the younger empires that are going to supplant it. All I knew was that I was stuck between my hatred of the empire I served and my rage against the evil-spirited little beasts who tried to make my job impossible. With one part of my mind I thought of the British Raj as an unbreakable tyranny, as something clamped down, in *saecula saeculorum*, upon the will of prostrate peoples; with another part I thought that the greatest joy in the world would be to drive a bayonet into a Buddhist priest's guts. Feelings like these are the normal by-products of imperialism; ask any Anglo-Indian official, if you can catch him off duty.

One day something happened which in a roundabout way was enlightening. It was a tiny incident in itself, but it gave me a better glimpse than I had had before of the real nature of imperialism—the real motives for which despotic governments act. Early one morning the sub-inspector at a police station the other end of the town rang me up on the phone and said that an elephant was ravaging the bazaar. Would I please come and do something about it? I did not know what I could do, but I wanted to see what was happening and I got on to a pony and started out. I took my rifle, an old .44 Winchester and much too small to kill an elephant, but I thought the noise might be useful *in terrorem*. Various Burmans stopped me on the way and told me about the elephant's doings. It was not, of course, a wild elephant, but a tame one which had gone "must." It had been chained up, as tame elephants always are when their attack of "must" is due, but on the previous night it had broken its chain and escaped. Its mahout, the only person who could manage it when it was in that state, had set out in pursuit, but had taken the wrong direction and was now twelve hours' journey away, and in the morning the elephant had suddenly reappeared in the town. The Burmese population had no weapons and were quite helpless against it. It had already destroyed somebody's bamboo hut, killed a cow and raided some fruit-stalls and devoured the stock; also it had met the municipal rubbish van, and, when the driver jumped out and took to his heels, had turned the van over and inflicted violences upon it.

The Burmese sub-inspector and some Indian constables were waiting for me in the quarter where the elephant had been seen. It was a very poor quarter, a labyrinth of squalid bamboo huts, thatched with palm-leaf, winding all over a steep hillside. I remember that it was a cloudy, stuffy morning at the beginning of the rains. We began questioning the people as to where the elephant had gone, and, as usual, failed to get any definite information. That is invariably the case in the East; a story always sounds clear enough at a distance, but the nearer you get to the scene of events the vaguer it becomes. Some of the people said that the elephant had gone in one direction, some said that he had gone in another, some professed not even to have heard of any elephant. I had almost made up my mind that the whole story was a pack of lies, when we heard yells a little distance away. There was a loud, scandalized cry of "Go away, child! Go away this instant!" and an old woman with a switch in her hand came round the corner of a hut, violently shooing away a crowd of naked children. Some more women followed, clicking their tongues and exclaiming; evidently there was something that the children ought not to have seen. I rounded the hut and saw a man's dead body sprawling in the mud. He was an Indian, a black Dravidian coolie, almost naked, and he could not have been dead many minutes. The people said that the elephant had come suddenly upon him round the corner of the hut, caught him with its trunk, put its foot on his back and ground him into the earth. This was the rainy season and the ground was soft, and his face had scored a trench a foot deep and a couple of yards long. He was lying on his belly with arms crucified and head sharply twisted to one side. His face was coated with mud, the eyes wide open, the teeth bared and grinning with an expression of unendurable agony. (Never tell me, by the way, that the dead look peaceful. Most of the corpses I have seen looked devilish.) The friction of the great beast's foot had stripped the skin from his back as neatly as one skins a rabbit. As soon as I saw the dead man I sent an orderly to a friend's house nearby to borrow an elephant rifle. I had already sent back the pony, not wanting it to go mad with fright and throw me if it smelt the elephant.

The orderly came back in a few minutes with a rifle and five cartridges, and meanwhile some Burmans had arrived and told us that the elephant was in the paddy fields below, only a few hundred yards away. As I started forward practically the whole population of the quarter flocked out of the houses and followed me. They had seen the rifle and were all shouting excitedly that I was going to shoot the elephant. They had not shown much interest in the elephant when he was merely ravaging their homes, but it was different now that he was going to be shot. It was a bit of fun to them, as it would be to an English crowd; besides they wanted the meat. It made me vaguely uneasy. I had no intention of shooting the elephant—I had merely sent for the rifle to defend myself if necessary—and it is always unnerving to have a crowd following you. I marched down the hill, looking and feeling a fool, with the rifle over my shoulder and an ever-growing army of people jostling at my heels. At the bottom, when you got away from the huts, there was a metalled road and beyond that a miry waste of paddy fields a thousand yards across, not yet ploughed but soggy from the first rains and dotted with coarse grass. The elephant was standing eight yards from the road, his left side towards us. He took not the slightest notice of the crowd's approach. He was tearing up bunches of grass, beating them against his knees to clean them and stuffing them into his mouth.

I had halted on the road. As soon as I saw the elephant I knew with perfect certainty that I ought not to shoot him. It is a serious matter to shoot a working elephant—it is comparable to destroying a huge and costly piece of machinery—and obviously one ought not to do it if it can possibly be avoided. And at that distance, peacefully eating, the elephant looked no more dangerous than a cow. I thought then and I think now that his attack of "must" was already passing off; in which case he would merely wander harmlessly about until the mahout came back and caught him. Moreover, I did not in the least want to shoot him. I decided that I would watch him for a little while to make sure that he did not turn savage again, and then go home.

But at that moment I glanced round at the crowd that had followed me. It was an immense crowd, two thousand at the least and growing every minute. It blocked the road for a long distance on either side. I looked at the sea of yellow faces above the garish clothes—faces all happy and excited over this bit of fun, all certain that the elephant was going to be shot. They were watching me as they would watch a conjurer about to perform a trick. They did not like me, but with the magical rifle in my hands I was momentarily worth watching. And suddenly I realized that I should have to shoot the elephant after all. The people expected it of me and I had got to do it; I could feel their two thousand wills pressing me forward, irresistibly. And it was at this moment, as I stood there with the rifle in my hands, that I first grasped the hollowness, the futility of the white man's dominion in the East. Here was I, the white man with his gun, standing in front of the unarmed native crowd—seemingly the leading actor of the piece; but in reality I was only an absurd puppet pushed to and fro by the will of those yellow faces behind. I perceived in this moment that when the white man turns tyrant it is his own freedom that he destroys. He becomes a sort of hollow, posing dummy, the conventionalized figure of a sahib. For it is the condition of his rule that he shall spend his life in trying to impress the "natives," and so in every crisis he has got to do what the "natives" expect of him. He wears a mask, and his face grows to fit it. I had got to shoot the elephant. I had committed myself to doing it when I sent for the rifle. A sahib has got to act like a sahib; he has got to appear resolute, to know his own mind and do definite things. To come all that way, rifle in hand, with two thousand people marching at my heels, and then to trail feebly away, having done nothing—no, that was impossible. The crowd would laugh at me.

And my whole life, every white man's life in the East, was one long struggle not to be laughed at.

But I did not want to shoot the elephant. I watched him beating his bunch of grass against his knees, with that preoccupied grandmotherly air that elephants have. It seemed to me that it would be murder to shoot him. At that age I was not squeamish about killing animals, but I had never shot an elephant and never wanted to. (Somehow it always seems worse to kill a *large* animal.) Besides, there was the beast's owner to be considered. Alive, the elephant was worth at least a hundred pounds; dead, he would only be worth the value of his tusks, five pounds, possibly. But I had got to act quickly. I turned to some experienced-looking Burmans who had been there when we arrived, and asked them how the elephant had been behaving. They all said the same thing: he took no notice of you if you left him alone, but he might charge if you went too close to him.

It was perfectly clear to me what I ought to do. I ought to walk up to within, say, twenty-five yards of the elephant and test his behaviour. If he charged I could shoot, if he took no notice of me it would be safe to leave him until the mahout came back. But also I knew that I was going to do no such thing. I was a poor shot with a rifle and the ground was soft mud into which one would sink at every step. If the elephant charged and I missed him, I should have about as much chance as a toad under a steam-roller. But even then I was not thinking particularly of my own skin, only of the watchful yellow faces behind. For at that moment, with the crowd watching me, I was not afraid in the ordinary sense, as I would have been if I had been alone. A white man mustn't be frightened in front of "natives"; and so, in general, he isn't frightened. The sole thought in my mind was that if anything went wrong those two thousand Burmans would see me pursued, caught, trampled on and reduced to a grinning corpse like that Indian up the hill. And if that happened it was quite probable that some of them would laugh. That would never do. There was only one alternative. I shoved the cartridges into the magazine and lay down on the road to get a better aim.

The crowd grew very still, and a deep, low, happy sigh, as of people who see the theatre curtain go up at last, breathed from innumerable throats. They were going to have their bit of fun after all. The rifle was a beautiful German thing with cross-hair sights. I did not then know that in shooting an elephant one should shoot to cut an imaginary bar running from ear-hole to ear-hole. I ought, therefore, as the elephant was sideways on, to have aimed straight at his ear-hole; actually I aimed several inches in front of this, thinking the brain would be further forward.

When I pulled the trigger I did not hear the bang or feel the kick—one never does when a shot goes home—but I heard the devilish roar of glee that went up from the crowd. In that instant, in too short a time, one would have thought, even for the bullet to get there, a mysterious, terrible change had come over the elephant. He neither stirred nor fell, but every line of his body had altered. He looked suddenly stricken, shrunken, immensely old, as though the frightful impact of the bullet had paralysed him without knocking him down. At last, after what seemed a long time—it might have been five seconds, I dare say—he sagged flabbily to his knees. His mouth slobbered. An enormous senility seemed to have settled upon him. One could have imagined him thousands of years old. I fired again into the same spot. At the second shot he did not collapse but climbed with desperate slowness to his feet and stood weakly upright, with legs sagging and head drooping. I fired a third time. That was the shot that did for him. You could see the agony of it jolt his whole body and knock the last remnant of strength from his legs. But in falling he seemed for a moment to rise, for as his hind legs collapsed beneath him he seemed to tower upwards like a huge rock toppling, his trunk reaching skywards like a tree. He trumpeted, for the first and only time. And then down he came, his belly towards me, with a crash that seemed to shake the ground even where I lay.

I got up. The Burmans were already racing past me across the mud. It was obvious that the elephant would never rise again, but he was not dead. He was breathing very rhythmically with long rattling gasps, his great mound of a side painfully rising and falling. His mouth was wide open—I could see far down into caverns of pale pink throat. I waited a long time for him to die, but his breathing did not weaken. Finally I fired my two remaining shots into the spot where I thought his heart must be. The thick blood welled out of him like red velvet, but still he did not die. His body did not even jerk when the shots hit him, the tortured breathing continued without a pause. He was dying, very slowly and in great agony, but in some world remote from me where not even a bullet could damage him further. I felt that I had got to put an end to that dreadful noise. It seemed dreadful to see the great beast lying there, powerless to move and yet powerless to die, and not even to be able to finish him. I sent back for my small rifle and poured shot after shot into his heart and down his throat. They seemed to make no impression. The tortured gasps continued as steadily as the ticking of a clock.

In the end I could not stand it any longer and went away. I heard later that it took him half an hour to die. Burmans were bringing dahs and baskets even before I left, and I was told they had stripped his body almost to the bones by the afternoon.

Afterwards, of course, there were endless discussions about the shooting of the elephant. The owner was furious, but he was only an Indian and could do nothing. Besides, legally I had done the right thing, for a mad elephant has to be killed, like a mad dog, if its owner fails to control it. Among the Europeans opinion was divided. The older men said I was right, the younger men said it was a damn shame to shoot an elephant for killing a coolie, because an elephant was worth more than any damn Coringhee coolie. And afterwards I was very glad that the coolie had been killed; it put me legally in the right and it gave me a sufficient pretext for shooting the elephant. I often wondered whether any of the others grasped that I had done it solely to avoid looking a fool.

THE JACK RABBIT DRIVE
–Robert McAlmon–

It was agreed upon by members of the community that the thousands of jack rabbits throughout the countryside must be exterminated, in part at least. Their burrowings and nibblings destroyed too much grain and property. So for two weeks the day set for a drive was given wide publicity.

Horace slipped out of the house through the kitchen, stopping there to sneak cookies from under Linda's eyes. At the moment, however, she was feeling in good humor, and her black face, already gleaming with perspiration, gleamed more with a tender smiling at his six-year-old guile, and she gave him six cookies, whereupon he went joyfully into the back yard to look hopefully about. Maybe Freddie was around to be played with. He didn't like Freddie much but he was better than nobody. Horace felt uncomfortable because his mother had put a new suit on him, and made him wear an overcoat, and if Billie Anderson saw him with his yellow hair slicked back Billie might call him "mamma's boy" and that would mean another fight, because he and Billie were supposed to have a great scrap someday to show which was the best fighter in town of their age.

It was somewhat sheepishly that he began to play with Sally Porter a few minutes later. She was more fun to be with than Freddie, if she only weren't a girl. She dared do anything, and wasn't nearly so scared of going blocks from home if she could without her mother seeing and calling her back to play on the Porters' front lawn. Horace didn't want to play there because every boy in the neighborhood could see, and Sally might want to play doll house, which Horace didn't mind if Billie Anderson wasn't apt to know about it. The Porter horse, that was to run in the County Fair races, was picketed on the lawn too, and he'd stepped on Horace's bare foot one day when Horace was petting him. That was no fun, you can bet. The horse didn't mean to maybe, but Horace didn't want that to happen again.

As playing on the lawn was no fun at all Horace and Sally were out in back of the barn, almost without thinking to get there. It was the

alley they were supposed not to play in too, because the nigger washer-
woman's kids played there, since their ma's shack sat on top of the
alley. Mrs. Darian told Horace there wasn't any harm in his playing
with the colored children, but Mrs. Porter wouldn't let Sally. They had
not been there long, however, before Horace got scared, remembering
that he'd killed one of those niggers' chickens by hitting it on the head
with a stone he'd thrown; except he hadn't really killed it. He had only
stunned it, because when he and the nigger kids, all scared of what
their mas would say, buried the rooster in the manure pile, it began
to flop and finally got up and ran away, dizzy in the head. Maybe Mrs.
Lincoln, the nigger woman, wasn't mad at him though, because she
had sent him an egg no bigger than a robin's that one of her hens had
laid, but he didn't know. Maybe she'd just sent it to please his mother
for whom she did washing.

"We gotta go somewhere else and play because I'm not going to
have them darkie kids butting in on us. I have an idea anyway. Billie
Anderson says you can get a cent a bottle for beer bottles from the
bartender at the saloon."

"Why you awful boy, Horace. If we did that we'd just get the hide
licked off us and you know it," Sally said, pretending great horror. "Why
mamma is always giving it to papa because he goes in there and if she
heard I did that! And she would because someone would tell her."

"Aw rats, don't be a fraidy cat."

"You know I ain't no fraidy cat."

"Maybe you ain't, but Freddie is. I ast him yesterday to look for beer
bottles with me and he wouldn't, and he cried and ran home and we
scrapped, and he was going to tell on me, but I didn't care. I told him

'Tattle-tale, tattle-tale,
Hanging to the bull's tail—'"

"You are the naughtiest boy," Sally said with triumphant righteous-
ness, and so daring Horace, encouraged him to the scandalous conclusion of the ditty. Sally believed it her duty to act shocked and refuse
to speak to Horace for a few seconds, but the strain of that soon told
on her, and being sure that no older person had heard Horace, she
relaxed to curiosity.

"Where do you suppose we can find some beer bottles?" she asked. "We could hide them and collect a lot and then maybe get in the back door of the saloon and Mr. Murphy wouldn't tell on us."

After an hour's search in the alleys Sally had found one bottle that might be a beer bottle, or even a whiskey bottle, and Horace had found three bottles that he was sure were beer bottles, as he was sure Sally's was only a pop bottle. So the two went around to the alley behind the main street until they came to the backshed entrance to the saloon. They were afraid to go in, but after a consultation decided they'd better go in together and both get lickings if they were caught.

"The men will take it more like a joke if you're there," Horace sagely informed Sally. "They always think girls don't know nothing."

Sidling up to the bar inside Sally looked discreetly wide-eyed and innocent as she piped up, "I'se got some beer bottles, Mr. Man. P'ease give me some pennies for them." Horace was too scared to notice much that Sally was putting on baby accents.

"Well, I'll be—" Murphy, the bartender, started to say, but checked his profanity. "You kids will get paddled if your families hear you're coming in here. You'd better beat it quick. You'll get me in trouble too if they hear I let you in."

"We want candy." Horace broke in, feeling more at ease as he sensed that Murphy was a companion in guilt. "Just this once buy these bottles." His heart was going at a terrific pace and he felt uncomfortable because of many strange men about the bar who had laughed raucously at him and Sally.

"Here's a nickel. Now quick and beat it, kiddies," Murphy said and handed Horace the money.

"Don't I get none too?" lisped Sally.

"Divide that, you two kids. You'll founder yourself on all day suckers or cheap chocolates if I give you more," Murphy explained good naturedly, leaning over to pat Sally's tow head, and to tweak at one of her braids. He relented, however, and slipped her a nickel too, so she and Horace went happily out of the saloon, in their glee carelessly going through the front door, when they quickly remembered and were scared.

"O golly, Sally. I'll bet yer pa can see us because his office is right across the street."

"It ain't papa I care about knowing. He wouldn't lick me and he wouldn't dare tell mamma on me either, because she'd say that was his blood coming out in me. That's what she always says when she licks me."

The children now felt completely involved in guilt and decided it wasn't any use resisting temptation any more that afternoon, so they bought some all day suckers, and gum, and chocolates. They walked down the main street and soon came to the edge of the town where Daly's pasture was. It was a warm autumn afternoon, but too chilly to sit on the bank of the pond long, and few minnows were to be seen in the muddy water. A few cows were grazing on the dry grass in the pasture, but the children saw that they didn't come too near.

"I wonder which gives the most milk, the papa or the mamma cow," Horace queried, remembering the cow his father had sold because she went dry.

"It ought to be the papa cow because that's how cows support themselves, and the papa ought to always support the family, but mamma says it ain't so with us, cause papa drinks up everything he makes. I like pap better though. He isn't cranky every minute of the day."

This problem did not interest Horace much. He was full of candy, and drowsy in the sun except that it was cold on his pants when he sat on the ground. As his mind wandered he remembered that his brother Ralph had spoken of a jack rabbit drive at the breakfast table. That had excited Horace, but his mother told him of course he couldn't watch anything so brutal.

"I tell you, Sally," Horace said, "there's a jack rabbit drive to end up at the corner down the road. Let's run down there and see if there's any sign of it."

Since ten o'clock in the morning groups of men and boys had been occupied with the jack rabbit drive. On every side for miles from town, farmers, farm boys, and all the countless dogs of the countryside had been scouring the land to scare up rabbits. The clamor of guns firing, dogs barking, men shouting and beating with clubs, and horses trampling about was calculated to terrify all the rabbits who came within the range of the two semicircles of inclosing rabbit hunters.

It was by now four o'clock in the afternoon and evening chill was coming into the air. Going to the corner fence Horace knew of, Sally and he soon began to discern noises of the drive off in the distance. Now and then there was an echo or re-echo of a gunshot. Faintly, as though imagined, the resonance of a shot would sound, though neither Sally nor Horace could verify any one report as the noises were becoming more clear and decisive, or their expectant senses made them alert.

"I saw Dingo, pa's half-breed hunter dog, tear up a rabbit's burrow once, and he just ripped that rabbit all to pieces," Sally said. "That made pa mad because it showed that Dingo was no good as a hunter to tear game to pieces. That rabbit squealed once when Dingo grabbed it but it just squealed once."

"Ralph said he bet all the rabbit burrows in the country would be dug open, there are so many dogs," Horace volunteered. "I've never seen a jack rabbit. Only them pet rabbits I had when I was a baby two years ago. Gosh, I was mad at mamma for making me wear skirts a whole year after Billie had been wearing pants, but it wasn't as bad as Freddie having to wear long hair up till just last month. His mamma wants to make a girlboy out of him."

Fifteen minutes passed, with sounds of the drive coming clearly to them, and again seeming to grow dimmer, until finally the resonance of noises became continually louder. The distinguishable bark of dogs could be heard: the baying of hounds, the yipe of fox terriers, the excited joyful bark of mongrels, and the general hysteria of all the dogs' excitement. It was infrequently that a gun was fired.

Suddenly there was a rush of men from across the fields on every side, and they were shouting at each other.

"Here you are, boys; here you are." "Get in on every side." "Get your clubs ready. Knock them out as fast as they come hurtling against the fence." "They'll be here in thousands inside of three minutes." "Kill 'em at one blow."

From the village, men, women, and children, too, had begun to arrive for the end-up of the drive, the sounds of which had echoed through the town for the last half-hour. A share of even the women from the village carried clubs, or limbs of trees, and all the men and boys in the drive were so armed. The hullabaloo grew greater, with cursings, leaping about, and rabbit-threatening gesticulations in mock display of what they'd do to the rabbits.

The rabbits began coming. Tearing along, panic-struck huge white jack rabbits catapulted across the prairie towards the fence corner. Men on horses, men on foot, and dogs with lapping slobbery tongues circled in on them. The rabbits hurled themselves on at leaps of twenty, thirty, or even forty feet in the case of the huge-sized jacks. Shrilly, above the pandemonium a shriek of rabbit pain sounded now and then as some dog captured a jack and ripped it to bits.

Horace and Sally, standing near the front of the spectators, watched feverishly. Rabbits smashed into the impenetrable fence to be beaten on the head by men or boys jumping about. Before struck, terror was making the rabbits squeal. A continuous ripping, tearing sound, punctuated by the thump, thump, thump of clubs against the light-boned heads of the rabbits, went on.

At one moment Horace saw a rabbit caught by a great lean greyhound. Within a second another dog had caught the same rabbit by another portion of its body. Horace heard the squeal of that rabbit, saw the look of rodent terror in its eyes, and—dizzy within himself—heard the rip of the body. A stunned feeling held him, watching as though hypnotized. He was biting his lips and twitching his face nervously, unaware of himself or of his reactions to what he was seeing. It didn't seem that what he was seeing was actual. The jack rabbits looked so powerful and electric as they came across the prairie, and so limp, like damp besmudged cotton, as they lay torn upon the ground with the yellow of their hides, and the red of their interiors, showing.

Shortly the thing was done with. Heaped in piles against the fence were more than a thousand rabbit bodies. Their dull, glazed, half-open eyes, Horace noticed. He lingered, half wondering if they might not move again. Surely something more was going to happen after all this excitement.

"What happens to rabbits when they're dead?" Horace wondered, dazedly curious, to Sally, having heard of death before, but never having realized what it might mean.

"Huh, listen to the kid. Say sonny, them jacks is dead, and dead they'll stay and not be destroying crops on us farmers," a heavy-set man said with rough good nature to Horace, who shrank within himself from the obscenity, to him, of the man's manner. Yet his wonder made him speak in mechanical bewilderment.

"But they were alive just a few minutes ago."

"Sure kid, but they ain't now. We saw to that."

Horace didn't know how to think, and maybe he was afraid but not in a way he could cry about, or that he could ask his mother about. What if something began chasing people like the rabbits had been chased?

Sally was ready to go home, though she was still looking fascinatedly at the pile of rabbits. Horace had a moment of aversion to her because she leaned over and touched one, and didn't seem to feel sorry for it. A farm boy picked up a little mutilated rabbit and handed it to her. "Here, girlie," he told her, patting her head, "take this home to your mamma and have her cook it for you. It's nicer than chicken."

Sally took the rabbit and started to follow Horace, who had walked ahead of her. She caught up to him.

"You aren't going to take that rabbit home, are you? You couldn't eat it, could you?"

"Why not? Mamma feeds us rabbits lots of times."

"But it's dead," Horace explained.

"Every meat you eat is. That's what happens to all the cows that get shipped out of the stock yard every week."

Horace's mind was stalled. He couldn't think. He changed the topic. "I'll bet them rabbits were stronger than you or me. I'll bet we couldn't have held one without its kicking away because a man I saw grab a live one could hardly hold it."

Sally, becoming conscious that Horace walked away from her because she was carrying the rabbit, threw it aside with a quick gesture and said, "Nasty dead thing."

"It isn't its fault it's nasty," Horace said.

"I think it's awful. The poor rabbits."

"I don't know whether it's awful or not. People said it was a good thing to get rid of them."

When Horace and Sally got back to their houses they separated. Horace went through the kitchen, not even noticing Linda. In the sitting room he avoided speaking to his mother and, taking up a picture book, buried himself in the big easy chair. There was much he wanted to know but he didn't want his mother to know he had seen the jack rabbit drive.

Continually his mind reverted to the rabbits, how their white furry flesh had been torn, their squeals, the fear in their eyes. As he sat trying to think his mind was filled, not with definite pictures of rabbits, but with a flood of nervous images of rabbit carnage that made him shudder and want to shut the thought out. But he didn't try to look at his book. He even felt impatient with his mother when she began talking to him and so prevented him from thinking about the rabbits. He liked to think that as he shuddered he was trying to shut out the white ripping and squealing image.

Through dinnertime Horace was very quiet, and his mother asked him if he didn't feel very well.

"Rats, sick," his brother Ralph said. "Don't baby him. He's probably been up to something and keeps quiet not to give himself away."

"Nonsense, Ralph," his mother answered. "I can see that the boy is pale, and his eyes have a feverish look. Don't think I don't know children better than my own son knows them. Think of your wanting to let him see the rabbit drive. At his age what would you have thought? He's been hearing about that brutal affair I'm sure."

Soon after dinner Horace was sent up to bed, where, after saying his prayers, he was left, and ducked his head under the covers as soon as his mother was out of the room and he was alone in darkness. He began to tell himself a long story about a rabbit drive, except that the rabbit drive would come later on in the story. He kept delaying it, wanting a very exciting situation to work up to. Gradually, however, sleep overtook him, in spite of his fear in the dark, out of which anything might come. Suppose a great jack rabbit leaped right on him through the open window. He wouldn't know what to do then. He lay still, except that at imagined sounds he peeked from under the covers. At one moment he was sure there was something standing at the foot of his bed, but he knew he'd get scolded and teased if he called out, or ran downstairs, and he would have to say of course he didn't believe in boogie mans. He wondered if Sally was scared in the dark too, if she really was, but maybe she wouldn't say so any more than he would.

He was standing way out in the dark fields, and everywhere rabbits were nibbling about him, so many that he could not walk without stepping on them. They nibbled at his feet too, trying to eat him up. And one came running terrifically to leap at him; and after him many others came, running straight at him to knock him down and cover his face and body with their cottony bodies. They would smother him like the two princes smothered by their uncle. He couldn't move and they kept coming. Awaking, he moaned, and then, knowing it was a dream, kept quiet with his fear. Looking out from under his covers he saw the moon shining through the window, so that he could see there was no one, only his coat, at the foot of his bed. Half of his room was almost in day lightness, but back there in the corner, or in the closet—

He wanted to cry, almost, but nobody he wanted would hear him, and if there was somebody back in the corner and they heard him they'd know he was afraid. He must not cry, so as to be able to speak if they came over to get him. He must tell them that they dare not touch him; that he wasn't scared.

At last he went to sleep again.

III

OTHER ANIMALS AS COMPANIONS
||||||||||||||||||||||||||

PILLING THE CAT
—Cleveland Amory—

In any case, I remember well the first time I ever gave Polar Bear a pill. It was late in February, sometime after I had come back from California. As is my wont in such matters, before embarking on such a major enterprise as giving him a pill, I had decided, rather than embarrass myself with Dr. Thompson, I would consult other authorities on this subject. To my surprise, I discovered that there were many articles on either the general or specific topic. The fact that there were so many, I recognized, was hardly a good sign. But I tackled them anyway.

My favorite was an article by Susan Easterly entitled "How to Pill Your Cat." The reason this was my favorite was that Ms. Easterly seemed to address her work to those of us who had, as she put it, a cat of "the independent type"—one whom she identified as one "not prone to doing what you would like him to do."

That certainly, I thought, was Polar Bear. Indeed, he was so far from being "prone" to doing what I would like him to do in such a situation as being pilled that I decided the article could indeed have been written just for him. Without further ado I seized it eagerly.

"First of all," Ms. Easterly wrote, "do not advance upon your cat with feelings of abject terror. Think positively and have the pill ready."

Those were fighting words, and my thoughts harkened back to my Boston ancestor Colonel William Prescott and the Battle of Bunker Hill. If there was one thing I was determined I would not show, it would be terror, and certainly not "abject" terror. Polar Bear would never, I resolved, no matter how difficult the operation to come, see the whites of my eyes. As for thinking positively, my thoughts that first time I advanced on Polar Bear were so positive that I really felt, at that moment, I could have pilled a leopard. And my pill, though well hidden in the palm of my left hand, secured by my fourth finger—so that he would see the rest of my fingers normally extended—was just where I wanted it.

The trouble was that Polar Bear had apparently thoughts which were far from positive. They were, in fact, so negative that I was convinced that he had, by some dastardly subterfuge, where my positives were concerned, broken the code. Indeed, as I advanced on him he seemed to know that not only was I up to something but also that whatever this something was, it was not something he wanted to have anything to do with. And furthermore, some way, somehow, he knew about the pill. As he retreated as negatively as I positively advanced, there was no mistaking the fact that his eyes were riveted on what I thought I had so deftly hidden.

At this juncture I decided that not to advance farther was definitely the better part of valor. Rather I felt I should just hold the line at the ground I had already taken, and dig in. Meanwhile, I turned again to Ms. Easterly. I was sure she would have wise counsel for this kind of stalemate. And I was right. The only trouble was her advice was all too reminiscent of the advice I had received from another source, as all those of you with good memories will recall, about my cat's bath.

"Wrap your cat in a large towel," Ms. Easterly had written, "leaving only the head exposed. This prevents loss of your blood due to flailing claws." I was fully prepared to give blood in reasonable amounts, but

I was by no means big on wrapping Polar Bear in a towel. And, I soon learned, after cornering him, neither was he. Nonetheless, I had vowed to follow Ms. Easterly's advice to the letter, and I proceeded to do so.

"Hold the cat firmly against you," Ms. Easterly's advice continued, "in the crook of your arm and on your lap. This allows both your hands to remain free."

Since one of my hands was limited by my arm crook, and the other one by the pill, they were hardly free, but I did my best. And I'm sure Ms. Easterly's advice worked like a charm with her cat—albeit I could not help suspecting that her cat must have been very small, very old, and very sick, if indeed alive at all, when she performed this maneuver. Or that perhaps she has a black belt in karate. In any case, her suggestion did not work with Polar Bear. He shot out of the towel like a dart out of a blowgun.

I am, however, no quitter. I caught him and recovered him—literally in fact with the towel—and this time, instead of my first gentle crook of the arm I held him in such a viselike grip that I elicited from him one of the most baleful "Aeiou"'s [sic] I had ever heard. I pretended, of course, that I hadn't heard it, meanwhile reading on by holding the article with my half-free pill hand.

"Place your hand over the cat's head," Ms. Easterly stalwartly continued, apparently at this time engaging a third hand, "using the thumb or forefinger, whichever is preferred, to grasp each corner of the cat's jaw. Apply slight pressure and its mouth will open."

Once more I took Ms. Easterly at her word as best I could, using the crook arm hand. I applied first, as she had suggested, slight pressure. Then I applied slightly more pressure. And finally I applied enough pressure to open the mouth of a crocodile.

The problem was that the mouth did not open. It did not open as much as a single solitary slit. Reluctantly I decided to modify Ms. Easterly's instructions. I took my index finger and, using it like an awl, worked my way into Polar Bear's mouth, a little back of his teeth. At last I had my whole finger in and across his mouth—like a bit in the mouth of a horse. And of course Polar Bear did just what a horse would do—he bit on the bit.

Go ahead, I told him, bite the hand that feeds you, the hand that's doing all this for your own good. He literally gagged on this line but I would not stop. Instead, at his very next gag, I used the opportunity to pop the pill into the back of his mouth.

"Close his mouth immediately," my instructions read, "stroke his throat and the natural reflex action will leave no doubt that the pill has been swallowed. Done properly and quickly, your cat will not even realize that he has ingested a pill."

I did the stroking perfectly. And then, just as I was congratulating myself on a masterful job masterfully performed, something hit me right between the eyes. Well, not exactly between the eyes but in fact on the nose—and it plopped from there to the floor.

It was, of course, the pill. Maybe some cats would not "even realize," as Ms. Easterly had put it, that they had "ingested a pill," but Polar Bear was not of their number. As a matter of fact he had, after firing his bull's-eye, once more jumped out of the towel to the floor and was quietly lying down licking his fancied wounds. From time to time, however, he would fix a by now extremely beady eye on me with just one obvious question on his mind. Would I, or would I not, be foolish enough to answer the bell for the next round? I stared right back at him. What did he think I was made of? Was his memory so short that it could not retain any of the saga of my past triumphs over his intransigence?

I took a deep breath and once more stood up. This time, almost in one masterful maneuver, I grabbed him, wrapped him in the towel, sawed open his mouth, and plopped in the pill. And this time also, after politely telling him to shut his mouth, then, with my hand, actually shutting it, I stroked his throat over and over until I was certain there was not the slightest possibility that he hadn't swallowed it. To make absolutely certain, however, I opened his mouth again, this time with surprising little resistance, I was pleased to note, and peered around inside. No pill anywhere.

I watched him as he went away to lick not only his fancied wounds but also, now, his pride. But I was a gracious winner. I went over, got down on my knees and scrubbed his ears and stomach. "You see, Polar

Bear," I told him, "that wasn't so bad after all, was it?" I also told him he couldn't possibly have even tasted the pill. And surely he must realize that he couldn't set himself up as judge and jury of what was best for him. Only I, and his vet, could do that.

As gracious a winner as I was, Polar Bear was, I was glad to see, a gracious loser. I was thinking about this when, out of the corner of my eye, I spotted a telltale white object on the rug behind him. No, I thought, it couldn't be. But of course it was. It was the pill.

For a long moment I said nothing. I just looked at the pill and then, slowly, back at him. Finally he too looked at the pill and then, equally slowly, back at me. There was no doubt about what he was doing—he was smiling.

I rose to my feet with as much of what dignity I had left as I could muster. All right, I thought, if all-out war was what he wanted, all-out war was what he would get. But, I warned him—and he could go to the bank on what I was saying—the next attack would come when he least expected it. I would bide my time and then I would go all out.

And I did just that. I bode in fact for a good long time, because I had made up my mind that a nighttime excursion, under cover of darkness, was my best chance for success. And that night, after he had jumped up on the bed and was fast asleep—using, as usual, about three-quarters of my king-sized bed—I struck. With one single but incredibly rapid motion—one which would have done credit to the late George Patton—I sat up, seized him, plunged the pill into his mouth, and this time not only stroked his throat but, as I did so, all but did the swallowing for him. It was not pretty, but war never is.

The point is that he did indeed that night swallow a pill. But to say he was furious is putting it mildly. If cats can be livid, livid he was. He obviously considered my actions as the greatest doublecross since Brutus stabbed Caesar. And to his way of thinking, even that dark deed, dastardly as it was, happened after all in broad daylight. What I had done to him had been done in the depths of the night.

Just the same, hard as it was to bear his wrath, the fact remained, from that day to this, or rather from that night to this, that is the way, with slight variations—as, for example, when he is sound asleep in the daytime—that I have administered all pills to him. Let sleeping dogs lie, they say. But where does it say that about sleeping cats?

LYING DOGGO
—*Bobbie Ann Mason*—

Grover Cleveland is growing feeble. His eyes are cloudy, and his muzzle is specked with white hairs. When he scoots along on the hardwood floors, he makes a sound like brushes on drums. He sleeps in front of the woodstove, and when he gets too hot he creeps across the floor.

When Nancy Culpepper married Jack Cleveland, she felt, in a way, that she was marrying a divorced man with a child. Grover was a young dog then. Jack had gotten him at the humane society shelter. He had picked the shyest, most endearing puppy in a boisterous litter. Later, he told Nancy that someone said he should have chosen an energetic one, because quiet puppies often have something wrong with them. That chance remark bothered Nancy; it could have applied to her as well. But that was years ago. Nancy and Jack are still married, and Grover has lived to be old. Now his arthritis stiffens his legs so that on some days he cannot get up. Jack has been talking of having Grover put to sleep.

"Why do you say 'put to sleep'?" their son, Robert, asks. "I know what you mean." Robert is nine. He is a serious boy, quiet, like Nancy.

"No reason. It's just the way people say it."

"They don't say they put *people* to sleep."

"It doesn't usually happen to people," Jack says.

"Don't you dare take him to the vet unless you let me go along. I don't want any funny stuff behind my back."

"Don't worry, Robert," Nancy says.

Later, in Jack's studio, while developing photographs of broken snow fences on hillsides, Jack says to Nancy, "There's a first time for everything, I guess."

"What?"

"Death. I never really knew anybody who died."

"You're forgetting my grandmother."

"I didn't really know your grandmother." Jack looks down at Grover's face in the developing fluid. Grover looks like a wolf in the snow on the hill. Jack says, "The only people I ever cared about who died were rock heroes."

———

Jack has been buying special foods for the dog—pork chops and liver, vitamin supplements. All the arthritis literature he has been able to find concerns people, but he says the same rules must apply to all mammals. Until Grover's hind legs gave way, Jack and Robert took Grover out for long, slow walks through the woods. Recently, a neighbor who keeps Alaskan malamutes stopped Nancy in the Super Duper and inquired about Grover. The neighbor wanted to know which kind of arthritis Grover had—osteo- or rheumatoid? The neighbor said he had rheumatoid and held out knobbed fingers. The doctor told him to avoid zucchini and to drink lots of water. Grover doesn't like zucchini, Nancy said.

Jack and Nancy and Robert all deal with Grover outside. It doesn't help that the temperature is dropping below twenty degrees. It feels even colder because they are conscious of the dog's difficulty. Nancy holds his head and shoulders while Jack supports his hind legs. Robert holds up Grover's tail.

Robert says, "I have an idea."

"What, sweetheart?" asks Nancy. In her arms, Grover lurches. Nancy squeezes against him and he whimpers.

"We could put a diaper on him."

"How would we clean him up?"

"They do that with chimpanzees," says Jack, "but it must be messy."

"You mean I didn't have an original idea?" Robert cries. "Curses, foiled again!" Robert has been reading comic books about masked villains.

"There aren't many original ideas," Jack says, letting go of Grover. "They just look original when you're young." Jack lifts Grover's hind legs again and grasps him under the stomach. "Let's try one more time, boy."

Grover looks at Nancy, pleading.

Nancy has been feeling that the dying of Grover marks a milestone in her marriage to Jack, a marriage that has somehow lasted almost fifteen years. She is seized with an irrational dread—that when the dog is gone, Jack will be gone too. Whenever Nancy and Jack are apart— during Nancy's frequent trips to see her family in Kentucky, or when Jack has gone away "to think"—Grover remains with Jack. Actually, Nancy knew Grover before she knew Jack. When Jack and Nancy were students, in Massachusetts, the dog was a familiar figure around campus. Nancy was drawn to the dog long before she noticed the shaggy-haired student in the sheepskin-lined corduroy jacket who was usually with him. Once, in a seminar on the Federalist period that Nancy was auditing, Grover had walked in, circled the room, and then walked out, as if performing some routine investigation, like the man who sprayed Nancy's apartment building for silverfish. Grover was a beautiful dog, a German shepherd, gray, dusted with a sooty topcoat. After the seminar, Nancy followed the dog out of the building, and she met Jack then. Eventually, when Nancy and Jack made love in his apartment in Amherst, Grover lay sprawled by the bed, both protective and quietly participatory. Later, they moved into a house in the country, and Nancy felt that she had an instant family. Once, for almost three months, Jack and Grover were gone. Jack left Nancy in California, pregnant and terrified, and went to stay at an Indian reservation in New Mexico. Nancy lived in a room on a street with palm trees. It was winter. It felt like a Kentucky October. She went to a park every day and watched people with their dogs, their children, and tried to comprehend that she was there, alone, a mile from the San Andreas fault, reluctant to return to Kentucky. "We need to decide where we stand with each other," Jack had said when he left. "Just when I start to think I know where you're at, you seem to disappear." Jack always seemed to stand back and watch her, as though he expected her to do something excitingly original. He expected her to be herself, not someone she thought people wanted her to be. That was a twist: he expected the unexpected. While Jack was away, Nancy indulged in crafts projects. At the Free University, she learned batik and macramé. On her own, she learned to crochet. She had never done anything like that before.

She threw away her file folders of history notes for the article she had wanted to write. Suddenly, making things with her hands was the only endeavor that made sense. She crocheted a bulky, shapeless sweater in a shell stitch for Jack. She made baby things, using large hooks. She did not realize that such heavy blankets were unsuitable for a baby until she saw Robert—a tiny, warped-looking creature, like one of her clumsily made crafts. When Jack returned, she was in a sprawling adobe hospital, nursing a baby the color of scalded skin. The old song "In My Adobe Hacienda" was going through her head. Jack stood over her behind an unfamiliar beard, grinning in disbelief, stroking the baby as though he were a new pet. Nancy felt she had fooled Jack into thinking she had done something original at last.

"Grover's dying to see you," he said to her. "They wouldn't let him in here."

"I'll be glad to see Grover," said Nancy. "I missed him."

She had missed, she realized then, his various expressions: the staccato barks of joy, the forceful, menacing barks at strangers, the eerie howls when he heard cat fights at night.

———

Those early years together were confused and dislocated. After leaving graduate school, at the beginning of the seventies, they lived in a number of places—sometimes on the road, with Grover, in a van—but after Robert was born they settled in Pennsylvania. Their life is orderly. Jack is a free-lance photographer, with his own studio at home. Nancy, unable to find a use for her degree in history, returned to school, taking education and administration courses. Now she is assistant principal of a small private elementary school, which Robert attends. Now and then Jack frets about becoming too middle-class. He has become semipolitical about energy, sometimes attending anti-nuclear power rallies. He has been building a sun space for his studio and has been insulating the house. "Retrofitting" is the term he uses for making the house energy-efficient.

"Insulation is his hobby," Nancy told an old friend from graduate school, Tom Green, who telephoned unexpectedly one day recently. "He insulates on weekends."

"Maybe he'll turn into a butterfly—he could insulate himself into a cocoon," said Tom, who Nancy always thought was funny. She had not seen him in ten years. He called to say he was sending a novel he had written—"about all the crazy stuff we did back then."

The dog is forcing Nancy to think of how Jack has changed in the years since then. He is losing his hair, but he doesn't seem concerned. Jack was always fanatical about being honest. He used to be insensitive about his directness. "I'm just being honest," he would say pleasantly, boyishly, when he hurt people's feelings. He told Nancy she was uptight, that no one ever knew what she thought, that she should be more expressive. He said she "played games" with people, hiding her feelings behind her coy Southern smile. He is more tolerant now, less judgmental. He used to criticize her for drinking Cokes and eating pastries. He didn't like her lipstick, and she stopped wearing it. But Nancy has changed too. She is too sophisticated now to eat fried foods and rich pies and cakes, indulging in them only when she goes to Kentucky. She uses makeup now—so sparingly that Jack does not notice. Her cool reserve, her shyness, has changed to cool assurance, with only the slightest shift. Inwardly, she has reorganized. "It's like retrofitting," she said to Jack once, but he didn't notice any irony.

It wasn't until two years ago that Nancy learned that he had lied to her when he told her he had been at the Beatles' Shea Stadium concert in 1966, just as she had, only two months before they met. When he confessed his lie, he claimed he had wanted to identify with her and impress her because he thought of her as someone so mysterious and aloof that he could not hold her attention. Nancy, who had in fact been intimidated by Jack's directness, was troubled to learn of his peculiar deception. It was out of character. She felt a part of her past had been ripped away. More recently, when John Lennon died, Nancy and Jack watched the silent vigil from Central Park on TV and cried in each other's arms. Everybody that week was saying that they had lost their youth.

Jack was right. That was the only sort of death they had known.

———

Grover lies on his side, stretching out near the fire, his head flat on one ear. His eyes are open, expressionless, and when Nancy speaks to him he doesn't respond.

"Come on, Grover!" cries Robert, tugging the dog's leg. "Are you dead?"

"Don't pull at him," Nancy says.

"He's lying doggo," says Jack.

"That's funny," says Robert. "What does that mean?"

"Dogs do that in the heat," Jack explains. "They save energy that way."

"But it's winter," says Robert. "I'm freezing." He's wearing a wool pullover and goose-down vest. Jack has the thermostat set on fifty-five, relying mainly on the woodstove to warm the house.

"I'm cold too," says Nancy. "I've been freezing since 1965, when I came North."

Jack crouches down beside the dog. "Grover, old boy. Please. Just give a little sign."

"If you don't get up, I won't give you your treat tonight," says Robert, wagging his finger at Grover.

"Let him rest," says Jack, who is twiddling some of Grover's fur between his fingers.

"Are you sure he's not dead?" Robert asks. He runs the zipper of his vest up and down.

"He's just pretending," says Nancy.

The tip of Grover's tail twitches, and Jack catches it, the way he might grab at a fluff of milkweed in the air.

Later, in the kitchen, Jack and Nancy are preparing for a dinner party. Jack is sipping whiskey. The woodstove has been burning all day, and the house is comfortably warm now. In the next room, Robert is lying on the rug in front of the stove with Grover. He is playing with a computer football game and watching *Mork and Mindy* at the same time. Robert likes to do several things at once, and lately he has included Grover in his multiple activities.

Jack says, "I think the only thing to do is just feed Grover pork chops and steaks and pet him a lot, and then when we can stand it, take him to the vet and get it over with."

"When can we stand it?"

"If I were in Grover's shape, I'd just want to be put out of my misery."

"Even if you were still conscious and could use your mind?"

"I guess so."

"I couldn't pull the plug on you," says Nancy, pointing a carrot at Jack. "You'd have to be screaming in agony."

"Would you want me to do it to you?"

"No. I can see right now that I'd be the type to hang on. I'd be just like my Granny. I think she just clung to life, long after her body was ready to die."

"Would you really be like that?"

"You said once I was just like her—repressed, uptight."

"I didn't mean that."

"You've been right about me before," Nancy says, reaching across Jack for a paring knife. "Look, all I mean is that it shouldn't be a matter of *our* convenience. If Grover needs assistance, then it's our problem. We're responsible."

"I'd want to be put out of my misery," Jack says.

During that evening, Nancy has the impression that Jack is talking more than usual. He does not notice the food. She has made chicken Marengo and is startled to realize how much it resembles chicken cacciatore, which she served the last time she had the same people over. The recipes are side by side in the cookbook, gradations on a theme. The dinner is for Stewart and Jan, who are going to Italy on a teaching exchange.

"Maybe I shouldn't even have made Italian," Nancy tells them apologetically. "You'll get enough of that in Italy. And it will be real."

Both Stewart and Jan say the chicken Marengo is wonderful. The olives are the right touch, Jan says. Ted and Laurie nod agreement. Jack pours more wine. The sound of a log falling in the woodstove reminds Nancy of the dog in the other room by the stove, and in her mind she stages a scene: finding the dog dead in the middle of the dinner party.

Afterward, they sit in the living room, with Grover lying there like a log too large for the stove. The guests talk idly. Ted has been sandblasting old paint off a brick fireplace, and Laurie complains about the gritty dust. Jack stokes the fire. The stove, hooked up through the fireplace, looks like a robot from an old science fiction movie. Nancy and Jack used to sit by the fireplace in Massachusetts, stoned, watching the blue frills of the flames, imagining that they were musical notes, visual textures of sounds on the stereo. Nobody they know smokes grass anymore. Now people sit around and talk about investments and proper flue linings. When Jack passes around the Grand Marnier, Nancy says, "In my grandparents' house years ago, we used to sit by their fireplace. They burned coal. They didn't call it a fireplace, though. They called it a grate."

"Coal burns more efficiently than wood," Jack says.

"Coal's a lot cheaper in this area," says Ted. "I wish I could switch."

"My grandparents had big stone fireplaces in their country house," says Jan, who comes from Connecticut. "They were so pleasant. I always looked forward to going there. Sometimes in the summer the evenings were cool and we'd have a fire. It was lovely."

"I remember being cold," says Nancy. "It was always very cold, even in the South."

"The heat just goes up the chimney in a fireplace," says Jack.

Nancy stares at Jack. She says, "I would stand in front of the fire until I was roasted. Then I would turn and roast the other side. In the evenings, my grandparents sat on the hearth and read the Bible. There wasn't anything *lovely* about it. They were trying to keep warm. Of course, nobody had heard of insulation."

"There goes Nancy, talking about her deprived childhood," Jack says with a laugh.

Nancy says, "Jack is so concerned about wasting energy. But when he goes out he never wears a hat." She looks at Jack. "Don't you know your body heat just flies out the top of your head? It's a chimney."

Surprised by her tone, she almost breaks into tears.

———

It is the following evening, and Jack is flipping through some contact sheets of a series on solar hot-water heaters he is doing for a magazine. Robert sheds his goose-down vest, and he and Grover, on the floor, simultaneously inch away from the fire. Nancy is trying to read the novel written by the friend from Amherst, but the book is boring. She would not have recognized her witty friend from the past in the turgid prose she is reading.

"It's a dump on the sixties," she tells Jack when he asks. "A really cynical look. All the characters are types."

"Are we in it?"

"No. I hope not. I think it's based on that Phil Baxter who cracked up at that party."

Grover raises his head, his eyes alert, and Robert jumps up, saying, "It's time for Grover's treat."

He shakes a Pet-Tab from a plastic bottle and holds it before Grover's nose. Grover bangs his tail against the rug as he crunches the pill.

Jack turns on the porch light and steps outside for a moment, returning with a shroud of cold air. "It's starting to snow," he says. "Come on out, Grover."

Grover struggles to stand, and Jack heaves the dog's hind legs over the threshold.

Later, in bed, Jack turns on his side and watches Nancy, reading her book, until she looks up at him.

"You read so much," he says. "You're always reading."

"Hmm."

"We used to have more fun. We used to be silly together."

"What do you want to do?"

"Just something silly."

"I can't think of anything silly." Nancy flips the page back, rereading. "God, this guy can't write. I used to think he was so clever."

In the dark, touching Jack tentatively, she says, "We've changed. We used to lie awake all night, thrilled just to touch each other."

"We've been busy. That's what happens. People get busy."

"That scares me," says Nancy. "Do you want to have another baby?"

"No. I want a dog." Jack rolls away from her, and Nancy can hear him breathing into his pillow. She waits to hear if he will cry. She recalls Jack returning to her in California after Robert was born. He brought a God's-eye, which he hung from the ceiling above Robert's crib, to protect him. Jack never wore the sweater Nancy made for him. Instead, Grover slept on it. Nancy gave the dog her granny-square afghan too, and eventually, when they moved back East, she got rid of the pathetic evidence of her creative period—the crochet hooks, the piles of yarn, some splotchy batik tapestries. Now most of the objects in the house are Jack's. He made the oak counters and the dining room table; he remodeled the studio; he chose the draperies; he photographed the pictures on the wall. If Jack were to leave again, there would be no way to remove his presence, the way the dog can disappear completely, with his sounds. Nancy revises the scene in her mind. The house is still there, but Nancy is not in it.

————

In the morning, there is a four-inch snow, with a drift blowing up the back-porch steps. From the kitchen window, Nancy watches her son float silently down the hill behind the house. At the end, he tumbles off his sled deliberately, wallowing in the snow, before standing up to wave, trying to catch her attention.

On the back porch, Nancy and Jack hold Grover over newspapers. Grover performs unselfconsciously now. Nancy says, "Maybe he can hang on, as long as we can do this."

"But look at him, Nancy," Jack says. "He's in misery."

Jack holds Grover's collar and helps him slide over the threshold. Grover aims for his place by the fire.

After the snowplow passes, late in the morning, Nancy drives Robert to the school on slushy roads, all the while lecturing him on the absurdity of raising money to buy official Boy Scout equipment, especially on a snowy Saturday. The Boy Scouts are selling water-savers for toilet tanks in order to earn money for camping gear.

"I thought Boy Scouts spent their time earning badges," says Nancy. "I thought you were supposed to learn about nature, instead of spending money on official Boy Scout pots and pans."

"This is nature," Robert says solemnly. "It's ecology. Saving water when you flush is ecology."

Later, Nancy and Jack walk in the woods together. Nancy walks behind Jack, stepping in his boot tracks. He shields her from the wind.

Her hair is blowing. They walk briskly up a hill and emerge on a ridge that overlooks a valley. In the distance they can see a housing development, a radio tower, a winding road. House trailers dot the hillsides. A snowplow is going up a road, like a zipper in the landscape.

Jack says, "I'm going to call the vet Monday."

Nancy gasps in cold air. She says, "Robert made us promise you won't do anything without letting him in on it. That goes for me too." When Jack doesn't respond, she says, "I'd want to hang on, even if I was in a coma. There must be some spark, in the deep recesses of the mind, some twitch, a flicker of a dream—"

"A twitch that could make life worth living?" Jack laughs bitterly.

"Yes." She points to the brilliantly colored sparkles the sun is making on the snow. "Those are the sparks I mean," she says. "In the brain somewhere, something like that. That would be beautiful."

"You're weird, Nancy."

"I learned it from you. I never would have noticed anything like that if I hadn't known you, if you hadn't got me stoned and made me look at your photographs." She stomps her feet in the snow. Her toes are cold. "You educated me. I was so out of it when I met you. One day I was listening to Hank Williams and shelling corn for the chickens and the next day I was expected to know what wines went with what. Talk about weird."

"You're exaggerating. That was years ago. You always exaggerate your background." He adds in a teasing tone, "Your humble origins."

"We've been together fifteen years," says Nancy. She stops him, holding his arm. Jack is squinting, looking at something in the distance. She goes on, "You said we didn't do anything silly anymore. What should we do, Jack? Should we make angels in the snow?"

Jack touches his rough glove to her face. "We shouldn't unless we really feel like it."

It was the same as Jack chiding her to be honest, to be expressive. The same old Jack, she thought, relieved.

———

"Come and look," Robert cries, bursting in the back door. He and Jack have been outside making a snowman. Nancy is rolling dough for a quiche. Jack will eat a quiche but not a custard pie, although they are virtually the same. She wipes her hands and goes to the door of the porch. She sees Grover swinging from the lower branch of the maple tree. Jack has rigged up a sling, so that the dog is supported in a harness, with the canvas from the back of a deck chair holding his stomach. His legs dangle free.

"Oh, Jack," Nancy calls. "The poor thing."

"I thought this might work," Jack explains. "A support for his hind legs." His arms cradle the dog's head. "I did it for you," he adds, looking at Nancy. "Don't push him, Robert. I don't think he wants to swing."

Grover looks amazingly patient, like a cat in a doll bonnet.

"He hates it," says Jack, unbuckling the harness.

"He can learn to like it," Robert says, his voice rising shrilly.

———

On the day that Jack has planned to take Grover to the veterinarian, Nancy runs into a crisis at work. One of the children has been exposed to hepatitis, and it is necessary to vaccinate all of them. Nancy has to arrange the details, which means staying late. She telephones Jack to ask him to pick up Robert after school.

"I don't know when I'll be home," she says. "This is an administrative nightmare. I have to call all the parents, get permissions, make arrangements with family doctors."

"What will we do about Grover?"

"Please postpone it. I want to be with you then."

"I want to get it over with," says Jack impatiently. "I hate to put Robert through another day of this."

"Robert will be glad of the extra time," Nancy insists. "So will I."

"I just want to face things," Jack says. "Don't you understand? I don't want to cling to the past like you're doing."

"Please wait for us," Nancy says, her voice calm and controlled.

On the telephone, Nancy is authoritative, a quick decision-maker. The problem at work is a reprieve. She feels free, on her own. During the afternoon, she works rapidly and efficiently, filing reports, consulting health authorities, notifying parents. She talks with the disease-control center in Atlanta, inquiring about guidelines. She checks on supplies of gamma globulin. She is so preoccupied that in the middle of the afternoon, when Robert suddenly appears in her office, she is startled, for a fleeting instant not recognizing him.

He says, "Kevin has a sore throat. Is that hepatitis?"

"It's probably just a cold. I'll talk to his mother." Nancy is holding Robert's arm, partly to keep him still, partly to steady herself.

"When do I have to get a shot?" Robert asks.

"Tomorrow."

"Do I have to?"

"Yes. It won't hurt, though."

"I guess it's a good thing this happened," Robert says bravely. "Now we get to have Grover another day." Robert spills his books on the floor and bends to pick them up. When he looks up, he says, "Daddy doesn't care about him. He just wants to get rid of him. He wants to kill him."

"Oh, Robert, that's not true," says Nancy. "He just doesn't want Grover to suffer."

"But Grover still has half a bottle of Pet-Tabs," Robert says. "What will we do with them?"

"I don't know," Nancy says. She hands Robert his numbers workbook. Like a tape loop, the face of her child as a stranger replays in her mind. Robert has her plain brown hair, her coloring, but his eyes are Jack's—demanding and eerily penetrating, eyes that could pin her to the wall.

After Robert leaves, Nancy lowers the venetian blinds. Her office is brilliantly lighted by the sun, through south-facing windows. The design was accidental, nothing to do with solar energy. It is an old building. Bars of light slant across her desk, like a formidable scene in a forties movie. Nancy's secretary goes home, but Nancy works on, contacting all the parents she couldn't get during working hours. One parent anxiously reports that her child has a swollen lymph node on his neck.

"No," Nancy says firmly. "That is *not* a symptom of hepatitis. But you should ask the doctor about that when you go in for the gamma globulin."

Gamma globulin. The phrase rolls off her tongue. She tries to remember an odd title of a movie about gamma rays. It comes to her as she is dialing the telephone: *The Effect of Gamma Rays on Man-in-the-Moon Marigolds*. She has never known what that title meant.

The office grows dim, and Nancy turns on the lights. The school is quiet, as though the threat of an infectious disease has emptied the corridors, leaving her in charge. She recalls another movie, *The Andromeda Strain*. Her work is like the thrill of watching drama, a threat held safely at a distance. Historians have to be detached, Nancy once said, defensively, to Jack, when he accused her of being unfriendly to shopkeepers and waiters. Where was all that Southern hospitality he had heard so much about? he wanted to know. It hits her now that historians are detached about the past, not the present. Jack has learned some of this detachment: he wants to let Grover go. Nancy thinks of the stark images in his recent photographs—snow, icicles, fences, the long shot of Grover on the hill like a stray wolf. Nancy had always liked Jack's pictures simply for what they were, but Jack didn't see the people or the objects in them. He saw illusions. The vulnerability of the image, he once said, was what he was after. The image was meant to evoke its own death, he told her.

By the time Nancy finishes the scheduling, the night maintenance crew has arrived, and the coffeepot they keep in a closet is perking. Nancy removes her contact lenses and changes into her fleece-lined boots. In the parking lot, she maneuvers cautiously along a path past a mountain of black-stained snow. It is so cold that she makes sparks on the vinyl car seat. The engine is cold, slow to turn over.

At home, Nancy is surprised to see balloons in the living room. The stove is blazing and Robert's face is red from the heat.

"We're having a party," he says. "For Grover."

"There's a surprise for you in the oven," says Jack, handing Nancy a glass of sherry. "Because you worked so hard."

"Grover had ice cream," Robert says. "We got Häagen-Dazs."

"He looks cheerful," Nancy says, sinking onto the couch next to Jack. Her glasses are fogged up. She removes them and wipes them with a Kleenex. When she puts them back on, she sees Grover looking at her, his head on his paws. His tail thumps. For the first time, Nancy feels ready to let the dog die.

When Nancy tells about the gamma globulin, the phrase has stopped rolling off her tongue so trippingly. She laughs. She is so tired she throbs with relief. She drinks the sherry too fast. Suddenly, she sits up straight and announces, "I've got a clue. I'm thinking of a parking lot."

"East or West?" Jack says. This is a game they used to play.

"West."

"Aha, I've got you," says Jack. "You're thinking of the parking lot at that hospital in Tucson."

"Hey, that's not fair going too fast," cries Robert. "I didn't get a chance to play."

"This was before you were born," Nancy says, running her fingers through Robert's hair. He is on the floor, leaning against her knees. "We were lying in the van for a week, thinking we were going to die. Oh, God!" Nancy laughs and covers her mouth with her hands.

"Why were you going to die?" Robert asks.

"We weren't really going to die." Both Nancy and Jack are laughing now at the memory, and Jack is pulling off his sweater. The hospital in Tucson wouldn't accept them because they weren't sick enough to hospitalize, but they were too sick to travel. They had nowhere to go. They had been on a month's trip through the West, then had stopped in Tucson and gotten jobs at a restaurant to make enough money to get home.

"Do you remember that doctor?" Jack says.

"I remember the look he gave us, like he didn't want us to pollute his hospital." Nancy laughs harder. She feels silly and relieved. Her hand, on Jack's knee, feels the fold of the long johns beneath his jeans. She cries, "I'll never forget how we stayed around that parking lot, thinking we were going to die."

"I couldn't have driven a block, I was so weak," Jack gasps. "

"You were yellow. *I* didn't get yellow."

"All we could do was pee and drink orange juice."

"And throw the pee out the window."

"Grover was so bored with us!"

Nancy says, "It's a good thing we couldn't eat. We would have spent all our money."

"Then we would have had to work at that filthy restaurant again. And get hepatitis again."

"And on and on, forever. We would still be there, like Charley on the MTA. Oh, Jack, do you *remember* that crazy restaurant? You had to wear a ten-gallon hat—"

Abruptly, Robert jerks away from Nancy and crawls on his knees across the room to examine Grover, who is stretched out on his side, his legs sticking out stiffly. Robert, his straight hair falling, bends his head to the dog's heart.

"He's not dead," Robert says, looking up at Nancy. "He's lying doggo."

"Passed out at his own party," Jack says, raising his glass. "Way to go, Grover!"

MY LIFE AS A WEST AFRICAN GRAY PARROT
–Leigh Buchanan Bienen–

I

The dark, I am in the dark. They have put the green cloth over my cage. I am in the dark once again. I smell the acrid felt. I smell the green of transitions, the particles of dust in the warp of the fabric which remind me of forests and terror. I am in the dark. I shall never fly again. Even my masterful imitation of the electric pencil sharpener will not pierce the dark. My master and mistress are talking in the corridor. "That will shut it up," she says, knocking the aluminum pan against the porcelain sink and causing me, as she knows, pain.

My cage sits on a squat wooden table in a room facing the kitchen. The smell of roasting pig sickens me, although the odor of tomatoes and basil reminds me of my duty to God. My mistress does not recognize my powers. She calls from the kitchen, "What do you know, plucked chicken?" A visitor thoughtfully suggests the parrot might like the door shut while she sniffles her way through the cutting of onions.

Worse, they leave open the water-closet door, shouting things to one another from within. The animal odors do not offend me but my master sprays a poisonous antiseptic on the fixtures which irritates my sensitive nostrils and threatens my divine coloration. The red of my tail will fade in fumes of ammonia or chlorine.

Like blood, the color of my red tail has its own startling quality. This extraordinary color makes my red feathers magical. The red is a vivid crimson which glows from across the room. The red is the source of my power, my beauty, which I possess only briefly. The red is set off by its contrast to the pearl gray of my breast. The ivory white skin around my eyes, and the gunmetal gray of my chipped beak. The feathers on my back shade to light gray at the root, leaving a line of charcoal along the knife's edge of my wing feathers.

It is difficult to remember how beautiful I once was. The silken gray feathers falling over a young, full breast in layers as delicate as the tracery of a waterfall, each hue of gray, each smudge of crimson in subtle harmony with the rest. Now only the surprising crimson remains, the purest blue-red of my tail and the hints of the same crimson in my remaining wing feathers. Now to my mistress's distress I have plucked my breast almost clean. Pink dots appear where the oval pinfeathers were. Tiny blood flecks materialize from my pores like crimson teardrops, but not like the crimson of my tail. This urge to destroy myself and my unbearable beauty comes over me in spurts and impedes my progress. In a rush I grab five, six or seven feathers and pull them out in a flurry. The pain is delicious. The mistress shrieks at me from the kitchen when she catches me at it: "Stop picking, filthy bird." But she cannot separate me from myself. Only I possess the engine to destroy my own beauty.

My master and mistress purchased me because they had been told I could talk. The owner of the pet store, a fat Indian with one milky blind eye, pulled out my red tail feathers and sold them one by one. He told my master and mistress I could talk, not because he believed it but because recently I had bitten his finger through to the knuckle. He believed a parrot's bite was a curse. This same fat Indian failed to mention the magical qualities which caused my feathers to be valued by those who bought and sold in windowless back rooms. My master and mistress praised my beauty with awe while the Indian, slumped in a small wooden chair in the back storeroom, wondered if he would catch a vile infection from my nasty bite.

The master and mistress proudly carried me home and installed me in a large cage on a table in the dining room, on top of a figured blue carpet and beside a tall window which let in the creamy winter light through white silk curtains. The cat came and curled up in a puddle of sunlight beneath my cage. At first the master and mistress fussed continually over my placement by the window. When the sun went down, at a remarkably early hour every afternoon, the master would jump up and pull the curtains shut. "The breeze will kill the bird," he shouted at his wife, as if she were not in the room. In reply she insisted that cold was no worry. She had seen pictures of parrots in the Jardin des Plantes shaking snowflakes off their wings. "But the draft, the draft, there must not be a draft," she shrieked. As the winter days shortened and became increasingly pale, this exchange was repeated. A small machine was installed in the dining room. Its angry red coils created a suffocating dryness which by itself almost catapulted me into my next incarnation. The heat radiating from those disagreeable wires bore no resemblance to the warmth of sunlight in my African jungle.

In those days a perch stood alongside my cage. On some afternoons, at the time when the winter light was strongest, my mistress would open the cage door allowing me to climb out onto the wooden perch, where I could stretch one wing then another slowly downward towards the floor. If the master was out, my mistress would sit down at the dining room table and recite speeches at me. The same sonorous words over and over. Her diction was beyond reproach on these occasions. Once she taped her voice and played it beside my cage for the entire day. I added to my repertoire the sibilant sounds of plastic across metal as the tape rewound itself on the white disc. Instead of her cultured tones I preferred the syncopated accents of the immigrant cleaning lady who muttered lilting obscenities as she scoured a shine into the inlaid tabletops in the living room.

During this early period I often whispered aloud, laughed, or simply whistled. The master and mistress were amazed when my laughter coincided with their amusement. They did not understand that laughter is a form of crying, that we laugh to keep our perception of the world from crumbling. My own laughter is a hollow chuckle, a sinister and frightening sound, recognizable as a laugh by its mirthlessness. When humans laugh they add wheezes and croaks to mask the sadness of laughter. My master and mistress do not yet understand that the highest form of communication is wordless, achieved by a glance upward or a bestial grunt, by the perception of a change in the rhythm of breathing, or by a blink of an eye, in my case the flicker of a brown membrane between lashless lids.

When visitors came into the dining room they used to remark, to the pleasure of my master and mistress: "Look! How it stares back at you." Meaning, they were surprised. My yellow eye pierced through whatever image they had manufactured of themselves, images of purpose and the aura of an imminent, important appointment which was constructed by a high, excited tone of voice. My yellow eyes can see behind a necklace of stones to the throb at the throat, behind thick tweed to the soft folds of the belly, to the dark roots of hair which has been falsely hennaed to a color which is a poor imitation of the red wings of the Amazonian parrot.

The guests were always amazed. At dinner advertising men and women in public relations were encouraged to speculate upon whether my mobile and bony throat (not yet exposed by picking) or my knobby, black tongue produced such extraordinary sounds. The mistress asked pensively: "Imagine how the bird speaks." The master replied with gravity: "The consonance between words and meaning is illusory."

At her urging they called in an expert in the field of Parrot Linguistics, a spectacled man who wore a Russian suit with wide, waving trousers. The mistress served him tea in a glass with a slice of lemon on the saucer. The man removed his thick glasses and examined the white papery skin surrounding my beak and nostrils. My beak was chipped, but he only commented, "I see nothing unusual about the beak or throat of this parrot."

"His tongue," my mistress urged, "look at his tongue. The bird has an exceptionally long and globular black tongue."

The expert had already donned his baggy jacket and removed his spectacles. "Yes," he said, "it is unusual for a bird to encompass such a wide range of laughter."

My imitations of the human voice exactly reproduced individual intonations. The precision of my imitation of the Polish servant rendered my mistress speechless with jealousy. Erroneously, the copywriters concluded mimicry was the source of my magic, and they congratulated my mistress on acquiring such a rare and amusing pet. In those early days of enthusiasm my mistress would wipe her finely manicured fingers upon a paper towel and scratch my skull, murmuring, "Now Polly, poor Polly, here Polly." In those days they both fed me tidbits from their table, corners of roast dripping with honey, a half-eaten peach with chunks of amber flesh still clinging to the pit, or the thigh bone of a chicken, a treat of which I remain inordinately fond. I would sidestep over, slide down the metal bars of my cage with my head lowered, and take the tidbit in one curled claw.

The mistress carefully saved all of my red feathers in those days, picking them out from the newspaper shreds with her long red fingernails. She put them in a box of tooled leather and closed the lid so that the incandescence of red would not startle a stranger who happened to walk into the room. Later they became so alienated from the source of my beauty, and so quarrelsome, they no longer took pleasure or strength from the color of my tail feathers. They even forgot to lock my cage and sometimes carelessly left the door open after shaking a few seeds hastily into my dish. During the earlier phase they were proud to possess me. They purchased bird encyclopedias and left them open on the table turned to pages with pictures of parrots. The painted drawing of the yellow-headed Amazon intrigued me and greatly contributed to my education. Feathers of the palest lemon cascaded down from the top of the head ending in a ring of creamier yellow around the neck. The white cockatoos also inspired envy, especially for the flecks of fine pink and light yellow which tinged their wings. I admired their crests, feathers as a flag to the world, and the white back feathers which had the sheen of ancient silk. Another source of wonder were the many-hued black parrots from South America, so advanced in beauty they are rarely glimpsed even by their own kind.

Now when they stand beside my cage, my master and mistress only discuss the price I will fetch. "Is it eight hundred dollars?" he asks. "The last advertisement in the paper had one listed at eight hundred dollars."

My mistress is greedier, but also more practical. "It will fetch more at an auction," she answers, "when people bid against each other in competition."

The refusal to acknowledge my sexual identity is a special humiliation. I laid an egg to announce my essentially female nature. Now that she hates and fears me, my mistress always refers to me in the impersonal third person. I have long since been moved away from the dining room, into a small dark room no bigger than a closet. The tiny unwashed window faces a bleak, blank wall of brick, and the door to a dark and dusty closet stands open behind my cage. The mistress uses my room for storage. The abandoned wire torso of a dress frame is a cage shaped in the outline of a woman. A broken vacuum cleaner lies coiled in permanent hibernation in one corner. Portraits of forgotten ancestors, who willed their property to other branches of the family, stand facing the wall. My cage is now cleaned only once a week. The room is too mean even to serve as an adequate storage facility. The fat, neutered gray cat no longer likes to visit me because there is no rug on the floor and the room is unheated. She curls herself in front of the refrigerator, where a small warm exhaust is continuously expelled from the motor. We exchange remarks about the deplorable spiritual condition of our custodians. The striped gray cat and I together speculate upon whether or not the master and mistress will in their next incarnation understand the power of red, as distinct from the power of blood, the sole power which now strikes fear in their hearts. Both the master and mistress show a measurable anger when the tiny flecks of blood appear against my gray skin. My blood is either light pink or a droplet of burgundy, both distinct from the singing crimson of my tail. When my mistress concluded that the picking was going to continue she began to think of ways to get rid of me. But she would not consider letting me go at a loss.

II

It is difficult for me to remember the jungle, the sun in Africa, or my days in the dark pet shop owned by the blind-eyed Indian. My journey must be almost finished, for only the young command memories. In my native jungle parrots are caught by blindfolded boys who climb to the treetops and rob the nests of their chicks. The mothers swoop down, diving with their gray and white heads tucked under, as they shriek their protest. They will attack and tear the flesh as the bald chicks disappear into a knotted cloth held in the teeth of a boy who shimmies down the trunk as fast as he can. The parrots beat their red-flecked wings around the heads of the nest robbers, biting an ear, frantically flying from branch to branch as they accompany the marauders to the edge of the forest with high-pitched screams. The village boys are blindfolded because they believe they will be struck blind if they look into a parrot's nest. To these people we have long been recognized as magic birds, lucky birds, or birds which carry a curse. And now we are almost extinct.

With six other featherless shivering chicks who died within a week I was brought to a pet shop in the middle of the urban sprawl which constitutes a city outside the jungle. The owner placed me in a cage on top of a teetering pile of small cages. One contained a banded snake with a festering hole in his side, another held a monkey with a crippled arm. There were also green parrots and yellow ones from neighboring forests.

Eventually I became an ornament in the compound of a king, living in a gilded cage on a vast veranda shaded by a roof of woven rattan. Every evening a servant boy peeled me an enormous rainbow-colored mango. My cage was a tall cylinder, large enough to fly across and decorated with tin bells and wooden totems. Visitors came especially to admire me from a distance. They did not press their faces within inches of my nostrils, oppressing me with the odor of skin. They stood back to gaze at my feathers and offered me meat. Like worshipers, they came in formal dress. The women were wrapped in cloth of bright blue, and the men wore flowing gold-embroidered gowns which swayed and brushed the floor as they walked rapidly towards me across the veranda. Another parrot was resident in this royal household. She taught me bearing, demeanor and style. She had been the property of kings through three generations. She remembered kings who had been forgotten by their heirs and successors, and her beautiful piercing whistle caused all those within earshot to stop talking and listen to her call. When she was found dead at the bottom of her cage one morning they buried her with incense and incantations, mourning her loss with ancient, certain ceremonies.

The royal family also had a dog, a brown cur with an extraordinarily long and ugly hairless tail. The dog had to be locked inside the royal compound, or he would have been eaten by the many hungry people outside the walls. The cur was fat, and the urchins who roamed the mud streets in packs would have snatched him for roasting or stewing. The animal was so dispirited and envious of the esteem in which parrots were held that he spent hours lying beside our large golden cage discussing philosophy. The youngest daughter of the king occasionally came barefoot onto the veranda and held his head on her lap while she fed him morsels of goat. Finally he became so fat and arthritic he could not climb the steps to the veranda. His view was that the vicissitudes of fate he suffered in this epoch were haphazard. In the next generation—he expressed this opinion while lying panting on the cool clay floor—it would be dogs with long tails, instead of birds with red feathers, who would be offered raw meat and worshiped for their wisdom. Who knows, he remarked with a supercilious snarl, whether or not the privileges you now enjoy because of your divine coloration will not be given to those with visible ears? He often called attention to his long, bald tail as if the tail by itself should have entitled him to all that he envied. On drowsy tropical afternoons my partner and I humored him by appearing to take these notions seriously.

III

It is true that when I strike I wound. I bit the finger of a small dirty boy to the bone when he poked a yardstick through the bars of my cage. His mother and my mistress were whispering in the kitchen, and they both ignored my shrieks of warning. The boy ran squawking in pain to his mother, and my embarrassed mistress banged the bars of my metal cage with a metal fork, shouting reproaches. The startled mother held her son to her breast and pressed a linen handkerchief of my master's to his limp finger. Furred tentacles of crimson stretched out along threads of cotton and silently eliminated the white between. The sniffling boy looked at me, where I was shivering in the farthest corner of my cage, and signaled his triumph.

I miss the treats, especially the blue-red marrow of chicken bones, which my mistress used to give me in an attempt to make me recite her name. In those days I used to climb upon the back of her hand. She held out her fist with the painted nails curled under, and I could feel her wince when I placed one gray claw and then the other against her skin. I uncoiled my talons to avoid cutting into the flesh of her hand and balanced myself by hooking onto the cage with my beak. She feared I would turn and strike for no reason, and her wrist would stiffen. At such times I was swept away by the sense of her as another living creature, myself at an earlier stage of development. This involuntary response filled me with sadness, for I thought of the generations and generations which remained before her, and I moved away from her hand and huddled on my perch, mourning as she soaped her hands at the kitchen sink. I no longer try to reach her, except with whistles and catcalls, for I know she has come to hate me. Sometimes I receive a reply. She will turn on the radio or rustle the newspaper in an answer.

If nothing else a cage has walls to climb. When my mistress enters the room I take my hooked beak and spill the seeds out of my plastic dish and onto the floor. I can spill almost all of my food in one angry gesture. My beak along the railings makes an insistent, drumming sound which never fails to evoke a click of annoyance from my mistress. When she leaves I slide down the bars and pick out sunflower seeds, the tiny grains of millet, and especially those very small twigs from among the shreds of newspaper. Sometimes my mistress and master discuss my fate in the corridor, using sign language. I can hear the faint rustle of sleeves as they gesture in the hallway. But I rarely listen. I am dreaming of my next life now. The cat curls up in front of the vent of the icebox. We plan together. She licks her paw, passes it over one ear, then her eye, softly.

I can still not resist music, especially the soprano tones. The high notes bring back memories of the sadness of being human. Until the music plays I can convince myself that I have reached a point where memories could no longer overcome me, a point where my feathers offer complete protection. But at the height of a melodic line I hide in the farthest corner of my cage, assaulted by emotions. The beauty of singing strikes home, into the depths of my parrot's heart. I relive my human life, the fears and promises of childhood, the exhilaration of striving, and the limited peace which settles in the breast on rare occasions. I surpass the highest notes with my own high-pitched shriek.

At first my mistress was delighted with these performances, calling the neighbors to witness. Later she shut the door when the radio played music, as if to keep me away from something. The music which I heard faintly from behind the closed door inspired me to dream, and when I sang I swooned, losing my footing on the perch, falling fluttering to the iron grate at the bottom of my cage. The music transported me back to the high trees of the rain forest where parrots flew from limb to limb high above the shrieking of monkeys, never leaving the shadowed protection of branches.

IV

The Attack. It came so startlingly that my screams of pain and fright escaped without thought. A large rat had crawled from the alleyway, through the old crumbling walls of our city house, into a crawlspace in the closet of my dark room. The door of my cage had been carelessly left open. The gray beast with brown ferret eyes slithered his soft fat body up the table leg and into my cage. He stuck his black snout into my food, spilling the seeds, and proceeded to stalk me with a cold-blooded ruthlessness born of generations of experience. In spite of his aged, spoiled softness, the beast struck swiftly, efficiently, with one bite after another, striking my wing, my leg, my throat, then pulling away from my reach. His rat snout twitched and the small dappled spots on his back quivered as he flattened himself to pounce once again at my neck, my throat. Shrieking, bleeding, I beat my wings helplessly against the inside of the cage. Feathers were everywhere. Blood splattered on the unclean walls from a bite on my chest, an open wound in my leg, and from a hole in my wing. In two bites he had pulled out all of my red tail feathers. Aiming for the eye of the lumbering beast—in spite of his waddling gait, I could not place a fatal blow he was so insulated with fat—I bit the soft rubbery flesh of his nose. I dug my claws into the well-fed muscular shoulder until he turned his head and with bared buck teeth bit off one talon and a large part of the toe above it. Wounded, he went into retreat, his hairless tail threading its way around the door frame of the closet.

The attack must have been brief although my wounds were many. The vision of relentless, reasonless destruction remained: a fat waddling beast baring rodent teeth as he came to trap me in the corner of my cage. Hours later my mistress returned and found me shivering and barely alive, crouched on the bottom of my cage. At the sight of the blood, the scattered red and gray feathers, my mistress was distraught, especially when she realized her personal carelessness had exposed me to a danger which neither of us realized had been ever present.

For days and nights I was only aware of the electric light clicking on and off at intervals. My mistress, perhaps only regretting the loss of her financial investment, sat beside my cage and wept with a depth of feeling which kindled surprise even in my semiconscious state. Other visitors came and peered at me anxiously through the bars. Those who had marveled at my feats of imitation came now to stand silently in front of my cage, disapprovingly clucking their tongues over the pity of it.

My bite wounds stopped bleeding almost immediately, but the shock to my spirit had been profound. Worse, a silent, raging infection daily gained upon me. Soon I could only rest my beak on the bottom rungs of my cage. Finally I could no longer stand. I simply crouched in a corner at the bottom of my cage and rested my head against the bars cursing the demon beast of destruction. I could no longer sing, speak or whistle. Every red feather was gone, and my wing and chest, where the feathers had been pulled out, were bare and covered with festering sores.

In the middle of the night my mistress took me to the veterinarian's hospital in the heart of the city, a large facility associated with an old and famous zoo. Although I could no longer raise my head, I felt no localized pain. A young man with a beard and a white coat picked me up in a towel, held me under a bright light, and put a stethoscope to my heart. With my last quantum of strength I flapped my mutilated wings in protest. Then the blessed darkness, my cage left on an antiseptic stainless-steel table, as the doctor switched off the bright light overhead behind him.

In the hospital it was impossible to distinguish night from day. The veterinarian in the white coat, his soft black eyes and his black beard made it difficult to determine his age, treated me with injections, ointments, and powerful medicines, monitoring my blood every few days. My leg was put in a splint and photographed. A milky white substance was applied to the open sores on my breast and wings. The veterinarian sat in front of my cage and talked softly to me as he wrote his day's reports in soft, smudgy pencil on a mimeographed form. When he looked up at me, so clinically, after scratching something on a paper attached to a clipboard, the vision of gray destruction was momentarily dispelled. Under his care I slowly began to regain my strength.

My mistress came to visit on occasion, although she hardly spoke or looked at me when she came. While I limped gingerly to the edge of the cage door, she would talk to the young girl whose function it was to inform the doctors of any unexpected events in the ward. In this large acrid room with concrete floors and row after row of cages, crises were frequent. Not all could be saved. My immediate neighbors were a white cat with cancer whose stomach had been shaved bare to expose a line of cross-stitches like teeth marks across her pale, pale pink skin, a dog whose back leg had been amputated so skillfully that if he stood in profile on his good side his silhouette looked whole, and a one-hundred-year-old yellow crested cockatoo whose anemia had been caused by a diet of nothing but sunflower seeds for over fifty years. She had been sent to the zoo for an evaluation by the heirs to an estate when she passed hands after the death of the old couple who bought her on their honeymoon in a pre-war London flea market.

During the latter part of my recuperation I was placed in a green-domed aviary in the zoo along with other tropical birds. The domed enclosure imitated the wild, which did not, I thought, properly prepare the displaced birds for spiritual progression through containment. Their instincts to fly, to be free, were inappropriately encouraged. Attitudes of confinement and limitation, required for passage onwards, were thwarted. In spite of my condition, I myself was overcome with a memory and desire for flight when I entered the dome, even though it had been years since I had been let out of my cage. The memory of flying overcame me with an exhilarating rush of recognition. To fly, to be free, to soar on a current of wind, seductive memories took over before I was able to re-establish the distance I had learned to impose at great cost to my spirit. The sunlight filtered through the green glass dome and through the imported foliage. I was unused to the soft, almost liquid light, unlike the dark chill of my room.

The tropical birds in the zoo immediately recognized that, unlike them, I had not been born in captivity. I was taken from the wild. Some had ancestors who were wild, but most, the exception being one all-black Amazonian parrot, were born in zoos, pet stores or aviaries. They could not hope to compete with my heritage as the idol of kings. Two other members of my own species displayed themselves on a palm branch near the top of the green glass dome, showing that even in these circumstances they had learned to restrain from flight. One had a fine assortment of red flecks in the wing he stretched downward for my inspection.

I continued to hop away on my good leg, flap my wings and shriek at the touch of a human, but I knew I owed my resuscitation to the skill and expertise of the dark-eyed doctor. Those gentle educated fingers had deduced what was needed to make me well. His knowledge was the opposite of mine, gained measuring things outside of himself, mine the mastery of the mysteries within.

The creamy chill of winter passed into the shy green of spring. The doctor considered me well enough to go home. My mistress came and carefully listened to his instructions. The doctor never commented upon the cause of my injury, but upon arriving back in the apartment I saw the hole in the closet wall had been hastily covered over with a piece of plywood and a few nails.

After my stay in the hospital my mistress began covering my cage at night, perhaps because my laughter in the dark unnerved her, perhaps to protect her investment. Those occasional shrieks at midnight, attempts to discover if there were kindred spirits in the neighborhood, might have been frightening. One evening the mistress bustled into my small room with a large piece of green felt. It was an especially unusual occurrence because she rarely came close to my cage now, asking the master or even a casual visitor to sprinkle a few seeds into my dish. The first time she walked in with the cover she threw it without warning over my cage as I hissed and flapped my wings. Then she slammed the door shut.

My age, my great age weighs heavily upon me when the cover floats down over the cage for the night. The cover stills my voice, blocks out my vision of even this closet where I will be confined for the rest of my parrot life, unless I am rescued by a stroke of fortune or sold again. If another epoch is coming when parrots are worshiped and fed mangoes and red meat, I do not think I will live to see it. My fate will be to die in this tiny cage, surrounded by my own filth, without love, and reliant upon a natural enemy for conversation. The snow outside makes the wall behind my cage as chill as the marble of tombstones, and I long for the damp warmth of the jungle. What joy have I except the joy of my own whistle? Sometimes the city birds answer my imitations of their calls. Soon I shall be beyond the need to communicate, at a level where I recognize that the attempt to pass messages between living things is as foolish as words. In my next life I will live for five hundred years in a form which is incapable of development or destruction. Perhaps then the dog with his long tail will have assumed my position as teacher, scholar and despised pet, and the cat will be left to sleep undisturbed in the limbo of sunlight.

The master and mistress are huddled together in bed now, happy to know I am temporarily silenced. I hear the creak of the springs, a cough, the single click of the light switch, which I answer perfectly. I shut one yellow eye and wait for the morning.

IV

OTHER ANIMALS AS PREY
||||||||||||||||||||||||||||||

THE PLEASURES OF HUNTING
–Ernest Hemingway–

Now it is pleasant to hunt something that you want very much over a long period of time, being outwitted, out-manœuvred, and failing at the end of each day, but having the hunt and knowing every time you are out that, sooner or later, your luck will change and that you will get the chance that you are seeking. But it is not pleasant to have a time limit by which you must get your kudu or perhaps never get it, nor even see one. It is not the way hunting should be. It is too much like those boys who used to be sent to Paris with two years in which to make good as writers or painters after which, if they had not made good, they could go home and into their fathers' business. The way to hunt is for as long as you live against as long as there is such and such an animal; just as the way to paint is as long as there is you and colors and canvas, and to write as long as you can live and there is pencil and paper or ink or any machine to do it with, or anything you care to write about, and you feel a fool, and you are a fool, to do it any other way. But here we were, now, caught by time, by the season, and by the

running out of our money, so that what should have been as much
fun to do each day whether you killed or not was being forced into
that most exciting perversion of life; the necessity of accomplishing
something in less time than should truly be allowed for its doing. So,
coming in at noon, up since two hours before daylight, with only three
days left, I was starting to be nervous about it. [. . .]

From the top of one rise we saw two kongoni showing yellow on a
hillside about a mile away and I motioned to Droop that we would go
after them. We started down and in a ravine jumped a waterbuck bull
and two cows. Waterbuck was the one animal we might get that I knew
was worthless as meat and I had shot a better head than this one carried. I had the sights on the buck as he tore away, remembered about
the worthless meat, and having the head, and did not shoot.

"No shoot kuro?" Droopy asked in Swahili. "*Doumi sana*. A good
bull."

I tried to tell him that I had a better one and that it was no good
to eat.

He grinned.

"*Piga kongoni m'uzuri.*"

"Piga" was a fine word. It sounded exactly as the command to
fire should sound or the announcement of a hit. "M'uzuri," meaning
good, well, better, had sounded too much like the name of a state for
a long time and walking I used to make up sentences in Swahili with
Arkansas and M'uzuri in them, but now it seemed natural, no longer
to be italicized, just as all the words came to seem the proper and
natural words and there was nothing odd or unseemly in the stretching of the ears, in the tribal scars, or in a man carrying a spear. The
tribal marks and the tattooed places seemed natural and handsome
adornments and I regretted not having any of my own. My own scars
were all informal, some irregular and sprawling, others simply puffy
welts. I had one on my forehead that people still commented on, asking if I had bumped my head; but Droop had handsome ones beside
his cheekbones and others, symmetrical and decorative, on his chest
and belly. I was thinking that I had one good one, a sort of embossed
Christmas tree, on the bottom of my right foot that only served to

wear out socks, when we jumped two reedbuck. They went off through the trees and then stood at sixty yards, the thin, graceful buck looking back, and I shot him high and a touch behind the shoulder. He gave a jump and went off very fast.

"Piga." Droopy smiled. We had both heard the whunk of the bullet.

"Kufa," I told him. "Dead."

But when we came up to him, lying on his side, his heart was still beating strongly, although to all appearances he was dead. Droopy had no skinning knife and I had only a penknife to stick him with. I felt for the heart behind the foreleg with my fingers and feeling it beating under the hide slipped the knife in but it was short and pushed the heart away. I could feel it, hot and rubbery against my fingers, and feel the knife push it, but I felt around and cut the big artery and the blood came hot against my fingers. Once bled, I started to open him, with the little knife, still showing off to Droopy, and emptying him neatly took out the liver, cut away the gall, and laying the liver on a hummock of grass, put the kidneys beside it.

Droopy asked for the knife. Now he was going to show me something. Skillfully he slit open the stomach and turned it inside, tripe side, out, emptying the grass in it on the ground, shook it, then put the liver and kidneys inside it and with the knife cut a switch from the tree the buck lay under and sewed the stomach together with the withe so that the tripe made a bag to carry the other delicacies in. Then he cut a pole and put the bag on the end of it, running it through the flaps, and put it over his shoulder in the way tramps carried their property in a handkerchief on the end of a stick in Blue Jay corn plaster advertisements when we were children. It was a good trick and I thought how I would show it to John Staib in Wyoming some time and he would smile his deaf man's smile (you had to throw pebbles at him to make him stop when you heard a bull bugle), and I knew what John would say. He would say, "By Godd, Urnust, dot's smardt."

Droop handed me the stick, then took off his single garment, made a sling and got the buck up on his back. I tried to help him and suggested by signs that we cut a pole and sling him, carrying him between us, but he wanted to carry him alone. So we started for camp, me with the tripe bag on the end of a stick over my shoulder, my rifle slung, and Droopy staggering steadily ahead, sweating heavily, under the buck. I tried to get him to hang him in a tree and leave him until we could send out a couple of porters, and to that end we put him in the crotch of a tree. But when Droop saw that I meant to go off and leave him there rather than simply allow him to drain he got him down onto his shoulders again and we went on into camp, the boys, around the cooking fire, all laughing at the tripe bag over my shoulder as we came in.

This was the kind of hunting that I liked. No riding in cars, the country broken up instead of the plains, and I was completely happy. I had been quite ill and had that pleasant feeling of getting stronger each day. I was underweight, had a great appetite for meat, and could eat all I wanted without feeling stuffy. Each day I sweated out whatever we drank sitting at the fire at night, and in the heat of the day, now, I lay in the shade with a breeze in the trees and read with no obligation and no compulsion to write, happy in knowing that at four o'clock we would be starting out to hunt again. I would not even write a letter. The only person I really cared about, except the children, was with me and I had no wish to share this life with anyone who was not there, only to live it, being completely happy and quite tired. I knew that I was shooting well and I had that feeling of well being and confidence that is so much more pleasant to have than to hear about. [. . .]

We followed Droopy into the thick, tall grass that was five feet above our heads, walking carefully on the game trail, stooping forward, trying to make no noise breathing. I was thinking of the buff the way I had seen them when we had gotten the three that time, how the old bull had come out of the bush, groggy as he was, and I could see the horns, the boss coming far down, the muzzle out, the little eyes, the roll of fat and muscle on his thin-haired, gray, scaly-hided neck, the heavy power and the rage in him, and I admired him and respected him, but he was slow, and all the while we shot I felt that it was fixed and that we had him. This was different, this was no rapid fire, no pouring it on him as he comes groggy into the open, if he comes now I must be quiet inside and put it down his nose as he comes with the head out. He will have to put the head down to hook, like any bull, and that will uncover the old place the boys wet their knuckles on and I will get one in there and then must go sideways into the grass and he would be Pop's from then on unless I could keep the rifle when I jumped. I was sure I could get that one in and jump if I could wait and watch his head come down. I knew I could do that and that the shot would kill him but how long would it take? That was the whole thing. How long would it take? Now, going forward, sure he was in here, I felt the elation, the best elation of all, of certain action to come, action in which you had something to do, in which you can kill and come out of it, doing something you are ignorant about and so not scared, no one to worry about and no responsibility except to perform something you feel sure you can perform, and I was walking softly ahead watching Droopy's back and remembering to keep the sweat out of my glasses when I heard a noise behind us and turned my head. It was P. O. M. with M'Cola coming on our tracks.

"For God's sake," Pop said. He was furious.

We got her back out of the grass and up onto the bank and made her realize that she must stay there. She had not understood that she was to stay behind. She had heard me whisper something but thought it was for her to come behind M'Cola.

"That spooked me," I said to Pop.

"She's like a little terrier," he said. "But it's not good enough."

We were looking out over that grass.

"Droop wants to go still," I said. "I'll go as far as he will. When he says no that lets us out. After all, I gut-shot the son of a bitch."

"Mustn't do anything silly, though."

"I can kill the son of a bitch if I get a shot at him. If he comes he's got to give me a shot."

The fright P. O. M. had given us about herself had made me noisy.

"Come on," said Pop. We followed Droopy back in and it got worse and worse and I do not know about Pop but about half way I changed to the big gun and kept the safety off and my hand over the trigger guard and I was plenty nervous by the time Droopy stopped and shook his head and whispered "Hapana." It had gotten so you could not see a foot ahead and it was all turns and twists. It was really bad and the sun was only on the hillside now. We both felt good because we had made Droopy do the calling off and I was relieved as well. What we had followed him into had made my fancy shooting plans seem very silly and I knew all we had in there was Pop to blast him over with the four-fifty number two after I'd maybe miss him with that lousy four-seventy. I had no confidence in anything but its noise any more.

We were back trailing when we heard the porters on the hillside shout and we ran crashing through the grass to try to get to a high enough place to see to shoot. They waved their arm and shouted that the buffalo had come out of the reeds and gone past them and then M'Cola and Droopy were pointing and Pop had me by the sleeve trying to pull me to where I could see them and then, in the sunlight, high up on the hillside against the rocks I saw two buffalo. They shone very black in the sun and one was much bigger than the other and I remember thinking this was our bull and that he had picked up a cow and she had made the pace and kept him going. Droop had handed me the Springfield and I slipped my arm through the sling and sighting, the buff now all seen through the aperture, I froze myself inside and held the bead on the top of his shoulder and as I started to squeeze he started running and I swung ahead of him and loosed off. I saw him lower his head and jump like a bucking horse as he comes out of the chutes and as I threw the shell, slammed the bolt forward and shot again, behind him as he went out of sight, I knew I had him. Droopy and I started to run and as we were running I heard a low bellow. I stopped and yelled at Pop, "Hear him? I've got him, I tell you!"

"You hit him," said Pop. "Yes."

"Goddamn it, I killed him. Didn't you hear him bellow?"

"No."

"Listen!" We stood listening and there it came, clear, a long, moaning, unmistakable bellow.

"By God," Pop said. It was a very sad noise.

M'Cola grabbed my hand and Droopy slapped my back and all laughing we started on a running scramble, sweating, rushing, up the ridge through the trees and over rocks. I had to stop for breath, my heart pounding, and wiped the sweat off my face and cleaned my glasses.

"Kufa!" M'Cola said, making the word for dead almost explosive in its force. "N'Dio! Kufa!"

"Kufa!" Droopy said grinning.

"Kufa!" M'Cola repeated and we shook hands again before we went on climbing. Then, ahead of us, we saw him, on his back, throat stretched out to the full, his weight on his horns, wedged against a tree. M'Cola put his finger in the bullet hole in the center of the shoulder and shook his head happily.

Pop and P. O. M. came up, followed by the porters.

"By God, he's a better bull than we thought," I said.

"He's not the same bull. This is a real bull. That must have been our bull with him."

"I thought he was with a cow. It was so far away I couldn't tell."

"It must have been four hundred yards. By God, you *can* shoot that little pipsqueak."

"When I saw him put his head down between his legs and buck I knew we had him. The light was wonderful on him."

"I knew you had hit him, and I knew he wasn't the same bull. So I thought we had two wounded buffalo to deal with. I didn't hear the first bellow."

"It was wonderful when we heard him bellow," P. O. M. said. "It's such a sad sound. It's like hearing a horn in the woods."

"It sounded awfully jolly to me," Pop said. "By God, we deserve a drink on this. That was a shot. Why didn't you ever tell us you could shoot?"

"Go to hell."

"You know he's a damned good tracker, too, and what kind of a bird shot?" he asked P. O. M.

"Isn't he a beautiful bull?" P. O. M. asked.

"He's a fine one. He's not old but it's a fine head."

We tried to take pictures but there was only the little box camera and the shutter stuck and there was a bitter argument about the shutter while the light failed, and I was nervous now, irritable, righteous, pompous about the shutter and inclined to be abused because we could get no picture. You cannot live on a plane of the sort of elation I had felt in the reeds and having killed, even when it is only a buffalo, you feel a little quiet inside. Killing is not a feeling that you share and I took a drink of water and told P. O. M. I was sorry I was such a bastard about the camera. She said it was all right and we were all right again looking at the buff with M'Cola making the cuts for the headskin and we standing close together and feeling fond of each other and understanding everything, camera and all. I took a drink of the whiskey and it had no taste and I felt no kick from it.

"Let me have another," I said. The second one was all right.

We were going on ahead to camp with the chased-by-a-rhino spearsman as guide and Droop was going to skin out the head and they were going to butcher and cache the meat in trees so the hyenas would not get it. They were afraid to travel in the dark and I told Droopy he could keep my big gun. He said he knew how to shoot so I took out the shells and put on the safety and handing it to him told him to shoot. He put it to his shoulder, shut the wrong eye, and pulled hard on the trigger, and again, and again. Then I showed him about the safety and had him put it on and off and snap the gun a couple of times. M'Cola became very superior during Droopy's struggle to fire with the safety on and Droopy seemed to get much smaller. I left him the gun and two cartridges and they were all busy butchering in the dusk when we followed the spearsman and the tracks of the smaller buff, which had no blood on them, up to the top of the hill and on our way toward home. We climbed around the tops of valleys, went across gulches, up and down ravines and finally came onto the main ridge, it dark and cold in the evening, the moon not yet up, we plodded along, all tired. Once M'Cola, in the dark, loaded with Pop's heavy gun and an assortment of water bottles, binoculars, and a musette bag of books, sung out a stream of what sounded like curses at the guide who was striding ahead.

"What's he say?" I asked Pop.

"He's telling him not to show off his speed. That there is an old man in the party."

"Who does he mean, you or himself?"

"Both of us."

We saw the moon come up, smoky red over the brown hills, and we came down through the chinky lights of the village, the mud houses all closed tight, and the smells of goats and sheep, and then across the stream and up the bare slope to where the fire was burning in front of our tents. It was a cold night with much wind.

SKETCHES FROM A HUNTER'S ALBUM
—Ivan Turgenev—

For a long while I could find no game; finally, a landrail flew out of an extensive oak thicket which was completely overgrown with wormwood. I fired: the bird turned over in the air and fell. Hearing the shot, Kasyan quickly covered his face with his hand and remained stock-still until I had reloaded my gun and picked up the shot bird. Just as I was preparing to move farther on, he came up to the place where the bird had fallen, bent down to the grass which had been sprinkled with several drops of blood, gave a shake of the head and looked at me in fright. Afterwards I heard him whispering: "A sin! 'Tis a sin, it is, a sin!"

Eventually the heat forced us to find shelter in the wood. I threw myself down beneath a tall hazel bush, above which a young and graceful maple had made a beautiful spread of its airy branches. Kasyan seated himself on the thick end of a felled birch. I looked at him. Leaves fluttered slightly high above, and their liquid, greenish shadows glided calmly to and fro over his puny figure, clad somehow or other in a dark cloth coat, and over his small face. He did not raise his head. Bored by his silence, I lay down on my back and began admiringly to watch the peaceful play of the entwined leaves against the high, clear sky. It is a remarkably pleasant occupation, to lie on one's back in a forest and look upwards! It seems that you are looking into a bottomless sea, that it is stretching out far and wide *below* you, that the trees are not rising from the earth but, as if they were the roots of enormous plants, are descending or falling steeply into those lucid, glassy waves, while the leaves on the trees glimmer like emeralds or thicken into a gold-tinted, almost jet-black greenery. Somewhere high, high up, at the very end of a delicate branch, a single leaf stands out motionless against a blue patch of translucent sky, and, beside it, another sways, resembling in its movement the ripplings upon the surface of a fishing reach, as if the movement were of its own making and not caused by the wind. Like magical underwater islands, round white clouds gently float into view and pass by, and then suddenly the whole of this sea, this radiant air, these branches and leaves suffused with sunlight, all of it suddenly begins to stream in the wind, shimmers with a fugitive brilliance, and a fresh, tremulous murmuration arises which is like the endless shallow splashing of oncoming ripples. You lie still and you go on watching: words cannot express the delight and quiet, and how sweet is the feeling that creeps over your heart. You go on watching, and that deep, clear azure brings a smile to your lips as innocent as the azure itself, as innocent as the clouds passing across it, and as if in company with them there passes through your mind a slow cavalcade of happy recollections, and it seems to you that all the while your gaze is traveling farther and farther away and drawing all of you with it into that calm, shining infinity, making it impossible for you to tear yourself away from those distant heights, from those distant depths. . . .

"Master, eh, master!" Kasyan suddenly said in his resonant voice.

I raised myself up in surprise; until that moment he had hardly answered any of my questions and now he had suddenly started talking of his own accord.

"What do you want?" I asked.

"Why is it now that you should be killing that wee bird?" he began, looking me directly in the face.

"How do you mean: why? A landrail is a game bird. You can eat it."

"No, it wasn't for that you were killing it, master. You won't be eating it! You were killing it for your own pleasure."

"But surely you yourself are used to eating a goose or a chicken, for example, aren't you?"

"Such birds are ordained by God for man to eat, but a landrail— that's a bird of the free air, a forest bird. And he's not the only one; aren't there many of them, every kind of beast of the forest and of the field, and river creature, and creature of the marsh and meadow and the heights and the depths—and a sin it is to be killing such a one, it should be let to live on the earth until its natural end. . . . But for man there is another food laid down; another food and another drink; bread is God's gift to man, and the waters from the heavens, and the tame creatures handed down from our fathers of old."

I looked at Kasyan in astonishment. His words flowed freely; he did not cast around for them, but spoke with quiet animation and a modest dignity, occasionally closing his eyes.

"So according to you it's also sinful to be killing fish?" I asked.

"A fish has cold blood," he protested with certainty, "it's a dumb creature. A fish doesn't know fear, doesn't know happiness: a fish is a creature without a tongue. A fish doesn't have feelings, it has no living blood in it. . . . Blood," he continued after a pause, "blood is holy! Blood does not see the light of God's sun, blood is hidden from the light. . . . And a great sin it is to show blood to the light of day, a great sin and cause to be fearful, oh, a great one it is!"

He gave a sigh and lowered his eyes. I must admit that I looked at the strange old man in complete amazement. His speech did not sound like the speech of a peasant: simple people did not talk like this, nor did ranters. This language, thoughtfully solemn and unusual as it was, I had never heard before.

HUNTING AT SEA
—*Laurens van der Post*—

Starting from a point where I was truly bewildered, dismayed and even mistrustful of the man, I soon discovered a far-ranging kind of fellow-feeling for kaspersen which uncovered unexpected depths of compassion and a sense of the importance of an understanding in the human spirit that is beyond censure and judgement. Also he taught me things about whales and the sea during the three seasons of spasmodic winter whaling that no-one else, I believe, could have done. [. . .]

What did he teach me? He taught me, of course, all that there was to know in those days about the life of a hunter at sea. He provided my imagination with the aboriginal point of departure in the evolution of man's relationship with the sea which is necessary for the sense of continuity with our primordial beginning. He passed on to me all that he knew about whales and their hunting—in greater depth than anyone else could have done because of his own compulsive interest in what he did. This interest of his ensured that in our discussions there was always two-way traffic between us. [. . .]

From the beginning to the end of my three seasons with this man I got more of the feel of the sea, and more experience of its role in the life and spirit of man, than I came to have in the many ships which I subsequently sailed in across the oceans of the world. It is something for which I remain intensely grateful.

One of the greatest of those moments, by some great good fortune, came on my very first day out at sea with Thor Kaspersen. He was still suffering from the physical after-effects of a long weekend of intense drinking and the subsequent shock of the sudden and total abstention that he never failed to observe at sea, and I was obviously and understandably an encumbrance to him on that first day. I was not surprised therefore that when the look-out appeared characteristically without any command, at the foot of the rope ladder to take up his position in the tub at the foremast, Kaspersen dismissed me from his side with a curt though impersonal suggestion: "You want see whales? You go with him and look damn good!"

With that he called out something in Norwegian to the burly farmer-sailor who already had a foot on the first rung of rope. Consequently the man waited and, after telling me to do exactly as he did—in serviceable English—led me up the ladder of the foremast. Soon we were up together in the tub at the crow's nest looking out over the dark blue water under the morning sky. It was a day without a single cloud and, as always, the sea heaved with the long, deep swell which is the everlasting thrust of life coming straight from the steady beat of the heart of that great ocean of history. There was not a ripple to mar the reflection of the day in its water, nor blur our vision of it. . . .

I had no experience of what we were looking for except, of course, the vicarious one that I had gained through reading books on whaling. But again, thanks largely to what I had learned from indigenous trackers, I did not impose any willful expectations during my watch over those immense, heaving but vacant waters. I remembered above all one of the basic tenets of their teachings: one kept one's eyes, as well as one's heart, free from any preconceived notions, so that whatever was to happen would find neither heart nor vision closed against it, and consequently the event could fall unimpeded into one's senses. My reward came after about an hour of watching the ocean. By then I had forced myself to take no further interest in the way our ship was constantly swinging like a pendulum from what seemed like one perilous pitch to another. At an acute angle to port of the tiny deck below us, one would be staring straight down into the sea and one could often then see the fin of a shark or the shadow of a great fish pass with infinite ease like that of a cloud over a field of grass in the deep, green-blue water below. Then we would swing back to another equally acute and dangerous angle over to starboard. But fortunately my eyes and mind were open to receive one of those happenings for which precisely such a suspension of the senses had been prescribed.

The surprise was so great that I could not, at first, quite believe in the event. Midway between the *Larsen II* and the horizon, and east-south-east of our port bow, it appeared as if the sea had suddenly come alive. It first breathed in deeply and then, from behind a high amber swell, it breathed out so powerfully that it sent a fountain of steam soaring upwards from the summit of one of its longest ranges of water. Briefly, the fountain stood there like a palm of silver in some mirage before the eyes of a traveler lost in a great wasteland. My lack of recognition, however, did not last a second and quickly transformed itself into a sense of being witness to something miraculous; so much so that I remember that the hair at the back of my head was tingling. Some reflex of my whole being made me grasp the sleeve of my companion's jacket violently and call out, hoarse with emotion, "My God, something is blowing there!"

He came about so fast that he nearly squeezed the breath out of me as he pushed me against the side of the tub. He was just in time to see the same samite-white fountain of life rise out of the trough between two great waves. Loud as my own call had sounded in my ears, it was as nothing compared to the voice of a Minotaur which broke from him. It sounded as if it had come straight out of the pit and drum of his stomach. As his shout in Norwegian of the first "blast" of the day fell on the deck below, our ship came to life. I saw Thor Kaspersen on the bridge look up with great speed at the crow's nest in order to take a bearing on the direction in which my companion was pointing and, at the same time, spin the wheel to point the ship in the right direction, setting the bells in the engine-room below to ring out the most imme-diate message: "Full speed ahead!"

I found myself marveling at the way in which the propeller bit into the water and sent the *Larsen II* jumping forward like a hunter whose rider has just seen his hounds flush a fox. As for the rest of this action that followed with equal speed and despatch, no detachment of the best brigade of Guards trained for a Trooping of the Colour could have carried out words of command as faultlessly as did the men of this ship.

The bo'sun was already at his station by the donkey-engine, winch and drum, on which a cable was wound and which led across the decks up to another yellow coil on the gunner's platform where the end was securely tied to a harpoon in the gun set and ready for firing. There, too, one of the crew was already checking that both harpoon gun and coils of the rope were arranged in perfect sequence and firing order. All this had sprung from an apparently indifferent, almost somnambu-lant moment in the progression of the ship towards the first blow of the whale. For the two of us in the crow's nest watching this blow, it was a transfiguration of a spout of silver into a white mist that drifted slowly sideways over the waters. It was, for me, the most magical blow of all the three that followed. But to my companion, who had watched everything through German field-glasses which he always wore round his neck, it was obviously just another business affair. He began to speak more to himself than to me, something to the effect that it was the blow of a Blue Whale, a big one too, and that it had "sounded" and would now remain submerged for at least twenty-five minutes if not more; he paused and reiterated with passion that it was indeed an unusually large whale, since it had left behind it so large a design of smoothed-out water where it had dived back deeply into the heart of the sea. Then, when he was quite satisfied that the ship was making exactly for the target on which his glasses were focused, he proceeded to shout down his deductions to the Captain on the bridge below.

All this combined to make me acutely aware of how every person in the ship, and even the ship itself, had been joined together in an overwhelming singleness of purpose. [. . .]

"Big, very big [. . .] but patch of water vanishing fast [. . .] must hurry [. . .] if we to arrive before it goes. Why ship so slow today? Don't they know patches don't last long, not even biggest ones? God in heaven! Thor Kaspersen can do better [. . .] and to hurry quicker [. . .] quicker. [. . .]"

[. . .] "Nearly twenty-five minutes: if he doesn't surface soon he will have gone."

The time passed and still no whale nor any sign of one appeared.

"He vanished—or he is extremely big and gone very deep to stay under for so long!"

My companion's whispers were full of doubt. Judging by the way I seemed to detect a lessening of concentration among the men on the deck below, it seemed to me that he represented the feeling of everyone except, of course, Kaspersen. Kaspersen was now crouching over his gun and expecting to shoot at any moment.

Just on half an hour, not a furlong away and straight ahead of us, the sea suddenly came alive and there arose the greatest blow of all. I saw it rise some thirty to forty feet into the air. Now that we were near, I realised I had never seen anything more beautiful and moving—a beauty indeed great enough to give the phenomenon of a kind of sanctity and make it inviolate and total in my imagination. As this, the highest of all the blows, established itself like a fountain in the air, it was followed by the reappearance of the whale, slowly and majestically arching itself over the crest of the swell. I had become so totally absorbed in what had now become for me an act of almost Biblical revelation, that the desperate reactions on the ship were of secondary importance. It seemed to me that we must be almost within firing range. Indeed, when the second blow came and that broad back reappeared so close, the crystal silence was suddenly shattered by a burst of gunshot, and in my line of vision appeared a cable with something heavy at the end of it, wriggling like the fastest of snakes towards the whale. It hit its target in the centre of the back just as it achieved the greatest arc over the sea. I winced in participation of the shock and pain of the harpoon's entry into the warm flesh and blood. At once a spurt of mist appeared where the harpoon had entered deep into the flesh of the whale, and a slighter and lesser thud from within the inner tabernacle of its body reached my ears.

A great sigh of relief and satisfaction broke from my companion. As if he had never doubted Thor Kaspersen at all, he explained, "Got him, harpoon, grenade and all! No gunner like him now or ever before!"

Then I had no time to ask him what he meant by "grenade." It was only later that I learnt that each harpoon carried a grenade between its flukes set to explode within seconds of hitting its target so that for both humanitarian and practical reasons it killed the whale as quickly as possible. But even so the sound of the gun and the explosion made me assume that there had been an instant killing. I soon realised I couldn't have been more wrong.

The whale, on being hit, sounded at once and dived with such power and speed that the coil of cable on the gunner's platform unwound so fast that the slack between it and the drum on the winch was spent almost at once. I watched the spring on the derrick through which the cable passed suddenly forced to take all the strain of the whale's steep dive. It stretched so violently that the gap in the coils widened alarmingly. The steel moaned, thinned and yawned so much that I feared it would snap. But the man beside the donkey-engine had begun to release his brake on the winch by pulling on the lever just in time to allow the cable to unwind and give neither too fast nor too slowly, but just enough to hold it taut enough to act as a brake on the whale's precipitous descent. I reacted with revulsion at what seemed the unfairness of it, for both winch and spring were the modern technological equivalents of "playing" one of the greatest of the sea creatures as if it were no more than a trout which had been deceived by a fly on some English river, and so had impaled itself on a hook. Since then I have never taken kindly to the thought of either when done for so-called sport. The moment, indeed, was the tip of the iceberg of a paradox remaining potentially below the surface of my imagination. [. . .]

On one hand I could not deny the excitement and the acceleration into a consummation of archaic joy which the process of stalking and hunting, even at sea, had evoked in me, although I was present now only as an observer. On the other hand, hard on these emotions came an equal and opposite revulsion which nearly overwhelmed me when the hunt, as now, was successful and one was faced with the acceptance of the fact that one had aided and abetted in an act of murder of such an unique manifestation of creation. The only dispensation of the paradox ever granted to me in the past, unaware as I had been of the immensity of it until revealed to me in this moment at sea, was that in hunting out of necessity, all revulsions were redeemed by the satisfaction one felt in bringing food home to the hungry. That such satisfaction was not an illusion, nor a form of special pleading in the court of natural conscience, was proved for me by the profound feeling of gratitude one invariably felt for the animal who had died in order to allow others to live. But this form of killing and this battle for survival going on down in the sea, far deeper than any Shakespearian Prospero could ever have sounded, what could this possibly have to do with the necessities which were essential for the redemption of the act of killing? Once, in the days when the Arctic and Northern seas were witnessing a similar elimination of their whales, it is probable that some of these essential preconditions of redemption of this sort of killing might have existed. But, in this increasingly technological moment of my youth, when control of life was passing more and more from nature to man, and when there were already available all sorts of artificial substitutes for the essential oils of which animals like the whale had once been the only source of supply, what, I asked myself bitterly, could justify such killing except the greed of man for money, and money, moreover, acquired in the easiest and cheapest way without regard to the consequences? Worse still, I was certain that our imperviousness to the consternation caused by such killing in the heart of nature could be the beginning of an enmity between man and the life which had brought him forth, that would imperil his future on earth itself. [. . .]

For some twenty minutes I watched the surface consequences of this struggle between the doomed whale and the master rod which the *Larsen II* had become in the hands of the supreme angler Thor Kaspersen. I watched with a mixture of equal extremes of excitement and distaste. As always, I was moved by the way in which an animal, without exception, never accepts defeat as long as a flicker of life vibrates within its being. Equally, it was now a point of honour for this great whale, doomed as it was, to go on fighting until not it itself but the life within it decided that primordial honour had been satisfied. As for myself, who could influence the affair as little as I could control the longing to do so, I thought that the whale had already fought long and hard enough to be free to be dismissed into the peace and company of all that had fought likewise before it.

The ship had long lost all the way given to it by its last burst of speed and was now totally at rest in the sea. She was swaying so widely from port to starboard and back again that I thought my companion and I would fall out of our tub, so I hung on as hard as I could to its edges. All I could see below were those shadows of great sharks and other beings of the sea passing now like the shadows not of cloud but of an unbelievable dream moving through the half light that the sun had made of the opaque water. All there below looked indeed as if the sea were carrying on business as usual. But not so *Larsen II*. As it lost the last of its way, it began to heel over towards the angle of the whale's desperate plunge.

The silence, every half minute or so, was broken by the sound of the winch being released to give the whale more line. Even the bows of the ship, with Kaspersen still standing at the gun with his back firmly averted, began to swing in the direction of the plunge. So it took all the bo'sun's skill at the wheel and the experienced judgement of the man at the winch to keep on playing the whale at an angle which would not get the harpoon cable entangled with the poop and gun platform of the ship. This Olympian tug-of-war between whale and ship went on for perhaps some twenty minutes. Then a deep

"Ah yes, he has seen the light at last!" was uttered by my companion. The expression, even at the time, seemed inappropriate enough to be almost blasphemous. An adaptation of Mark Antony's "And I am bound for the dark," would have been a more precise and dignified comment on its condition. But it was apt enough to the extent that the pull between the whale and the spring through which the cable passed to the ship had suddenly slackened and the winch itself was sent spinning rapidly to take in the excess.

The whale surfaced—still alive but with its flank covered in blood. It was fighting not so much the cable and harpoon but life within itself which was leaving it for good. In the process, it was thrashing and beating the waves with that beautifully carved tail; perhaps one of the finest and most precious ornaments and decorations worn in the brave order of the animal kingdom. It was my first experience of what whalers call, so aptly, "the flurry of death." Indeed, soon the thrashing ceased and the whale floated inert on the surface. It was as if a black grave-stone had been raised on the surface of the sea as sign of the guilt of the everlasting Cain in man.

The whale was immediately hauled to the side of the ship. The two crew members with the long steel lances joined forces to cut deep openings into the side of the whale. At the same time they produced a long rubber tube with a nozzle at the end, inserted the nozzle into the holes they had made and set the donkey-engine going again to pump it full of air, so that once the nozzles were withdrawn and the holes securely plugged, it would be able to float by itself like a buoy on the water. It was only then that I realised how huge an animal it was. My companion informed me that at a guess it could be between a hundred and a hundred and twenty tons in weight.

We watched it being lashed firmly to the side of the ship by the head, the middle and the tail. That tail, which had been so alive and violent a moment before, was now still and cold as moonlit marble. The dead whale had parallel grooves in its skin which ran from chin to tail and were there, according to my companion, to allow for expansion to fill it with the breath it needed for diving so deeply and for so long.

Once all this was complete, Thor Kaspersen signalled to me whether I would not now like to come and join him on the bridge. But somehow, for the moment, I had taken against him and all the others below. Despite my own part in the affair, I preferred to stay up there in the tub where I could have myself to myself. This I made plain with an abrupt, almost offensive, signal. Even so, Kaspersen still had thought for our welfare, because he sent the cook up the rope-ladder to hand to us a huge flask of hot, sweet tea, mugs and sandwiches made of thick slices of Norwegian cheese between even thicker slices of brown rye bread.

As the day was still young we continued our hunting and, before sunset, we had killed two more whales in a similar manner. In the first fall of darkness we began heading back to harbour, with enough light to show me two things that have stayed with me ever since. First, there were suddenly great white sharks of the Indian Ocean to follow us brazenly on our way, every now and then turning upside down so that the strange, phantom-white of their bellies, and that angle of death implicit in the line of their jaws set underneath their faces, showed up quite clearly like a grin on a skeleton. Upside down they pulled huge chunks of flesh out of the whales we were taking back to port, with an expertise that no pack of hunting dogs, whom I thought supreme masters of the art, could have equalled. Most of all I remember a baby whale, wary and nervous as it was of the sharks, following us at some distance, compelled because its mother was one of the whales tied to the ship's impervious flanks. It kept us company until, forlorn and desperate, it too was lost in the final fall of night. [. . .]

THE GRAY CHIEFTAIN
–Charles A. Eastman–

On the westernmost verge of Cedar Butte stood Haykinshkah and his mate. They looked steadily toward the setting sun, over a landscape which up to that time had scarcely been viewed by man—the inner circle of the Bad Lands.

Cedar Butte guards the southernmost entrance to that wonderland, standing fully a thousand feet above the surrounding country, and nearly half a mile long by a quarter of a mile wide. The summit is a level, grassy plain, its edges heavily fringed with venerable cedars. To attempt the ascent of this Butte is like trying to scale the walls of Babylon, for its sides are high and all but inaccessible. Near the top there are hanging lands or terraces and innumerable precipitous points, with here and there deep chimneys or abysses in the solid rock. There are many hidden recesses and more than one secret entrance to this ancient castle of the gray chieftain and his ancestors, but to assail it successfully requires more than common skill and spirit.

Many a coyote had gone up as high as the second leaping-bridge and there abandoned the attempt. Old grizzly had once or twice begun the ascent with doubt and misgiving, but soon discovered his mistake, and made clumsy haste to descend before he should tumble into an abyss from which no one ever returns. Only Igmutanka, the mountain-lion, had achieved the summit, and at every ascent he had been well repaid; yet even he seldom chose to risk such a climb, when there were many fine hunting-grounds in safer neighborhoods.

So it was that Cedar Butte had been the peaceful home of the big spoonhorns for untold ages. To be sure, some of the younger and more adventurous members of the clan would depart from time to time to found a new family, but the wiser and more conservative were content to remain in their stronghold. There stood the two patriarchs, looking down complacently upon the herds of buffalo, antelope, and elk that peopled the lower plains. While the sun hovered over the western hills, a coyote on a near-by eminence gave his accustomed call to his mate. This served as a signal to all the wild hunters of the plains to set up their inharmonious evening serenade, to which the herbivorous kindred paid but little attention. The phlegmatic spoonhorn pair listened to it all with a fine air of indifference, like that of one who sits upon his own balcony, superior to the passing noises of the street.

It was a charming moonlight night upon the cedar-fringed plain, and there the old chief presently joined the others in feast and play. His mate sought out a secret resting-place. She followed the next gulch, which was a perfect labyrinth of caves and pockets, and after leaping two chasms she reached her favorite spot. Here the gulch made a square turn, affording a fine view of the country through a window-like open-ing. Above and below this were perpendicular walls, and at the bottom a small cavity, left by the root of a pine which had long since fallen and crumbled into dust. To this led a narrow terrace—so narrow that man or beast would hesitate before venturing upon it. The place was her own by right of daring and discovery, and the mother's instinct had brought her here to-night, for the pangs of deadly sickness were upon her.

In a little while relief came, and the ewe stood over a new-born lamb, licking tenderly the damp, silky hair, and trimming the little hoofs of their cartilaginous points. The world was quiet now, and those whose business it is to hunt or feed at night must do so in silence, for such is the law of the plains. The wearied mother slept in peace.

The sun was well above the butte when she awoke, although it was cool and shadowy still in her concealed abode. She gave suck to the lamb and caressed it for some time before she reluctantly prepared its cradle, according to the custom of her people. She made a little pocket in the side of the cave and gently put her baby in. Then she covered him all up, save the nose and eyes, with dry soil. She put her nose to his little sensitive ear and breathed into it warm love and cau-tion, and he felt and understood that he must keep his eyes closed and breathe gently, lest bear or wolf or man should spy him out when they had found her trail. Again she put her warm, loving nose to his eyes, then patted a little more earth on his body and smoothed it off. The tachinchana closed his eyes in obedience, and she left him for the plain above in search of food and sunlight.

———

At a little before dawn, two wild hunters left their camp and set out for Cedar Butte. Their movements were marked by unusual care and secrecy. Presently they hid their ponies in a deep ravine and groped their way up through the difficult Bad Lands, now and then pausing to listen. The two were close friends and rival hunters of their tribe.

"I think, friend, you have mistaken the haunts of the spoonhorn," remarked Wacootay, as the pair came upon one of the lower terraces. He said this rather to test his friend, for it was their habit thus to criticise and question each other's judgment, in order to extract from each other fresh observations. What the one did not know about the habits of the animals they hunted in common the other could usually supply.

"This is his home—I know it," replied Grayfoot. "And in this thing the animals are much like ourselves. They will not leave an old haunt unless forced to do so either by lack of food or overwhelming danger."

They had already passed on to the next terrace and leaped a chasm to gain the opposite side of the butte, when Grayfoot suddenly whispered, "In ahjin!" (Stop!). Both men listened attentively. "Tap, tap, tap," an almost metallic sound came to them from around the perpendicular wall of rock.

"He is chipping his horns!" exclaimed the hunter, overjoyed to surprise the chieftain at this his secret occupation. "Poor beast, they are now too long for him, so that he cannot reach the short grass to feed. Some of them die starving, when they have not the strength to do the hard bucking against the rock to shorten their horns. He chooses this time, when he thinks no one will hear him, and he even leaves his own clan when it is necessary for him to do this. Come, let us crawl up on him unawares."

They proceeded cautiously and with catlike steps around the next projection, and stood upon a narrow strip of slanting terrace. At short intervals the pounding noise continued, but strain their eyes as they might they could see nothing. Yet they knew that a few paces from them, in the darkness, the old ram was painfully driving his horns against the solid rock. Finally they lay flat upon the ground under a dead cedar, the color of whose trunk and that of the scanty soil somewhat resembled their clothing, and on their heads they had stuck some bunches of sage-bush, to conceal them from the eyes of the spoonhorn.

With the first gray of the approaching dawn the two hunters looked eagerly about them. There stood, in all his majesty, heightened by the wild grandeur of his surroundings, the gray chieftain of the Cedar Butte! He had no thought of being observed at that hour. Entirely unsuspicious of danger, he stood alone upon a pedestal-like terrace, from which vantage-point it was his wont to survey the surrounding country every morning. If the secret must be told, he had done so for years, ever since he became the head chief of the Cedar Butte clan.

It is the custom of their tribe that when a ram attains the age of five years he is entitled to a clan of his own, and thereafter must defend his right and supremacy against all comers. His experience and knowledge are the guide of his clan. In view of all this, the gray chieftain had been very thorough in his observations. There was not an object anywhere near the shape of bear, wolf, or man for miles around his kingdom that was not noted, as well as the relative positions of rocks and conspicuous trees.

The best time for Haykinshkah to make his daily observations is at sunrise and sunset, when the air is usually clear and objects appear distinct. Between these times the clan feed and settle down to chew their cud and sleep, yet some are always on the alert to catch a passing stranger within their field of observation. But the old chief spoonhorn pays very little attention. His duty is done. He may be nestled in a gulch just big enough to hold him, either sound asleep or leisurely chewing his cud. The younger members of the clan take their position upon the upper terraces and under the shade of projecting rocks, after a whole night's feasting and play upon the plain.

As spoonhorn stood motionless, looking away off toward the distant hills, the plain below appeared from this elevated point very smooth and sheetlike, and every moving object a mere speck. His form and color were not very different from the dirty gray rocks and clay of the butte.

Wacootay broke the silence. "I know of no animal that stands so long without movement, unless it is the turtle. I think he is the largest ram I have ever seen."

"I am sure he did not chip where he stands now," remarked Grayfoot. "This chipping-place is a monastery to the priests of the spoonhorn tribe. It is their medicine-lodge. I have more than once approached the spot, but could never find the secret entrance."

"Shall I shoot him now?" whispered his partner in the chase.

"No, do not do it. He is a real chief. He looks mysterious and noble. Let us know him better. Besides, if we kill him now we shall never see him again. Look! he will fall to that deep gulch ten trees' length below, where no one can get at him."

As Grayfoot spoke the animal shifted his position, facing them squarely. The two men closed their eyes and wrinkled their motionless faces into the semblance of two lifeless mummies. The old sage of the mountains was apparently deceived, but after a few moments he got down from his lofty position and disappeared around a point of rock.

"I never care to shoot an animal while he is giving me a chance to know his ways," explained Grayfoot. "We have plenty of buffalo meat. We are not hungry. All we want is spoons. We can get one or two sheep by-and-by, if we have more wit than they."

To this speech Wacootay agreed, for his curiosity was now fully aroused by Grayfoot's view, although he had never thought of it in just that way before. It had always been the desire for meat which had chiefly moved him in the matter of the hunt.

Having readjusted their sage wigs, the hunters made the circuit of the abyss that divided them from the ram, and as they looked for his trail they noticed the tracks of a large ewe leading down toward the inaccessible gulches.

"Ah, she has some secret down there! She never leaves her clan like this unless it is to steal away on a personal affair of her own."

So saying, Grayfoot with his fellow tracked the ewe's footprint along the verge of a deep gulf with much trouble and patience. The hunter's curiosity and a strong desire to know her secret impelled the former to lead the way.

"What will be our profit, if one slips and goes down into the gulch, never to be seen again?" remarked Wacootay, as they approached a leaping-place. The chasm below was of a great depth and dark. "It is not wise for us to follow farther; this ewe has no horns that can be made in to spoons."

"Come, friend; it is when one is doubting that mishaps are apt to occur," urged his companion.

"Koda, heyu yo!" exclaimed Wacootay, the next moment, in distress.

"Hehehe, koda! Hold fast!" cried the other.

Wacootay's moccasined foot had slipped on the narrow trail, and in the twinkling of an eye he had almost gone down a precipice of a hundred feet; but with a desperate launch forward he caught the bough of an overhanging cedar and swung by his hands over the abyss.

Quickly Grayfoot pulled both their bows from the quivers. He first tied himself to the trunk of the cedar with his packing-strap, which always hung from his belt. Then he held both the bows toward his friend, who, not without difficulty, changed his hold from the cedar bough to the bows. After a short but determined effort, the two men stood side by side once more upon the narrow foothold of the terrace. Without a word they followed the ewe's track to the cave.

Here she had lain last night. Both men began to search for other marks, but they found not so much as a sign of scratching anywhere. They examined the ground closely without any success. All at once a faint "Ba-a-a!" came from almost under their feet. They saw a puff of smokelike dust as the little creature called for its mother. It had felt the footsteps of the hunters and mistaken them for those of its own folk.

Wacootay hastily dug into the place with his hands and found the soil loose. Soon he uncovered a little lamb. "Ba-a-a!" it cried again, and quick as a flash the ewe appeared, stamping the ground in wrath.

Wacootay seized an arrow and fitted it to the string, but his companion checked him.

"No, no, my friend! It is not the skin or meat that we are looking for. We want horn for ladles and spoons. The mother is right. We must let her babe alone."

The wild hunters silently retreated, and the ewe ran swiftly to the spot and took her lamb away.

"So it is," said Grayfoot, after a long silence, "all the tribes of earth have some common feeling. I believe they are people as much as we are. The Great Mystery has made them what they are. Although they do not speak our tongue, we often seem to understand their thought. It is not right to take the life of any of them unless necessity compels us to do so.

"You know," he continued, "the ewe conceals her lamb in this way until she has trained it to escape from its enemies by leaping up or down from terrace to terrace. I have seen her teaching the yearlings and two-year-olds to dive down the face of a cliff which was fully twice the height of a man. They strike on the head and the two fore-feet. The ram falls largely upon his horns, which are curved in such a way as to protect them from injury. The body rebounds slightly, and they get upon their feet as easily as if they had struck a pillow. At first the yearlings hesitate and almost lose their balance, but the mother makes them repeat the performance until they have accomplished it to her satisfaction.

"They are trained to leap chasms on all fours, and finally the upward jump, which is a more difficult feat. If the height is not great they can clear it neatly, but if it is too high for that they will catch the rocky ledge with their fore-feet and pull themselves up like a man.

"In assisting their young to gain upper terraces they show much ingenuity. I once saw them make a ladder of their bodies. The biggest ram stood braced against the steep wall as high as his body could reach, head placed between his fore-feet, while the next biggest one rode his hind parts, and so on until the little ones could walk upon their broad backs to the top. We know that all animals make their young practise such feats as are necessary to their safety and advantage, and thus it is that these people are so well fitted to their peculiar mode of life.

"How often we are outwitted by the animals we hunt! The Great Mystery gives them this chance to save their lives by eluding the hunter, when they have no weapons of defence. The ewe has seen us, and she has doubtless warned all the clan of danger."

But there was one that she did not see. When the old chief left his clan to go to the secret place for chipping his horns, the place where many a past monarch of the Bad Lands has performed that painful operation, he did not intend to rejoin them immediately. It was customary with him at this time to seek solitude and sleep.

The two hunters found and carefully examined the tracks of the fleeing clan. The old ram was not among them. As they followed the trail along the terrace, they came to a leaping-place which did not appear to be generally used. Grayfoot stopped and kneeled down to examine the ground below.

"Ho!" he exclaimed; "the old chief has gone down this trail but has not returned. He is lying down near the chipping-place, if there is no other outlet."

Both men leaped to the next terrace below, and followed the secret pass into a rocky amphitheatre, opening out from the terrace upon which they had first seen the old ram. Here he lay asleep.

Wacootay pulled an arrow from his quiver.

"Yes," said his friend. "Shoot now! A warrior is always a warrior—and we are looking for horn for spoons."

The old chief awoke to behold the most dreaded hunter—man—on the very threshold of his sanctuary. Wildly he sprang upward to gain the top of the cliff; but Wacootay was expert and quick in the use of his weapon. He had sent into his side a shaft that was deadly. The monarch's fore-hoofs caught the edge—he struggled bravely for a moment, then fell limp to the rocky floor.

"He is dead. My friend, the noblest of chiefs is dead!" exclaimed Grayfoot, as he stood over him, in great admiration and respect for the gray chieftain.

V

OTHER ANIMALS AS TOOLS

IIIIIIIIIIIIIIIIIIIIIIIIII

THE DEAD BODY AND THE LIVING BRAIN
–Oriana Fallaci–

Libby had eaten her last meal the night before: orange, banana, monkey chow. While eating, she had observed us with curiosity. Her hands resembled the hands of a newly born child, her face seemed almost human. Perhaps because of her eyes. They were so sad, so defenseless. We had called her Libby because Dr. Maurice Albin, the anesthetist, had told us she had no name, we could give her the name we liked best, and because she accepted it immediately. You said, "Libby!" and she jumped; then she leaned her head on her shoulder. Dr. Albin had also told us that Libby had been born in India and was almost three years old, an age comparable to that of a seven-year-old girl. The rhesuses live 30 years, and she was a rhesus. Prof. Robert White uses the rhesuses because they are not expensive; they cost between $80 and $100. Chimpanzees, larger and easier to experiment with, cost up to $2,000 each.

After the meal, a veterinarian had come, and with as much ceremony as they use for the condemned, he had checked to be sure Libby was in good health. It would be a difficult operation, and her body should function as perfectly as a rocket going to the moon. A hundred times before, the experiment had ended in failure, and though Professor White became the first man in the entire history of medicine to succeed, the undertaking still bordered on science fiction. Libby was about to die in order to demonstrate that her brain could live isolated from her body and that, so isolated, it could still think.

————

At eight in the morning, Dr. Albin came to anesthetize Libby. In a cage near hers, a big monkey screamed ferociously, shaking the bars; in the adjoining rooms, dogs barked. Jim and Paul Austin, two assistants of Professor White's, grasped her and kept her on a table. Libby struggled powerfully, and it took time to immobilize her. The anesthetic consisted of 25 milligrams of pentothal. Dr. Albin injected it with a special plastic-covered needle. It was a big needle, and Libby cried, looking at it with surprise in her eyes. But she fell asleep very quickly, her little hands open as if to ask for mercy. Jim Austin began to shave her abdomen and her head. On her head, you could now see the electrodes that Dr. Leo Massopust, the neurophysiologist, had placed there six months before to measure the brain waves. The wires were red and yellow. The top of the skull, which had been removed, had been replaced with a kind of cement used by dentists. It was nine o'clock when Jim took her to surgery. He held her in his arms as if she were a baby.

————

Surgery was filled with computers and polygraphs. The atmosphere was tense, as it is before the blast-off of a rocket. Dr. Massopust was there, and Dr. Lee Wolin, the experimental psychologist, and Dr. David Yashol, the assistant of Professor White, and Dr. Satoru Kadoya, a Japanese who dedicates his life to the study of individual cells. Robert White came later. He was tall and strong and jolly. His teeth grasped a lighted pipe, and his eyes shone with a mysterious happiness. There is always a mysterious happiness in the look of a scientist who faces something that is considered impossible. Or a blasphemous challenge? Professor White is 41 years old and has spent half those years studying the brain. Because of this, perhaps, he seems to be much older: he has very few hairs, and those few are white. His colleagues admire his genius; his enemies hate him because he experiments on monkeys and dogs. When you ask him whether he's sorry to kill them, he answers: "Sure I am. Nobody gets immunized to the sight of someone who dies, man or monkey or dog. Death always disturbs me. My work isn't to bring death. It is to preserve life."

On the table in surgery, there was a little cot, and Libby was placed there. First, her wrists were tied, then her ankles. Dr. Albin inserted a tube in her femoral artery; the polygraph moved and indicated that her blood pressure was good. Her temperature and brain activity were also good. A secretary arrived with coffee and donuts for all. While drinking his coffee, Professor White explained that the brain of a monkey is similar to that of a man, differing only in size. Therefore, the procedure for isolating a human brain would be identical. In both cases, the danger lies in loss of blood; without blood, the brain dies in three minutes. And, unlike the heart, it cannot be resuscitated. What makes you what you are—a unique, irreplaceable being—thought, is the first thing that goes, and it never comes back. That's why the brain is a mystery. The operation we were going to see was to be an exploration of this mystery and of the despair of man, who knows much about the large cosmos he lives in, but little about the small cosmos that lives in his brain.

——

The journey started at ten a.m., when Professor White incised the skin of Libby's neck, uncovered the tissues and began to get rid of them, using a cautery that cut and burned at the same time. The first five hours of the operation would be spent like this, in demolishing Libby's head: muscle after muscle, nerve after nerve, vessel after vessel, slowly, patiently, implacably, until all would disappear like garbage among the dirty pads, and what would remain of Libby would be a body attached to a skull. A very difficult thing for any good surgeon, it seemed very easy for Professor White. He worked while smoking his pipe, chatting with us. The conversation was the sort you'd hear in a cocktail lounge: about Hugh Hefner, Svetlana Alliluyeva, the Red Guards. Libby went on sleeping. To keep her asleep, Dr. Albin injected those 25 milligrams of pentothal every 45 minutes. And because of that, you felt grateful to him.

————

By noon, Libby's neck had almost disappeared. Professor White cut her tracheal tube, quickly inserting the mechanical respirator. During this transfer, her heart lost some palpitations, her blood pressure precipitated, and there were worried looks, nervous gestures. But the machine worked well, the pressure went back to normal. Professor White attacked Libby's jaws, Libby's mouth, hypnotizing using his fingers. The fingers of a surgeon are so enchanting, more than those of a jeweler or a pianist. There is always a moment when they seem to be the fingers of a priest celebrating a Mass. And because of this, perhaps, you didn't cry for Libby. Not even now that those fingers were stealing her nose, her left eye, her right eye, and her features no longer existed. In their place was a smell of burnt flesh. Professor White looked tired. Perspiration clouded his glasses. Jim Austin wiped the sweat off his forehead with a pad. I asked him: "Would you call this animal alive?" He answered: "Why not?" The pressure, the temperature, the brain waves were perfect, though Libby couldn't see any more, or hear, or speak. She had finally become what he needed: a clean skull on a body. And he could now face the last part of the journey, the impossible part.

————

The blood that feeds the brain reaches it through four major vessels: the two carotid arteries and the two vertebral arteries. The vertebral vessels are inside the bony spinal column and the paired carotids are in the fleshy portion of the neck. The carotid arteries are the most important because they bring to the brain 80 percent of the blood. At three p.m., these four vessels were intact, Libby's head was still attached to the body. It was obvious that, once the head was cut off from the body, Libby's brain would have to be fed by the blood of another animal or by blood flowing through a mechanical system. On other occasions, Professor White had used a mechanical system; today, he would use another animal, the donor. To connect the carotids with the donor, Professor White employs this method: He inserts a T-shaped cannula into each carotid. The small branches of the T go inside the vessel, the stem of the T goes inside the tube connected to the femoral artery of the donor.

At 3:30, Professor White tied each carotid in two places, made a small cut between the ligations, inserted the T cannula through the cut, plugged the stem of the T cannula, which was not yet connected with the donor, undid the ligations and let the blood flow again in the carotids. Then he stopped and said: "Now, follow me. You must understand that, as in any hydraulic system, when the donor supplies this brain through the T cannula, he will have to receive in return as much blood as he has donated. Otherwise, the procedure would feed the brain while exsanguinating the donor. In order to return the blood to the donor, I must close Libby's vertebral arteries. If I don't, it would be as if you had four tubes, and while you put water in two tubes, you lost it through the other two. OK? The next part of the operation will consequently consist of sacrificing Libby's vertebral arteries. I will cut them a moment before cutting the spinal cord and the vertebrae; that is, a moment before the decapitation. At the same point, I will open the line connecting Libby's carotid with the donor. And all this will have to happen in less than three minutes." Then he said to Jim and Paul:

"Please bring the donor." Jim and Paul silently slipped out.

———

The donor was a big monkey, five times the size of Libby. Taking him out of the cage and anesthetizing him had been a real struggle. While Jim and Paul carried him, he slept, his neck and arms imprisoned by a sort of pillory. He had been wounded around the mouth, and he was ugly. You couldn't like him, even while thinking that he, too, had had a rough life. They had already used him six times, exposing his femoral artery. His body was full of scars. Professor White explained that the donor had to be big in order to feed Libby's brain the same quantity of blood that it had received before, when she had all her arteries. Then a deep silence fell, as it does just before a rocket takes off. The dramatic moment had come, the moment when the countdown cannot be interrupted, the numbers run faster and faster. Minus fifteen . . . minus fourteen . . . minus thirteen . . . minus twelve. . . .

Libby was turned on her stomach. Professor White removed a fragment of the bone that protects the spinal cord, gently dissected the
membrane that surrounds it. With a curved needle, he probed the
vertebral arteries, found them, tied them up. Jim was again wiping the
sweat from his forehead. The sweat had increased.

Minus ten . . . minus nine . . . minus eight . . . minus seven . . .
minus six. . . . Now, Libby's brain was fed only by her carotids, and it
received the necessary 80 percent of blood. The Professor had to be
very quick or her brain would be damaged, her death would be useless,
his work would be wasted. As quickly as lightning, he cut the vertebral
arteries, he ligated the carotid arteries under the T cannulae, he murmured, "Open the line," and unplugged the stem of the T cannulae,
connecting them with the donor. Then he caught the shears.

Minus five, four, three, two, one, lift-off! The shears opened, closed
over the veins, and the spinal cord, and the vertebrae, and below the
ligations of the carotids. A fountain of blood splashed the hands and
faces of the men, who didn't even notice. Then, like a glorious invisible flame, the blood of the big monkey flowed into Libby's carotids,
sprinkled her beheaded brain, came out to drip from the severed jugu-
lar veins into a recipient from which it returned to the big monkey. It
had taken less than three minutes, and from that moment, Libby was
only a Thought protected by a solid bone shell that Professor White
lifted anxiously, panting.

————

While this happened, no one paid any attention to Libby's body,
which was lying lifeless. Professor White might have fed it, too, with
blood, and made it survive without a head. But Professor White didn't
choose to, and so the body lay there, forgotten, until Paul untied it and
put it down on the floor. It was nothing now. All that Libby had been,
her joys and her fears, her reactions and her memories, the jungle
where she had been born, the net in which she had been captured, the
cage in which she had been imprisoned, her last meal, the last flashing
of her eyes when Dr. Albin had hurt her with the needle, everything
was still living inside that brain without flesh, connected with wires,
with tubes, with cannulae. As if she were a rocket, during the last three

minutes, Professor White had lost contact with her. She had entered infinity and didn't transmit any signal to Earth. The Pressure Monitoring Machine didn't move, or the Temperature Monitoring Machine, and the computers did not receive the electrical waves. But soon they did, as before, better than before, and Dr. Massopust said, "The brain activity is largely better than when the brain had a body."

"Dr. Massopust, how can you assert that he [the brain] thinks?"

"We know it through the instruments, the EEG traces. These wires indicate they are connected with a functional brain. No doubt about it. I even suspect that without his senses, he can think more quickly. What kind of thinking, I don't know. I guess he is primarily a memory, a repository for information stored when he had his flesh; he cannot develop further because he no longer has the nourishment of experience. Yet this, too, is a new experience."

"Dr. Wolin, he is now in a state of sleep or of drowsiness because of the anesthesia. When awake, would he be aware of the nothingness in which he is floating? Would he suffer?"

"I suppose that, waking, he would feel like an individual subjected to complete paralysis, because when a man is paralyzed, he is aware of the senses' absence. Yes, I assume that this monkey knows the absence of the flesh. But with no physical pain, because all the nerves have been cut off. Psychological suffering, I don't know. I have no idea if he would feel happy or unhappy or lonely."

My questions and his answers sounded useless, because the only one who could answer me was Libby's brain, which was able to think, but was not able to communicate with us any more. My God, what is a brain that is only a brain? Pure silence? Pure tragedy?

The brain lived and thought until nine o'clock. Actually, it could have lived as long as Professor White wished; once, he had kept a brain alive for days and days, using the machinery instead of a donor. This time, he allowed the brain only five hours, more than enough time to collect the information he was after. Professor White wanted to know, for example, how much oxygen and glucose the brain needed, what kind of wastes it ejected, how long it could survive when cooled. This last question was very important because of its relevance to operations on the human brain in people suffering from heart disease. Professor White believes that cooling the brain may prevent stroke. So he covered the brain with a cellophane bag, filled the bag with ice, cooled the brain to 14° centigrade, closed the circuit connecting it to the big monkey, and the brain survived without blood for half an hour. Then he opened the circuit again, and removed the ice, and the brain returned to normal. Until nine o'clock, when Professor White said, "OK. It's late. Let's go home." And, with a slight, casual movement, he severed the connections; he killed it.

The brain did not die at once. It took those three minutes. It died slowly, like the death of a fire that goes down little by little, and gets smaller and smaller, and now it is only the ghost of a flame that burns out, and now it is only a point of light, shining less, and less, and now it is extinguished, even the ashes vanish into nothing. It died when it didn't think any more. And so the big monkey was sewn up again, and disinfected, and returned to his cage; Professor White took Libby's skull, then the tweezers, broke the skull piece by piece, and showed the brain to us. It was a ball of jelly, a beautiful orange color. The photographer said: "Professor White, could you hold it for a photo?"

"If you like," he answered.

And he raised his hand, which opened the way the valves of an oyster open, and there the brain lay, like a pearl.

"It's only tissue, isn't it?" I said.

"Oh, no. It's much more," he said. "It was a perfume, and now it's an empty bottle from which the perfume has escaped. But the fragrance is still there."

He was speaking, obviously, of the soul.

DOCTOR RAT
—William Kotzwinkle—

"Doctor Rat. Doctor Rat . . ."

A young female calling to me from her cage. She needs my special counseling, as she's all in a tizzy about the bandages on her belly. "Yes, my dear, are your bandages too tight?"

"They cut a hole in my stomach!"

"Yes, of course. It's so that they'll be able to insert a plastic window there in order to watch your embryonic ratlings develop."

"I hate it! I'll gnaw it off! I'll bite through the bandages!"

"Please, my dear, don't be hysterical." I must say she's not showing the scientific attitude at all. We've got to have that window there, so that we can insert a thin hair through it and tickle the little ratlings as they grow inside her. It's part of a new program, for which I'm preparing extensive notes. A great deal can be learned by tickling an embryo with a hair, but naturally only the most advanced graduate students are qualified for such tickling. How, then, can we expect this female rat to have any appreciation of the fine points of the Stomach-window Program? Nonetheless, it is my duty to make her more receptive to the learned hair.

"Please don't let them hurt me, please . . ."

I think a little song might cheer her up:

> *"Oh scaly skin and dandruff*
> *with hemorrhagic sores,*
> *come and look inside us,*
> *they've provided us with doors!"*

I must move along here to the next cage, where a special magnesium diet has caused fatal clonic convulsions:

> *"Oh loss of hair and nervousness,*
> *diarrhea too,*
> *goiter and spasticity*
> *combined with Asian flu!"*

"Doctor Rat, I can no longer eat!"

"Aren't you the lad whose teeth have been trained to grow into a complete circle, piercing the roof of the mouth?"

"A nightmare, Doctor Rat. My mouth's a nightmare."

"We're watching you with keen interest, my boy. There's a chance the teeth may actually grow right up and pierce your brain. Come along and sing with me! Sing:

*"Irregular ovulation and
destruction of the thymus
chronic lymphedema and
amputation of the penis!"*

Excuse me, the Learned Professor has picked me up and is tying a string around my upper incisors at the moment. I am now permitted to hang by my teeth in the air as part of a new Insight Therapy Program—what fun, swinging back and forth here.

"Fight them, Doctor Rat! Bite them!"

A young radical rat shouting from his cage. Thus has our youth been corrupted by that goddamn blabber-mouth dog with his intuition-pictures. A rat may be waiting for decapitation, and suddenly he will see an intuitive play of pictures in his brain, sent there by this infernal dog on the treadmill. The rat will seem to participate in the scene, running with the wild dogs. The high intelligence of the dogs makes them very potent broadcasters, and being here under stress conditions adds power to their wavelength. Our lab is buzzing with revolutionary feelings. "You cock-sucking cur, how dare you sow dissent among these happy rats!"

The revolutionary mutt looks at me with red and squinting eyes. You perceived the subtlety of his broadcast, didn't you, with his sly insinuations of some sort of freedom to be gained by following a peculiar scent? But I know the truth and I'm shouting it to all: "The scent is five percent formaline, Brother Rats, and the only freedom you'll ever have is death! Death is freedom, that's the slogan!"

"Hurray for Doctor Rat!"

"You tell 'em, Doc."

"Thank you, friends and fellow supporters, thank you for your confidence. As you know, the rat is man's best friend. You've seen the advertisements in *Modern Psychology Magazine*: 'The Rat Is Our Friend.' Are we going to allow this wonderful friendship to go down the drain along with the cerebrospinal fluid? A rat must give his all! That's our purpose, that's why we're here on earth!"

My throat is certainly getting inflamed from all this. But I can't allow seventy-five years of laboratory experimentation to be pushed aside by a few revolutionary voices. This dog is in a powerful position, however, running here in our midst, tongue hanging out, legs flopping as the treadmill turns him, on and on. I've told the Learned Professor to jack up the heat in the dog's cage, so we can be finished with him soon. But the Learned Pro turns a deaf ear toward everything I say.

In the meantime, the dog has made numerous converts to his revolutionary cause. The whole Hemorrhagic Sore Cage has gone over to him. And I taught those ungrateful rats how to sing! What betrayal!

"Brother Rats, how can you be so easily swayed by this dirty dog? Look there, to your left. Look at the recipient rat on the surgical table. He's having a hole bored in his head. Listen to him screaming. The fresh tumor is being plunged into his brain tissue. In two or three weeks he'll be groveling around, the tumor increasing, obstructing all his bodily movements. That's reality, foolish rats. That's scientific reality, not a lot of stupid doggie drivel."

"Ah, go chase your tail, Doc. You're washed up around here!"

Those rats need to be shocked a few times down Maze Alleys A and D. They've lost all respect for my office. But I'm happy to see one of those rowdy rebel leaders being led to the cardiac puncture table. He's struggling, his teeth showing white and vicious.

"Fellow rat, now that your supreme scientific moment has come, don't you want to have a change of heart? Give your all to science happily. Set an example for these other young rats."

Several revolutionaries quickly move in front of me. "Don't say another word, Rat. Don't mock him in his agony."

"Mocking? Who's mocking? I'm here to eulogize the fellow, to write him up in glowing terms in the Newsletter. If you'll permit me to pass . . ."

The rebels block the way. The Learned Professor is feeling the rat's chest for the point of maximum palpitation. There, he's got it now, his thumb and forefinger on the fourth, fifth, and sixth ribs.

Now comes the needle, 26-gauge, half an inch long. The plunger is grasped and the needle is pushed slowly into the rat's heart. The Learned Pro will be withdrawing about 10 cc's of blood and that should finish this rebel off.

Good heavens! The blood is squirting right out of the rat's heart into the Learned Professor's eye! The Learned Pro is looking around puzzled as the blood drips down his cheek. I certainly won't be able to use this item in my Newsletter.

Everywhere around me—little accidents, little problems. It's the effect of the revolutionary dogs, and I fear it's going to spread like wildfire. [. . .]

———

My front paws are tied, but my rear legs are free on the treadmill and forced to run, to go nowhere inside a glass cage. My tongue is hanging out, my body weary. The men have heated the glass cage I'm in, so that it seems I'm running beneath the blazing sun, on and on, going nowhere.

I've been on this treadmill all week, and still I'm running, on and on, saliva dripping heavily from my mouth, mixed with bitter bile. The men stand and watch me as I run. I'm caught here, tied and heated, choking with thirst, my body soaked with sweat, my insides churning with pain. Hot like a desert, on and on I run . . .

. . . run . . . run . . . run . . . run . . . run as the wheel keeps turning, keeps clicking. Bright hot coils surround me on all sides, baking me, my cage an oven.

Run. Tongue out, dry and cracked. Run. Legs burning, my skin blistering, I retch up my bilious guts.

Run . . . run . . . run . . . run . . . run. Run, dogs, run. Run through the day . . . run through the night . . . run through the endless desert heat . . . heat without water . . . wheel without end . . . my eyes are on fire, my tongue is swollen, my throat is bubbling.

Run, dogs, run! Free yourselves! Run out into the sun. We're meeting at the edge of town. See us circling there. Join us there! Come, dogs, come!

———

"Oh, you disgusting dog! Go back to the alleyway you came from and stop shaming the good citizens of this laboratory with your perverted view of life!"

I think I've finally gotten through to the Learned Professor. He turned up the heat in the dog's cage this morning. The dog's skin is cracking with blisters and his mouth is foaming. He'll soon drop. But the Learned P. has twenty-five more dogs standing by to take their turn on the treadmill. And every one of them is a potential revolutionary! "What have you dogs got to complain about! You get your bowl of fox chow every morning, don't you? What could be nicer than that?"

They just stare at their leader, watching him as he flops along, his legs slapping up and down as the treadmill turns beneath him. Can you see the cloud of forms emanating from him? His revolutionary program billows and drifts all over our laboratory, infiltrating its way into every cage. See it there—dogs floating in the air, in full command of the intuitive band. They've taken over the central station. Their broadcast is reaching into the minds and hearts of every animal foolish enough to tune in. The noble function of intuition, through which the age-old secrets of our race are transmitted, is now in the hands of a revolutionary gang of mutts.

"I implore you, fellow rats and fellow animals everywhere—turn to another channel! We're running a film strip today on mechanical injuries to the teeth of canines. It's very informative, you'll see how to fracture a hound's tooth and bring about some marvelous hypoplastic defects. These will result in slowing the growth of all the other teeth in a dog, and I say that's a good thing! Dogs have too many teeth. They're vicious and dangerous and . . ."

It's so hard to get their interest. The dog's program is more subtly suggestive. It works on the weakness of my fellow rats. They don't realize that we're the friends of man, that we're here to serve humanity selflessly in every way we can. For only in man does one find the divine spark. The rest of us live in darkness, without souls.

"You're all just basic models, fellow rats! Don't you understand the meaning of that? A basic model has no feelings, has no spirit. Man is able to twist us and starve us and cut off our tails because that's the law! Haven't you read St. Thomas Aquinas? Animals have no soul!"

I'm growing hoarse trying to get the truth across to the Experimental Radiation Cage. All the rats in there have clubbed paws and absent toes and you'd think they'd be able to listen to reason. But no—they're sitting there, staring into space, entranced by the dog's broadcast.

"Five percent formaline, that's the scent! Believe me, fellow rats, there is no magic scent in the air. Look there—the dog has collapsed on the treadmill, his legs flopping lifelessly. He's dead! Look at the eyes rolled into his head and his body thumping along. He's dead! And death is the only freedom!"

The Learned Professor and his graduate assistants have opened the dog's cage and are taking him away. His body is thin and dehydrated, but his infernal message goes on!

"Plug your ears, rats. Don't listen!"

The Learned Prof is leading another dog into the glass chamber, tying his front paws to the rack. Now the power is switched on again and the treadmill is turning once more and another martyr is being created! Professor, I beg of you, get those dogs out of here!

He doesn't hear me. Professor, you're playing right into their hands! Don't let him run along in sight of all the other animals. Because the fumes of revolution are rising out of him already. Can't you see!

No, the L.P. doesn't see the powerful images pouring forth from that damned dog. But we can! We see dogs of all kinds, leaving their homes, leaving their posts, running away. They run in the air all around us as the intuitive picture grows brighter. The dog has conjured up trees and dusty roads and sparkling streams. A terrible power is at work in our laboratory, obliterating the wire cages and the operating tables and the exercise wheels. All of the marvelous equipment is being submerged behind a woodland scene.

"Don't look, fellow rats, don't look! Concentrate instead on the Shock Discrimination Box. Look at your fellow rats in there, jumping in the air after touching the electric grid. They're being driven slowly insane. They're going to receive their Mad Doctor's diploma soon. Isn't that worth working for? Chronically disordered behavior isn't something we get for nothing, just because we're rats. We have to earn our neurosis. Come over here and join in with those rats being tormented by the Disturbing Bell Stimuli. You know how sensitive our ears are; they're the perfect instrument for mankind to work with. I'd like you to observe carefully now—that's it, don't look at the disgusting doggie broadcast—observe how your fellow rat is being skillfully used. A bell is being rung alongside his head while his cage is oscillated in the air in an arc of 180 degrees. It's enough to make anybody feel strange, wouldn't you say? Swinging back and forth, with bells ringing all around you, you start to feel tense and frightened. Look, look, look at how the bell is being brought nearer, then moved away, now near again, threatening and retreating once more. Now, now! There, the rat has gone into a seizure, running around his cage and bumping into the walls. Look at him rolling over on his side with his legs kicking in the air. His body is trembling, and he has ticlike movements of the head. He's a candidate for a Mad Doctor's degree! Congratulations, my boy! We'll be throwing a pressed biscuit banquet in your honor a little later on!"

Well, now, here's a distinct improvement: The Learned Professor is bringing out his cigarette lighter. I hadn't thought we'd be doing this experiment again, but of course we've got to repeat these experiments in order to validate our findings.

The graduate assistant has selected a floppy-eared cocker spaniel for the experiment. Another assistant ties down the cocker's paws. Excellent, very smooth work. You young folks are Doctor Rat's pride and joy.

The nice doggie-woggie is all strapped down. And he won't be doing much revolutionary broadcasting, I guarantee.

The Learned Professor is flicking his lighter—he's got it lit—now he adjusts it so that it shoots out a long tongue of flame.

Doggie-woggie is looking at the flame, now looking at the Professor. Oh, you'll like this one, Doggie!

The Learned Professor brings the flame right into the dog's nostril, shoots it right up there. Excellent, well-aimed. The cocker is being forced to *inhale the flame.* Now the assistant lights his own lighter and both nostrils are filled with fire, as the dog's mouth snaps open in a soundless howl. [. . .]

That's it, Doggie, take a good deep noseful of fire. You'll like it.

This is the sort of experiment that doesn't cause much trouble. The dog is too panicked to send out any revolutionary signals. I wish I could say the same for our Pain Threshold Experiment over in the corner. It's not going well at all, because it proceeds at a slow, steady pace. Anything that lingers that way gives the dog a chance to concentrate, to produce the revolutionary signal.

Shall we look at the experiment more closely? One of our graduate assistants has been working for the past hour. He has a rawhide mallet.

Watch closely now: The assistant raises the mallet and whacks the dog in the leg with it. Another assistant keeps count. That's blow number 573. The dog will receive exactly a thousand blows on the leg. [. . .]

———

We lift our heads and howl, and the wild dogs lead us onward. Through the forest we race once again, with the dew upon us. The variety of smells is wonderfully sweet. How did I ever forsake this for a life of captivity, a life of subservience? I sold my soul for comfort, for security, for a leash. But there are others less eager than I.

"This is folly. Our masters are calling us!"

"Rid yourself of illusions!" cries a wild dog, leaping like a streak of light and then going far ahead.

We emerge from the forest onto a dirt road and run down it, in the warm summer air. It's a small and winding road, leading through farmland. Ahead of us, floating on the air, is the scent of man. We surge forward, afraid of nothing. Our numbers are great now, and we run on over the hill, catching sight of the man below. He's working with a horse who pulls a fallen tree along the road.

The man hears our howling and turns toward us. Seeing the torrent of teeth and tails he turns and runs into the forest. The work horse, still dragging his log, tries to follow the man, but the log catches in a tangle of smaller trees and the horse can't move. We see his trembling muscles and his frightened eyes.

"Come with us!" we cry. "Can't you smell what's in the air?"

The horse struggles to follow his master. If the wonderful smell has reached him, he gives no sign of it. He's securely in the traces, he's forgotten his nature. Realizing he's lost, we race past him then and on up the road with the warm dust beneath our paws and the smell inside our nose.

TERMINAL PROCEDURE
–M. *Pabst Battin*–

Much is not clear about the way the dogs died. Events on the periphery of the deaths, like points on undulating, outward-moving circles, recede into liquid uncertainty. The origins of the event are obscure, and its effects dwindle onward into indeterminacy. Causality cannot be established, and responsibility becomes a meaningless conceit, of no concern and no question.

Yet at the center remains the event itself, and it is fully clear: the dogs died.

PHASE 1

If we look, we can see the place where the dogs died: a small laboratory, assigned to an associate named Boaz, in a sprawling research institute. The place has not changed; it is the same simple, almost square room, hidden in an obscure wing of an old building far to one side of the institute's grounds. We see the usual furniture of science: two bulky wooden desks, an untidy bookcase, and a flimsy file cabinet cramped together on one wall; on the other side of the room, flanked by its recording and control apparatus, the soundproof experimental box. On the floor beside the box, centered on a stained and yellowed newspaper, is a small tin water dish.

The lab has not changed since the dogs died there, except that the stack of data tapes grows no higher, and a half cup of black coffee left in a mug marked Maia has dried into a thick brown crust. And there is a small stain, left by a few drops of blood-tinged fluid on the tile floor, which the janitor, if he has come at all, must have missed.

The lab has not changed. There is no one there now, but if we look back we can distinguish two figures: the researcher Boaz, and his assistant, a girl named Maia. They move, they talk, they look together at the clock, though that is all we see; the causes are obscure. We cannot tell, for instance, what brought Boaz to neuropsychological research: whether he was groomed, as the eldest, most promising son of a well-established family, in the finest schools for an eminent career in science; whether he was impelled to the study of mental phenomena by a scrupulously sublimated attraction to a particular professor; whether he chose psychology simply to spite his nervous mother; or whether his penchant for experimentation was born in the alley, nailing half-conscious rats to the boards of a tenement fence. Nor does it matter: he is here. We can watch him in his laboratory, though his past be indeterminate and his future uncertain: we see him not as the product

of any painstaking development, nor as a process toward some inef-
fable goal, but simply as himself.

We see what Boaz does before the dogs die: we see him in his
laboratory, shuffling through stacks of graphs, drawn meticulously on
green-ruled paper, running his fingers down the index columns in the
back of a thick black-bound book; we see him sprawling in a swivel
chair, talking with his assistant, the girl Maia or perhaps by telephone
with his wife; he sprawls back, his hand hanging idly over the arm of
the swivel chair. One of the dogs is sleeping beneath the chair; Boaz's
hand finds the dog, and his fingers play beneath the rope lead around
the dog's neck. The dog moves just enough so that Boaz's fingers can
scratch all of its neck, no more.

There is only one window in the laboratory, and it is obscured at
the top by an uneven venetian blind, at the bottom by an old and noisy
air conditioner. They will turn the air conditioner on in the afternoon,
Boaz and the girl Maia, even though it is not summer: it will grow hot
in the small square room with the door closed, hot and heavy with the
odors of the dogs. They will have to keep the door to the lab closed so
that the office workers across the hall do not see, and so that the dogs
do not break loose and escape down the long colorless corridors. And
they will think too, that the throaty hunt of the air conditioner will
cover the noise of the dogs, so that the office workers across the hall
do not hear.

But the office workers asked anyway, when Boaz and Maia came
back afterward to the lab, what they had done to the dogs.

"We had to give them a little shot," said Boaz.

"Oh," said the office workers. Uncertainly, some of them smoothed
thick hands across the flat planks of their girdles. "We thought something was wrong."

"Nothing is wrong. It was just a little shot," repeated Boaz.

"They don't seem to like it very much," said the worker whose
office door is just to the right across the hall from the lab. The worker
whose office is directly across the hall is ill; her door has remained
closed for a month now, maybe more. "They made a lot of noise."

"It's not getting the shot they mind so much," counters Boaz, his hand involuntarily pulling at his chin. "It's what's in the shot. When the fluid is forced into the tissue, it creates pressure. . . ."

The office workers understand. Some of them remember from the inoculations they had to have when they went to Europe, or from the preoperative injections given them when they had their root canals or their hysterectomies. They are not sure just how they know, but each is certain of the prick-pain of the needle itself, then the slow hard swelling within the flesh . . . yes, they understand, the needle does not hurt so much as the fluid. That is why the dogs made so much noise.

The office workers nod, and turn back into their separate rooms.

PHASE 2

There we have it, some of the scene the afternoon the dogs died. We saw the researcher, Boaz, as he parried the anxious questions of the women who work across the hall, but we missed the girl Maia, his assistant. Perhaps she had just stepped out, down the long corridor to the bathroom, to comb her straight black hair back out of her face—when she came to work that morning her hair was hanging loose, but by the time the dogs were dead she had bound it back, severely, with a thin rubber band—or perhaps when we looked she was hidden by the door of the soundproof experimental box. The box, after all, is very large, a double-walled cube of steel, insulated so well that even a dog, whose sense of hearing is much more acute than any man's, can hear nothing, nothing at all outside the box, nor can anyone outside hear even the loudest noise of a dog within. Maia might have easily been standing behind the box. Beside the box is the recording and control apparatus, a complex construction of knobs and dials and levers, displaying a small oscilloscope screen and twin reels of recording tape. She might have been watching from behind the apparatus, peering out between its irregular protrusions. Or perhaps she had stepped behind the box to put the rubber hand in her hair, for she is always just a little shy of Boaz's gaze and is not eager to invite any intimacies. In any case, she was there the afternoon the dogs died.

Of course she was there: it was part of her job. She must have known; she must have been told when she was hired to be Boaz's assistant what would happen to the dogs. Surely the institute's personnel officer, a conscientious man exactingly aware of the protective regulations, had felt obliged to tell her that the job involved handling experimental animals on which terminal neurological studies were to be performed. Or maybe Boaz had told her.

"Sit down, Maia," Boaz may have said, a gruff edge exposed in his low voice. "I am going to tell you exactly what these experiments are about, so you won't have any questions and so you won't say I didn't tell you."

She sat, crossing her thin legs, in the swivel chair, and smiled just slightly at him.

"The man in Personnel said you were doing basic research in comparative conditioning. Using dogs. My job would be to take care of the dogs and run the conditioning experiments. That's all he said."

"Let me explain," Boaz begins, rather stiffly. "There has been a lot of neurological research done on how the brain codes things. And there's been a lot of research on how animals react and learn in particular situations, but that kind of behavioral research says nothing about what happens in the brain. Not many attempts have been made to correlate a specific behavioral event with a neural event."

"And that's what you're trying to do."

"Yes," said Boaz. "It's worth doing."

She tosses her head lightly. "Well, I'm glad of *that*," she says, a little fliply.

He leans forward in the swivel chair. "You must understand that this research is significant," he warns, "and that it's important that we do it just this way."

She does not answer, and he begins again to explain. "What we're trying to find out is what patterns of electrical activity occur in the brain during certain types of conditioning or learning. So we have electrodes implanted in the dog's brain, and then we record the population of neural cells that fire while the dog is being conditioned."

Boaz must have watched her as he talked; he must have noticed how small a girl she is, small and slender, made smaller by the large swivel chair. Perhaps she was wearing her thin black hair free that beginning day, or perhaps it was knotted up with a long paisley scarf, but surely Boaz must have noticed her eyes: wide eyes rimmed in black mascara, eyes so wide she looked as if she might cry at any moment.

"Each dog spends an hour in the experimental box every third day, learning how to react to a given stimulus situation. It will take the dogs three or four months, maybe longer, to complete their conditioning, and then—" He hesitates, watching her wide eyes.

She looks at him, saying nothing.

"Stereotaxic implantation is very difficult," he says distantly, "because you never can be sure just where the electrodes are."

She sits silent, listening.

"An electrode is nothing but a piece of conductive wire, inserted directly into the brain through a tiny hole bored in the skull. The shaft end is cemented to a terminal for the monitoring equipment, called a pedestal, and the pedestal itself is affixed to the skull directly over the cortex region. The pedestal anchors the electrodes, and—"

"Do they hurt?" Maia interrupts.

"What?" he stops, a little annoyed.

"The electrodes. Do they hurt the dog?"

"There are no pain receptors in the brain," Boaz answers flatly. "Does it bother you?"

"No, I just wanted to know." She pulls a long strand of hair out of her face. "I just wanted to know, that's all. Go on with your story."

"This is not a story, Maia."

"I know," she answers quickly. "I'm sorry."

"The problem," he begins again, "is to determine just where the electrodes are. It's not easy to implant them precisely, and there's only one way to determine exactly where they are."

"What's that?"

"By direct inspection of the neural region." He talks more quickly, enunciating the syllables almost too clearly, as if to conceal in scientific jargon something he does not quite want her to understand.

She sits still, saying nothing.

"The procedure is terminal," he says at last.

"I knew that," she says flatly, and Boaz realizes that she is not going to cry, that her eyes are wide all the time.

"I am going to tell you how we are going to do the termination," he says, "just so you'll know."

Maia sits motionless. "All right."

"After the dog has completed its conditioning program, we give it a double or triple dose of anesthetic. Then we open the chest cavity while circulation is still functioning, and by inserting a tube directly into the heart, we can pump fluids up into the capillaries in the brain. We use a saline solution first to flush the blood out, and then a Formalin fixative. The Formalin prevents decomposition."

"Keeps it from spoiling," Maia translates, partly to herself and partly so that Boaz will know she understands.

"Then we remove the head, and put it in a preservative. Anytime after that we can remove and section the brain."

Maia sits quietly, as if forming questions. "Do you do all this?" she asks finally.

"No, no indeed," says Boaz, almost amused by her suggestion, "not when there are people around the institute who are really experienced at that sort of thing—"

"Who?"

"Some physiologists in the animal-surgery laboratory, over on the other side of the institute. It's all arranged."

"All we do is bring the dogs?"

"That's all."

She still sits quietly, though her fingers comb unevenly through her long thin hair, or twist the ends of the paisley scarf.

"Why are you telling me all this?" she asks, after a long time, her voice even and clear. "Not just so I'll know."

"Yes," he said, "so you'll know. So you won't ever have to say you didn't know what we were doing."

"I'm not a coward," she says slowly, deliberately.

"Good," says Boaz, his mouth achieving a smile.

She smiles easily back.

It is possible that sometime after the experiments were terminated and the dogs were dead Maia came back to the lab, perhaps still employed, to help Boaz write up the results of the experiments, or just to retrieve the little china pot she had used to brew coffee. Perhaps she came for no reason at all, just wandering in, opening the door by chance, to see the small square room again. Her eyes must have traveled over the walls, over the neat graphs Boaz had drawn of the dogs' performance in the box, graphs he had tacked to the walls, graphs with the dogs' names. Mustard, Monroe, Eggyolk, Isabel, graphs with the dogs' names. Frenchfry, Faulkner, Yoghurt, Trotsky, Theresa, 23 dogs, 23 names, Hubert, Pablo, Pianissimo; her eyes must have wandered over the untidy bookcase, the flimsy file cabinet holding old research proposals and reprints of other neuropsychological studies on dogs, mostly brown mongrel dogs, dogs with names, for it is customary in the biological sciences to name laboratory dogs, though cats and rats and mice are given only numbers, over the cabinet full of electronic scraps, bits of electrode wire and odd-numbered dials and snipped lengths of exposed film, over the old brown desks where she and Boaz had sat, talking or not talking while the dogs ran their trials in the experimental box. And when she came back, Maia may have stepped across the stained floor to the sound-proof box, put a thin hand out to touch the metal sides of the huge box; she may have opened first the outer door, pressed the heavy handle down, and then the inner door, as heavy as the first, and perhaps she stepped inside the box, as she would have with a dog, any dog, with Mustard or Muffin or Petunia, to see one last time the stout canvas harness in which she would have strapped the dog, Pablo, maybe, or Theresa, the dangling wires ready to connect to the pedestal cemented to the center of the skull, and other wires to be taped to the dog's wrist to administer graduated levels of electric shock; perhaps she would finger the slender bar to which the dog's foreleg would be tied so that when the dog lifted its leg in the response expected of it, the bar would move and record the leg lift on the dual spools of tape turning slowly at the top of the recording apparatus outside. Perhaps Maia, her eyes still rimmed in black and her hair falling free, would sit motionless in the soundproof silence of the box, or perhaps she simply turns away, steps down out of the empty box, and lets the door bang heavily shut behind her.

Or perhaps she did not come back.

Still later, much later, Maia shows someone a photograph, though the circumstances are so remote from the center that almost none of the details are clear. It may be in responding to the courtship of a new lover that Maia takes the small, square photograph, its corners bent, from her purse, as if by that one picture to explain herself; or perhaps she reminisces with her family, leafing through a dusty album of her single years. Perhaps she shows the photo to a colleague, laughing over cocktails at a convention of neuropsychologists, where Boaz will be honored for his work; or perhaps she sits alone, on the hard edge of a hospital bed, and shows the picture to herself. But the photograph itself, since it was taken much closer to the center, is quite clear; it is a snapshot, taken presumably by Boaz, of Maia on the lawn behind the lab, running in from the kennels with two of the dogs. The dogs strain ahead on their leads, their noses to the ground, but Maia is only allowing herself to be tugged, her head tossed back, her hair loose in the wind, her face laughing.

As she studies the photograph, Maia binds her black hair back with a rubber band. But she is too far from the center now, and we cannot see if there is any expression on her face.

PHASE 3

Still, some things are already clear. It is certain, for instance, that both Boaz and the girl knew what they were doing. Boaz knows because he designed the experiments, or at the very least took them over from some other researcher; in any case he knows: exact determination of the location of the electrodes is essential to correct analysis of the experimental data. That is what he knows.

And Maia knows too, knows that the dogs she runs through the experiments will eventually be put to sleep, have fluids perfused through their brains, have their heads severed, soaked in preservative, and their brains removed. But Maia also knows that however protracted the surgeries, the dogs will feel none of it; their conscious end will be swift, sleepy, painless. She finds nothing wrong with the plan.

And the dogs? Do they know? No, they are just dogs; they do not know anything more complex than immediate attention or actual pain. They are just dogs, common mongrel dogs, their coats dull and their markings irregular. Their breath is sour from the standard kennel diet, and the electrode pedestals protrude like plastic cancers from their heads. But their tails beat against the sides of the wooden desks when Maia brings them in from the kennels, and one jumps up to lick her hand.

Ah, yes, the one that licks her hand is Mustard. He is just a little smaller than most of the dogs, but smarter, sharper, and his coat is an almost yellowish brown—which is why, of course, Maia named him Mustard. She has just brought him into the lab; they have run breathless together across the wide green lawn, and after his hour in the box, they will run back again, loping free across the green grass to the kennel. But now Maia has looped the rope lead through the handle of the file drawer. Mustard paces nervously, keeping as far from the experimental box as possible; the rope pulls the file drawer out, then back, then out again. Annoyed, Boaz drums on the surface of his desk.

Maia presses a button on the recording apparatus; she speaks into it, her voice small but clear: "Now running Mustard. Avoidance conditioning. Number of trials: 50. Prestimulus interval 2.0, poststimulus interval 5.0 seconds." As she speaks, she twists the numbered dials on the face of the control apparatus, setting it to sound the stimulus tone and record the dog's behavior. "Shock duration .5, shock intensity 2.25 milliamps . . ." Then it is ready, and she turns toward Mustard.

She loosens the rope lead from the file cabinet, and pulls the dog toward the box. He struggles back, but the rope lead tightens, like a choke, and he has no choice. Maia lifts him up onto the platform inside the box; he struggles, but she is stronger, and she straps the canvas harness around his body. He struggles still, but now he cannot escape. She ties his right foreleg to the movable leg-lift bar; he pulls on it a few times, as if he remembers what response is expected of him, and the bar makes a little clicking noise outside the box.

Then Maia reaches for a thin coil of wire hanging from the ceiling of the box; there is a flat patch at the end of it, a sensor to measure electromyogram potentials in the muscles, and with adhesive tape she fixes the patch to a shaved area on the side of Mustard's leg. Finally, she tapes two small silver disks, attached to the end of a red wire, to the wrist joint of Mustard's foreleg, just above the footpad and below the dewclaw. It is the terminal that will give him the shock. She tightens the stomach strap.

"Good doggie," she murmurs, and she rubs the underside of his neck, just for a moment, before she puts the head restraint on him. Finally, when the restraining collar is in place and his head is secured so that he cannot move it, she plugs the wire leads into the pedestal in his head.

She stands back, checking: Mustard is strapped firmly in position, unable to move anything except his right foreleg and his tail.

"Good doggie," she says to him again. He is the cleverest of all the dogs. "Do a good job, Mustard, and you'll be the first one through." She hesitates, suddenly aware of her own words, and looks at Boaz. He looks back, as if to call her bluff.

She takes it. "Do a good job, Mustard," she promises, "and you'll be the first one to get your head cut off."

Boaz smiles into his papers, and Maia closes the inner door of the box. Mustard barks, but the sound is very flat, muffled by the door; after Maia has closed the outer door, she can hear nothing more. She looks in through the triple-thick window; Mustard, she can see, is still barking, but the straps are holding well. She turns to the control panel; it is all set, and she flips a single switch. The two tape reels at the top of the recording apparatus begin to turn, in unison, and the conditioned stimulus, a single clear tone, sounds. Then there is a clicking noise, the noise made by the bar as Mustard lifts his leg, and finally the rapid clatter of the printer, recording the data of the trial.

Then it is quiet. If we look in through the window, we will see Mustard standing motionless, his tail still and his eyes fixed dully on the wall of the box in front of him. The tone sounds again; this time he fails to lift his leg, and after precisely five seconds the shock is presented. He jerks his leg rapidly, since that is the only movement he can make, and then holds his leg up, unaware that the terminal is taped to his wrist and cannot be avoided. He struggles in the harness, but the canvas is tough, unyielding, and he cannot free himself. He drools heavily.

——

It is difficult to tell just how much more time elapsed before the end came, though surely Maia could figure it out from the dogs' records, from the protocol sheets or the data tapes or even the learning graphs taped to the walls. And it is hard to say just when they realized that the end had come: that some of the dogs had learned as much as the design of the experiment required, and that the experimental data on them was complete.

It may have been Boaz, sitting engrossed over long columns of figures recorded by the apparatus, who sees first that three of the dogs are finished. Or it may have been Maia, watching each of her dogs through the thick window of the box, who sees the end: Mustard, frail Theresa, and Pablo. Or perhaps they did not realize it at all; perhaps Boaz simply telephoned the animal-surgery laboratory.

He swivels outward from the telephone. "Tomorrow," he says to Maia, "be here early. We'll do them first thing in the morning."

She is puzzled. "I thought you said the physiologists were going to do it."

"They will," Boaz assures her, "all except for the anesthetic. We do that, here."

"How can we do it here? Wouldn't it be easier to do it there, then we wouldn't have to carry them . . . ?"

"No. Besides, that's the way we made the arrangements. We anesthetize the dogs here, and once they're out, put them in my car, drive over to the main building, and load them on a gurney at the shipping door. That way the physiology people won't have live dogs running around their sterile laboratory, and they won't have to waste a lot of time waiting for the anesthetic to take effect. It doesn't always work, you know."

"Why not?"

"You calculate the dosage according to the weight and condition of the dog. But you have to be sure not to give it too much, otherwise you'll kill it outright, so sometimes you end up giving it not quite enough."

"What happens then?"

Boaz smiles, tolerant of her question. "You just start all over again, that's all. That's another reason we're doing it here, in case we have to do any of the dogs twice."

Maia thinks for a moment. "I suppose it's nicer for the dogs to let them go to sleep in a place that's familiar, not with a lot of strange people standing around," she muses.

"I suppose so," says Boaz, without interest.

"Do I have to go with you to the surgery?"

He looks at her, and his gaze is suddenly kind. "No, Maia, you don't, not if you don't want to. I'll just need you here in the morning to help with the anesthetic."

She does not respond.

"Just hold some paws, that's all. It's just one little shot."

"All right," she says finally.

———

You see that they were quite calm about it beforehand, Boaz and the girl. After all, there was nothing unusual about the situation; their procedures were perfectly routine in experimental psychology, and they were executing these procedures as well as they could.

But afterward, after they had anesthetized the dogs and loaded them into the back seat of the car, Boaz saw that his hands were shaking.

Maia too may have seen his hands tremble, but she said nothing; she sat beside Boaz, immobile and silent. He knew the roads of the institute grounds well, and he had tried the great curve down the hill at every speed from 30 to 80, but his hands shook too much, he did not really see the road, he missed the turn. The car spun back off the road and slid, tilted, into a ditch; as it stopped Boaz heard a sliding noise, and then the heavy thump of a body falling to the floor. He turned quickly; it was Theresa, her leg bent back double beneath her body. He lurched over the seat to help her, but then he realized it made no difference. And he realized that Maia had not moved during the accident, not at all; she sat unmoving, her eyes glassy and hollow.

At the same moment Boaz saw a car pull off the road behind them, to help. He leapt out, strangely alarmed, as the car pulled up toward them. No, he thought, go away, and he ran toward the approaching car, "I'm all right," he yelled, his voice cracking, to the would-be samaritan, "I'm all right," his arms flailing, "go away, I'm all right," flailing, beating off the samaritan, and then, just for a moment, he saw himself: a madman, protecting an almost catatonic girl and three half-dead dogs.

Then he caught himself. "Thank you," he said to the driver, a bewildered student. "I think I can get it out of the ditch myself."

The record does not show how they got to the surgery lab: whether the student towed them out of the ditch, or whether Boaz scraped together branches from the woods and forced them into the mud under the wheels for traction; it is not important whether they took the usual route or another, back behind the pond; it is not clear how long Maia's state lasted, or when Boaz's hands stopped shaking, but the chief physiologist, a severe woman, said later that they were both present for the perfusion and termination procedure. She did say, when asked, that they were both rather quiet during the procedure, that she had expected Boaz, in particular, to be more interested in the findings—though of course they would all be recorded in detail and he would be able to study them later. She had attributed their silence to the natural squeamishness of those not accustomed to observing surgery, she said, and she quite understood. Besides, she guessed that Maia had grown fond of the dogs.

PHASE 4

It seems, then, that something must have upset them. Boaz was calm beforehand, calm and completely scientific, but afterward he ran his car off the road—a road he knew well—in broad daylight, without speeding.

And Maia? Wasn't she calm? She had been calm with the dogs that morning: she had done nothing unusual. She went out to the kennels, out behind the building, just as usual, quietly stepping through the early grass; the dogs heard her coming, and all 23 began to bark. She opened the wooden gate to the fence surrounding the kennels; the dogs leapt up, each in its own wire pen, to greet her. She began her duties at once, going from one pen to the next with the long-handled shovel, scooping out the little piles of excrement; then she hosed out the floors of the cages. Last she filled the dishes with water and with food, though she did not fill the dishes in the cages of Mustard, or Theresa, or Pablo. She walked the three back, each tugging in a different direction on its leash, across the lawn to the laboratory.

But Boaz was not ready. He had not been able to find the right kind of needle for the syringe. He had left a note for Maia, saying he'd gone over to the surgery lab to get a new needle. He might not be back until after lunch: she should wait.

So Maia was alone in the laboratory, with Mustard and Theresa and Pablo. She opened the drawer of her desk, and took out her sandwich. Ham sandwich, made from ham she had baked for someone, her boyfriend perhaps, or her father, or just herself. She folded out the square of waxed paper, opened the sandwich. Three slices of ham. Three heavy slices of thick, old ham, mottled with sinews that seemed to shimmer green. She wasn't hungry. Maybe the ham was spoiled; maybe the dark yellow mayonnaise was spoiled too. It would make her sick; no, she would not eat the ham, she would give it to the dogs; it would make them sick too, it would make no difference. She wasn't hungry, not at all.

She was suddenly aware of a dog's head in her lap. It was Pablo, nuzzling in between her knees, attracted by the sandwich. He was not an affectionate dog, but now he nuzzled up, his long flat head in her lap, his limp ears falling loosely over her knees. His smell surrounded her, the thick, sour smell of unclean animal. His eyes stared at hers, as if to plead for the sandwich, and her own eyes fixed on the pedestal in his forehead. Her hand moved up through the dirty fur to stroke the back of his head, but her eyes remained on the pedestal: a plastic cap as big around as a dime, protruding almost an inch from his skull. The skin had been slit lengthwise along his head, but it had not healed well; it had remained spread apart, like half-open lips, for about four inches. She could see the sloping base of the pedestal, where it was cemented to the exposed skull;

she could see edges of light-red flesh beneath the retracted skin. Pablo had had several infections, and even now a thin yellow pus oozed out from beneath the open skin, collecting in dirty black clots at the edges of the wound. She had tried to keep the opening as clear as she could, and from habit she reminded herself to put on more of the antibiotic ointment, but she realized there was no point in it: within an hour, or at the most two, she would see Pablo's head sitting not in her lap but in a stainless steel basin.

Almost reluctant to touch them, she lifts the slices of ham from her sandwich. She gives one to Pablo, the second to Theresa; Mustard jumps up and snatches his from the desk. She steadies herself against its edge, unwilling now to scold.

She considers the bread of her sandwich, not the ham, just the bread; she wonders if she ought to eat the bread, if she ought to eat something, so that she won't feel weak later on, later on at the surgery lab, when they are cutting into the chests of the dogs, when they are inserting the thin tube into the heart, still beating, into the heart still beating, so that it can pump the fluids into the brain, beating, beating slowly . . . she must eat the bread, she decides, so that she won't feel weak, so that . . .

Then she hears Boaz returning. Her stomach knots sharply, and she is glad she has eaten nothing. She gives the bread, too, to the dogs.

Boaz brings the new needle. He unwraps it, fits it carefully onto the syringe, and from his pocket takes a small rubber-sealed bottle: Nembutal. He has already calculated the dosage; it will be three times the normal amount. He picks the bottle up in one hand, inverts it, and pierces the needle upward through the rubber seal; he draws the plunger out, watching the syringe fill slowly with the clear fluid. When it is full, he withdraws the needle from the bottle, and puts them both on his desk.

"Ready, Maia?"

She looks at him; his face is firm, impassive, strange, and she wonders if she has ever seen him before. She wonders suddenly where he came from, if he was a rich child or a tramp, whether he could conjugate a Latin verb or skin a rat, whether he ever thought of death, and if he ever had a dog.

"Ready, Maia?"

She starts. "Yes. I'm ready," she answers, and together they begin. It is not easy; Maia must hold the dog, while Boaz injects the anesthetic. They do Theresa first, as if to practice on the weakest of the dogs, then Pablo and finally Mustard, and by the time they have finished with Mustard, the drug is already beginning to affect Theresa.

—

Afterward, there is nothing to do but watch; Maia pours two mugs of coffee from the little china pot, and she and Boaz sit in the chairs at their desks, swiveled outward. The dogs move free around the room, though always at a distance from the experimental box, as if they do not understand why they are not tied to the file drawer or harnessed up inside the box. Theresa is already distinctly slower, as if burdened by some weight; she lies for a moment on a pile of rags in the corner, and Mustard sniffs uncertainly beneath her tail. She struggles up again, but her hind legs drag; she pulls herself forward a little, then turns and drags her legs back toward the pile of rags. She does not reach it. Maia sees her fall; unsure, she stands, aware that Boaz is watching her, and pulls Theresa gently over to the rags, so that her head and forepaws rest upon them. Maia looks into the dog's eyes, as if perhaps expecting gratitude, but they are growing glassy. Theresa pulls for breath in short small shallow gasps, but as the drug overcomes her, her breaths grow long and wholly automatic. She does not move again.

"One down," observes Boaz, his voice flat.

"And two to go," answers Maia, her tone equally artificial. They do not look at each other.

Mustard and Pablo, heavier, healthier dogs, take longer to succumb; they stumble and dance, they slide down and fight back up, their legs slipping out from under them as they stagger sideways; they slurp water from the tin dish until they can no longer control their tongues, they whimper and thrash their tails and roll their heads, and in the end they too go down in motionless forms, their eyes glazed, their tongues hanging thick and still, their respiration so slow and even that it can barely be detected.

"Let's go," says Boaz finally, and Maia says nothing. She moves mechanically to open the door of the lab, and Boaz carries first Theresa,

then Pablo, and then Mustard past the open doors of the office workers, outside to his car.

PHASE 5

Wait. We saw, fairly clearly, what happened just beforehand: how Boaz
got the right needle for the syringe and Maia fed her sandwich to the
dogs, and we observed them together afterward, sitting silent in the
lab, watching the dogs struggle down. But we have missed something
between; we must have flinched, as one does in the face of the sun,
letting our eyes close and turn away. If we are to see clearly, we must
look back one last time.

We have seen them moving toward the center, Boaz and the girl,
Maia. They have glanced at the clock, though they have not read it; it
is early afternoon now, and on the other side of the campus people are
waiting for them. Maia has loosened Theresa's leash from the drawer
of the file cabinet; she has stood for a moment, uncertainly, in the
middle of the room; now she sits, slowly, on the floor beside the dog.
The filled syringe lies waiting on the desk; Boaz takes it and squats on
the floor beside them. He puts the syringe on the floor, aware there is
no need for sterile precautions, and looks just once at Maia. Together,
they turn Theresa over so that she is lying on her back, Maia at her
head, Boaz at her tail. Maia places her own thin leg over the dog's
chest, to pin her down, and grasps her forelegs tightly, just above the
elbow joint. Boaz shifts, uneasily, from squatting to kneeling, and picks
the syringe up from the floor.

Watch: we see Boaz at the center now, as he kneels over Theresa,
positioning the syringe over her belly. We see his back first, clearly; a
small red mole on the back of his neck, then the fine creases of adult
skin; we see the cross-woven threads of his cotton work shirt. We circle
around his collar, and we count three anomalous whiskers, not more
than an eighth of an inch long, that his razor has missed this morning. We see each separate stub of hair, closely shaven, we note the tiny
pocks and minute lines of his skin, drawn in tight lines toward his
mouth. We see small round beads of sweat across his upper lip, and
others on his temples. If we are still, we sense the anxious pace of his

heartbeat and feel the tight constriction of his breath. And then we see what he sees: the uneven edges of his fingernails, the coarse and calloused surfaces of his fingers, gripping the slim barrel of the syringe. He sees the slant-sharpened needle, poised. The drug must be injected directly into the peritoneum, he knows, and he chooses a place to the side of Theresa's abdomen and low, just above her back leg, where there are no internal organs that might be punctured. The hair on Theresa's belly is thin, and the needle rests directly on her pale skin. Her body moves a little as she struggles, but we see Maia holding her, her thin bare legs clamped across Theresa's chest, her small hands tight around the forelegs.

And we see Maia, too, we see the separate strands of her black hair, falling now into her face, into the face of the dog beneath her. It is thin hair, without curl or gloss. We see her round black-rimmed eyes, but they do not answer: they watch the floor, the cold tile floor, see the inexact angles of the edges of the tiles and the small fissures cracking between them; they study the scuffs and scratches, the streaks of dull gray color, the tiny pits and dents, the uneven seepages of mastic, the yellowed film of ancient wax. She looks once at Boaz and finds him watching her, his eyes wide, staring; her eyes recoil.

Her eyes recoil from his, and then she feels the dog jerk, she can almost feel the needle through the dog, the needle plunging into the soft belly, and she clamps her hands more tightly as the dog's throat arches back, yelping. She is afraid she will lose her grip, that the dog will struggle free and bite her, and she looks once more at Boaz, sees him fight to keep the dog's hind legs clamped between his knees, sees the syringe flap in the thrashing stomach, sees that it is still full, sees Boaz break, sweating heavily now, sees him break, lose hold of the syringe. It flaps wildly, and he grabs it, pulls it out.

The syringe is still full; the fluid is not in Theresa.

Boaz draws back, wipes his arm across his forehead. "I thought it would be easier," he says, unsure, afraid. His eyes plead.

But her eyes do not answer his. "Don't you know how to do this?" she asks, deliberately, almost coldly.

"Inject the anesthetic directly into the peritoneum," he recites mechanically, like a rote-learning schoolboy. "Be sure to avoid the internal organs. . . ."

"Haven't you done this before?" she asks, her voice kinder now.

"No."

"Then could we get somebody else to do it for us, somebody who knows how?" Maia's thin voice is hopeful.

Boaz turns on her. "I thought you weren't a coward."

She does not answer. She sees him pick the syringe up off the floor, the tip of its needle tinged with blood, and as she tightens her grip on the dog, she sees him hold it high, then thrust it hard into the abdomen. The dog howls again, hard and long. Maia's arms are suddenly weak, and she sees Boaz, his face sweating, his eyes narrow. She sees his hand move around on the syringe so that his thumb is on the plunger and he can press the fluid out of the syringe; she sees it, sees Boaz's thumb press the plunger, slowly, sees the Nembutal move slowly out of the syringe, through the needle, into Theresa, and she looks down into Theresa's face, sees the brown eyes wide and motionless with terror, feels the huge howl of pain welling up from her throat, from her bowels, a constant, motionless howl, frozen, frozen in pain, and Maia sees forever down in Theresa's open mouth, sees the brown-stained teeth and the flattened tongue, sees all the soft pale-red glistening surfaces of her throat, motionless in an eternity of pain.

———

No, much is not clear about the way the dogs died. Events on the periphery of the deaths, like points on outward-flowing circles, recede into ambiguity. The origins of the fact are obscure, its effects indeterminate. Causality has not been traced, at least not securely: dare we impute responsibility? Responsibility? To Boaz, or the thin girl Maia? No, responsibility is an empty conceit: of no concern, no consequence.

At the center there is only the fact: the dogs died.

VI

OTHER ANIMALS AS FOOD
IIIIIIIIIIIIIIIIIIIIIIIIIIII

THE SLAUGHTERER
—Isaac Bashevis Singer—

Yoineh Meir should have become the Kolomir rabbi. His father and his grandfather had both sat in the rabbinical chair in Kolomir. However, the followers of the Kuzmir court had set up a stubborn opposition: this time they would not allow a Hassid from Trisk to become the town's rabbi. They bribed the district official and sent a petition to the governor. After long wrangling, the Kuzmir Hassidim finally had their way and installed a rabbi of their own. In order not to leave Yoineh Meir without a source of earnings, they appointed him the town's ritual slaughterer.

When Yoineh Meir heard of this, he turned even paler than usual. He protested that slaughtering was not for him. He was softhearted; he could not bear the sight of blood. But everybody banded together to persuade him—the leaders of the community; the members of the Trisk synagogue; his father-in-law, Reb Getz Frampoler; and Reitze Doshe, his wife. The new rabbi, Reb Sholem Levi Halberstam, also pressed him to accept. Reb Sholem Levi, a grandson of the Sondz rabbi, was troubled about the sin of taking away another's livelihood; he did not want the younger man to be without bread. The Trisk rabbi, Reb Yakov Leibele, wrote a letter to Yoineh Meir saying that man may not be more compassionate than the Almighty, the Source of all compassion. When you slaughter an animal with a pure knife and with piety, you liberate the soul that resides in it. For it is well known that the souls of saints often transmigrate into the bodies of cows, fowl, and fish to do penance for some offense.

After the rabbi's letter, Yoineh Meir gave in. He had been ordained a long time ago. Now he set himself to studying the laws of slaughter as expounded in the *Grain of the Ox*, the *Shulchan Aruch*, and the Commentaries. The first paragraph of the *Grain of the Ox* says that the ritual slaughterer must be a God-fearing man, and Yoineh Meir devoted himself to the Law with more zeal than ever.

Yoineh Meir—small, thin, with a pale face, a tiny yellow beard on the tip of his chin, a crooked nose, a sunken mouth, and yellow frightened eyes set too close together—was renowned for his piety. When he prayed, he put on three pairs of phylacteries: those of Rashi, those of Rabbi Tam, and those of Rabbi Sherira Gaon. Soon after he had completed his term of board at the home of his father-in-law, he began to keep all fast days and to get up for midnight service.

His wife, Reitze Doshe, already lamented that Yoineh Meir was not of this world. She complained to her mother that he never spoke a word to her and paid her no attention, even on her clean days. He came to her only on the nights after she had visited the ritual bath, once a month. She said that he did not remember the names of his own daughters.

After he agreed to become the ritual slaughterer, Yoineh Meir imposed new rigors upon himself. He ate less and less. He almost stopped speaking. When a beggar came to the door, Yoineh Meir ran to welcome him and gave him his last groschen. The truth is that becoming a slaughterer plunged Yoineh Meir into melancholy, but he did not dare to oppose the rabbi's will. It was meant to be, Yoineh Meir said to himself; it was his destiny to cause torment and to suffer torment. And only heaven knew how much Yoineh Meir suffered.

Yoineh Meir was afraid that he might faint as he slaughtered his first fowl, or that his hand might not be steady. At the same time, somewhere in his heart, he hoped that he would commit an error. This would release him from the rabbi's command. However, everything went according to rule.

Many times a day, Yoineh Meir repeated to himself the rabbi's words: "A man may not be more compassionate than the Source of all compassion." The Torah says, "Thou shalt kill of thy herd and thy flock as I have commanded thee." Moses was instructed on Mount Sinai in the ways of slaughtering and of opening the animal in search of impurities. It is all a mystery of mysteries—life, death, man, beast. Those that are not slaughtered die anyway of various diseases, often ailing for weeks or months. In the forest, the beasts devour one another. In the seas, fish swallow fish. The Kolomir poorhouse is full of cripples and paralytics who lie there for years, befouling themselves. No man can escape the sorrows of this world.

And yet Yoineh Meir could find no consolation. Every tremor of the slaughtered fowl was answered by a tremor in Yoineh Meir's own bowels. The killing of every beast, great or small, caused him as much pain as though he were cutting his own throat. Of all the punishments that could have been visited upon him, slaughtering was the worst.

———

Barely three months had passed since Yoineh Meir had become a slaughterer, but the time seemed to stretch endlessly. He felt as though he were immersed in blood and lymph. His ears were beset by the squawking of hens, the crowing of roosters, the gobbling of geese, the lowing of oxen, the mooing and bleating of calves and goats; wings fluttered, claws tapped on the floor. The bodies refused to know any justification or excuse—every body resisted in its own fashion, tried to escape, and seemed to argue with the Creator to its last breath.

And Yoineh Meir's own mind raged with questions. Verily, in order to create the world, the Infinite One had had to shrink His light; there could be no free choice without pain. But since the beasts were not endowed with free choice, why should they have to suffer? Yoineh Meir watched, trembling, as the butchers chopped the cows with their axes and skinned them before they had heaved their last breath. The women plucked the feathers from the chickens while they were still alive.

It is the custom that the slaughterer receives the spleen and tripe of every cow. Yoineh Meir's house overflowed with meat. Reitze Doshe boiled soups in pots as huge as cauldrons. In the large kitchen there was a constant frenzy of cooking, roasting, frying, baking, stirring, and skimming. Reitze Doshe was pregnant again, and her stomach protruded into a point. Big and stout, she had five sisters, all as bulky as herself. Her sisters came with their children. Every day, his mother-in-law, Reitze Doshe's mother, brought new pastries and delicacies of her own baking. A woman must not let her voice be heard, but Reitze Doshe's maidservant, the daughter of a water carrier, sang songs, pattered around barefoot, with her hair down, and laughed so loudly that the noise resounded in every room.

Yoineh Meir wanted to escape from the material world, but the material world pursued him. The smell of the slaughterhouse would not leave his nostrils. He tried to forget himself in the Torah, but he found that the Torah itself was full of earthly matters. He took to the Cabala, though he knew that no man may delve into the mysteries until he reaches the age of forty. Nevertheless, he continued to leaf through the *Treatise of the Hassidim*, *The Orchard*, the *Book of Creation*, and *The Tree of Life*. There, in the higher spheres, there was no death, no slaughtering, no pain, no stomachs and intestines, no hearts or lungs or livers, no membranes, and no impurities.

This particular night, Yoineh Meir went to the window and looked up into the sky. The moon spread a radiance around it. The stars flashed and twinkled, each with its own heavenly secret. Somewhere above the World of Deeds, above the constellations, Angels were flying, and Seraphim, and Holy Wheels, and Holy Beasts. In Paradise, the mysteries of the Torah were revealed to souls. Every holy zaddik inherited three hundred and ten worlds and wove crowns for the Divine Presence. The nearer to the Throne of Glory, the brighter the light, the purer the radiance, the fewer the unholy host.

Yoineh Meir knew that man may not ask for death, but deep within himself he longed for the end. He had developed a repugnance for everything that had to do with the body. He could not even bring himself to go to the ritual bath with the other men. Under every skin he saw blood. Every neck reminded Yoineh Meir of the knife. Human beings, like beasts, had loins, veins, guts, buttocks. One slash of the knife and those solid householders would drop like oxen. As the Talmud says, all that is meant to be burned is already as good as burned. If the end of man was corruption, worms, and stench, then he was nothing but a piece of putrid flesh to start with.

Yoineh Meir understood now why the sages of old had likened the body to a cage—a prison where the soul sits captive, longing for the day of its release. It was only now that he truly grasped the meaning of the words of the Talmud: "Very good, this is death." Yet man was forbidden to break out of his prison. He must wait for the jailer to remove the chains, to open the gate.

Yoineh Meir returned to his bed. All his life he had slept on a feather bed, under a feather quilt, resting his head on a pillow; now he was suddenly aware that he was lying on feathers and down plucked from fowl. In the other bed, next to Yoineh Meir's, Reitze Doshe was snoring. From time to time a whistle came from her nostrils and a bubble formed on her lips. Yoineh Meir's daughters kept going to the slop pail, their bare feet pattering on the floor. They slept together, and sometimes they whispered and giggled half the night.

Yoineh Meir had longed for sons who would study the Torah, but Reitze Doshe bore girl after girl. While they were small, Yoineh Meir occasionally gave them a pinch on the cheek. Whenever he attended a circumcision, he would bring them a piece of cake. Sometimes he would even kiss one of the little ones on the head. But now they were grown. They seemed to have taken after their mother. They had spread out in width. Reitze Doshe complained that they ate too much and were getting too fat. They stole tidbits from the pots. The eldest, Bashe, was already sought in marriage. At one moment, the girls quarreled and insulted each other, at the next they combed each other's hair and plaited it into braids. They were forever babbling about dresses, shoes, stockings, jackets, panties. They cried and they laughed. They looked for lice, they fought, they washed, they kissed.

When Yoineh Meir tried to chide them, Reitze Doshe cried, "Don't butt in! Let the children alone!" Or she would scold, "You had better see to it that your daughters shouldn't have to go around barefoot and naked!"

Why did they need so many things? Why was it necessary to clothe and adorn the body so much, Yoineh Meir would wonder to himself.

Before he had become a slaughterer, he was seldom at home and hardly knew what went on there. But now he began to stay at home, and he saw what they were doing. The girls would run off to pick berries and mushrooms; they associated with the daughters of common homes. They brought home baskets of dry twigs. Reitze Doshe made jam. Tailors came for fittings. Shoemakers measured the women's feet. Reitze Doshe and her mother argued about Bashe's dowry. Yoineh Meir heard talk about a silk dress, a velvet dress, all sorts of skirts, cloaks, fur coats.

Now that he lay awake, all those words reechoed in his ears. They were rolling in luxury because he, Yoineh Meir, had begun to earn money. Somewhere in Reitze Doshe's womb a new child was growing, but Yoineh Meir sensed clearly that it would be another girl. "Well, one must welcome whatever heaven sends," he warned himself.

He had covered himself, but now he felt too hot. The pillow under his head became strangely hard, as though there were a stone among the feathers. He, Yoineh Meir, was himself a body: feet, a belly, a chest, elbows. There was a stabbing in his entrails. His palate felt dry.

Yoineh Meir sat up. "Father in heaven, I cannot breathe!"

2.

Elul is a month of repentance. In former years, Elul would bring with it a sense of exalted serenity. Yoineh Meir loved the cool breezes that came from the woods and the harvested fields. He could gaze for a long time at the pale-blue sky with its scattered clouds that reminded him of the flax in which the citrons for the Feast of Tabernacles were wrapped. Gossamer floated in the air. On the trees the leaves turned saffron yellow. In the twittering of the birds he heard the melancholy of the Solemn Days, when man takes an accounting of his soul.

But to a slaughterer Elul is quite another matter. A great many beasts are slaughtered for the New Year. Before the Day of Atonement, everybody offers a sacrificial fowl. In every courtyard, cocks crowed and hens cackled, and all of them had to be put to death. Then comes the Feast of Booths, the Day of the Willow Twigs, the Feast of Azereth, the Day of Rejoicing in the Law, the Sabbath of Genesis. Each holiday brings its own slaughter. Millions of fowl and cattle now alive were doomed to be killed.

Yoineh Meir no longer slept at night. If he dozed off, he was immediately beset by nightmares. Cows assumed human shape, with beards and side locks, and skullcaps over their horns. Yoineh Meir would be slaughtering a calf, but it would turn into a girl. Her neck throbbed, and she pleaded to be saved. She ran to the study house and spattered the courtyard with her blood. He even dreamed that he had slaughtered Reitze Doshe instead of a sheep.

In one of his nightmares, he heard a human voice come from a slaughtered goat. The goat, with his throat slit, jumped on Yoineh Meir and tried to butt him, cursing in Hebrew and Aramaic, spitting and foaming at him. Yoineh Meir awakened in a sweat. A cock crowed like a bell. Others answered, like a congregation answering the cantor. It seemed to Yoineh Meir that the fowl were crying out questions, protesting, lamenting in chorus the misfortune that loomed over them.

Yoineh Meir could not rest. He sat up, grasped his side locks with both hands, and rocked.

Reitze Doshe woke up. "What's the matter?"

"Nothing, nothing."

"What are you rocking for?"

"Let me be."

"You frighten me!"

After a while Reitze Doshe began to snore again. Yoineh Meir got out of bed, washed his hands, and dressed. He wanted to put ash on his forehead and recite the midnight prayer, but his lips refused to utter the holy words. How could he mourn the destruction of the Temple when a carnage was being readied here in Kolomir, and he, Yoineh Meir, was the Titus, the Nebuchadnezzar!

The air in the house was stifling. It smelled of sweat, fat, dirty underwear, urine. One of his daughters muttered something in her sleep, another one moaned. The beds creaked. A rustling came from the closets. In the coop under the stove were the sacrificial fowls that Reitze Doshe had locked up for the Day of Atonement. Yoineh Meir heard the scratching of a mouse, the chirping of a cricket. It seemed to him that he could hear the worms burrowing through the ceiling and the floor. Innumerable creatures surrounded man, each with its own nature, its own claims on the Creator.

Yoineh Meir went out into the yard. Here everything was cool and fresh. The dew had formed. In the sky, the midnight stars were glittering. Yoineh Meir inhaled deeply. He walked on the wet grass, among the leaves and shrubs. His socks grew damp above his slippers. He came to a tree and stopped. In the branches there seemed to be some nests. He heard the twittering of awakened fledglings. Frogs croaked in the swamp beyond the hill. "Don't they sleep at all, those frogs?" Yoineh Meir asked himself. "They have the voices of men."

Since Yoineh Meir had begun to slaughter, his thoughts were obsessed with living creatures. He grappled with all sorts of questions. Where did flies come from? Were they born out of their mother's womb, or did they hatch from eggs? If all the flies died out in winter, where did the new ones come from in summer? And the owl that nested under the synagogue roof—what did it do when the frosts came? Did it remain there? Did it fly away to warm countries? And how could anything live in the burning frost, when it was scarcely possible to keep warm under the quilt?

An unfamiliar love welled up in Yoineh Meir for all that crawls and flies, breeds and swarms. Even the mice—was it their fault that they were mice? What wrong does a mouse do? All it wants is a crumb of bread or a bit of cheese. Then why is the cat such an enemy to it?

Yoineh Meir rocked back and forth in the dark. The rabbi may be right. Man cannot and must not have more compassion than the Master of the universe. Yet he, Yoineh Meir, was sick with pity. How could one pray for life for the coming year, or for a favorable writ in Heaven, when one was robbing others of the breath of life?

Yoineh Meir thought that the Messiah Himself could not redeem the world as long as injustice was done to beasts. By rights, everything should rise from the dead: every calf, fish, gnat, butterfly. Even in the worm that crawls in the earth there glows a divine spark. When you slaughter a creature, you slaughter God. . . .

"Woe is me, I am losing my mind!" Yoineh Meir muttered.

A week before the New Year, there was a rush of slaughtering. All day long, Yoineh Meir stood near a pit, slaughtering hens, roosters, geese, ducks. Women pushed, argued, tried to get to the slaughterer first. Others joked, laughed, bantered. Feathers flew, the yard was full of quacking, gabbling, the screaming of roosters. Now and then a fowl cried out like a human being.

Yoineh Meir was filled with a gripping pain. Until this day he had still hoped that he would get accustomed to slaughtering. But now he knew that if he continued for a hundred years his suffering would not cease. His knees shook. His belly felt distended. His mouth was flooded with bitter fluids. Reitze Doshe and her sisters were also in the yard, talking with the women, wishing each a blessed New Year, and voicing the pious hope that they would meet again next year.

Yoineh Meir feared that he was no longer slaughtering according to the Law. At one moment, a blackness swam before his eyes; at the next, everything turned golden green. He constantly tested the knife blade on the nail of his forefinger to make sure it was not nicked. Every fifteen minutes he had to go to urinate. Mosquitoes bit him. Crows cawed at him from among the branches.

He stood there until sundown, and the pit became filled with blood.

After the evening prayers, Reitze Doshe served Yoineh Meir buckwheat soup with pot roast. But though he had not tasted any food since morning, he could not eat. His throat felt constricted, there was a lump in his gullet, and he could scarcely swallow the first bite. He recited the Shema of Rabbi Isaac Luria, made his confession, and beat his breast like a man who was mortally sick.

Yoineh Meir thought that he would be unable to sleep that night, but his eyes closed as soon as his head was on the pillow and he had recited the last benediction before sleep. It seemed to him that he was examining a slaughtered cow for impurities, slitting open its belly, tearing out the lungs and blowing them up. What did it mean? For this was usually the butcher's task. The lungs grew larger and larger; they covered the whole table and swelled upward toward the ceiling. Yoineh Meir ceased blowing, but the lobes continued to expand by themselves. The smaller lobe, the one that is called "the thief," shook and fluttered, as if trying to break away. Suddenly a whistling, a coughing, a growling lamentation broke from the windpipe. A dybbuk began to speak, shout, sing, pour out a stream of verses, quotations from the Talmud, passages from the Zohar. The lungs rose up and flew, flapping like wings. Yoineh Meir wanted to escape, but the door was barred by a black bull with red eyes and pointed horns. The bull wheezed and opened a maw full of long teeth.

Yoineh Meir shuddered and woke up. His body was bathed in sweat. His skull felt swollen and filled with sand. His feet lay on the straw pallet, inert as logs. He made an effort and sat up. He put on his robe and went out. The night hung heavy and impenetrable, thick with the darkness of the hour before sunrise. From time to time a gust of air came from somewhere, like a sigh of someone unseen.

A tingling ran down Yoineh Meir's spine, as though someone brushed it with a feather. Something in him wept and mocked. "Well, and what if the rabbi said so?" he spoke to himself. "And even if God Almighty had commanded, what of that? I'll do without rewards in the world to come! I want no Paradise, no Leviathan, no Wild Ox! Let them stretch me on a bed of nails. Let them throw me into the Hollow of the Sling. I'll have none of your favors, God! I am no longer afraid of your Judgment! I am a betrayer of Israel, a willful transgressor!" Yoineh Meir cried. "I have more compassion than God Almighty— more, more! He is a cruel God, a Man of War, a God of Vengeance. I will not serve Him. It is an abandoned world!" Yoineh Meir laughed, but tears ran down his cheeks in scalding drops.

Yoineh Meir went to the pantry where he kept his knives, his whetstone, the circumcision knife. He gathered them all and dropped them into the pit of the outhouse. He knew that he was blaspheming, that he was desecrating the holy instruments, that he was mad, but he no longer wished to be sane.

He went outside and began to walk toward the river, the bridge, the wood. His prayer shawl and phylacteries? He needed none! The parchment was taken from the hide of a cow. The cases of the phylacteries were made of calf's leather. The Torah itself was made of animal skin. "Father in Heaven, Thou art a slaughterer!" a voice cried in Yoineh Meir. "Thou art a slaughterer and the Angel of Death! The whole world is a slaughterhouse!"

A slipper fell off Yoineh Meir's foot, but he let it lie, striding on in one slipper and one sock. He began to call, shout, sing. I am driving myself out of my mind, he thought. But this is itself a mark of madness. . . .

He had opened a door to his brain, and madness flowed in, flooding everything. From moment to moment, Yoineh Meir grew more rebellious. He threw away his skullcap, grasped his prayer fringes and ripped them off, tore off pieces of his vest. A strength possessed him, the recklessness of one who had cast away all burdens.

Dogs chased him, barking, but he drove them off. Doors were flung open. Men ran out barefoot, with feathers clinging to their skullcaps. Women came out in their petticoats and nightcaps. All of them shouted, tried to bar his way, but Yoineh Meir evaded them.

The sky turned red as blood, and a round skull pushed up out of the bloody sea as out of the womb of a woman in childbirth.

Someone had gone to tell the butchers that Yoineh Meir had lost his mind. They came running with sticks and rope, but Yoineh Meir was already over the bridge and was hurrying across the harvested fields. He ran and vomited. He fell and rose, bruised by the stubble. Shepherds who take the horses out to graze at night mocked him and threw horse dung at him. The cows at pasture ran after him. Bells tolled as for a fire.

Yoineh Meir heard shouts, screams, the stamping of running feet. The earth began to slope and Yoineh Meir rolled downhill. He reached the wood, leaped over tufts of moss, rocks, running brooks. Yoineh Meir knew the truth: this was not the river before him; it was a bloody swamp. Blood ran from the sun, staining the tree trunks. From the branches hung intestines, livers, kidneys. The forequarters of beasts rose to their feet and sprayed him with gall and slime. Yoineh Meir could not escape. Myriads of cows and fowls encircled him, ready to take revenge for every cut, every wound, every slit gullet, every plucked feather. With bleeding throats, they all chanted, "Everyone may kill, and every killing is permitted."

Yoineh Meir broke into a wail that echoed through the wood in many voices. He raised his fist to heaven: "Fiend! Murderer! Devouring beast!"

———

For two days the butchers searched for him, but they did not find him. Then Zeinvel, who owned the watermill, arrived in town with the news that Yoineh Meir's body had turned up in the river by the dam. He had drowned.

The members of the burial society immediately went to bring the corpse. There were many witnesses to testify that Yoineh Meir had behaved like a madman, and the rabbi ruled that the deceased was not a suicide. The body of the dead man was cleansed and given burial near the graves of his father and his grandfather. The rabbi himself delivered the eulogy.

Because it was the holiday season and there was danger that Kolomir might remain without meat, the community hastily dispatched two messengers to bring a new slaughterer.

IT WAS A DIFFERENT DAY
WHEN THEY KILLED THE PIG
–João Ubaldo Ribeiro–

When they killed the pig it was a different day because long before everyone knew that this was the day they were going to kill the pig. It was known even many days beforehand, although one could never be really sure, because the grownups spoke about the pig in a vague and imprecise manner. In fact, the day they killed the pig happened for the first time in a never well remembered way. One day, for the first time, it seemed everybody woke up early. And the older people knew that this was the day for killing the pig, and it was usually what they talked about as they prepared clay bowls and stretched cords for sausages and told stories of past pigs, the best pigs this land had ever seen, the best in town. So those older people could say with simpleness: Today is the day they are going to kill the pig. A simpleness which contrasted with the eyes of the younger children, whose first thought as they left their beds was whether they were still on vacation or not, or whether it was Sunday or not; for those boys and girls, when they noticed the same inexperience in the eyes of another their age, passed along the information almost breathlessly and glanced sideways as if they were conspiring. Today they are going to kill the pig. And maybe it was one of those subjects that deserved a glare from the grownups when harped upon, one of those secret subjects that made the room fall silent and provoked unknown gestures in the older people if a child entered the room. But the day for killing the pig was always a sunny day, and for some reason on that day the children were left freer than usual. Then, as time passed, the children would wake up already knowing that the pig was going to be killed, and maybe if they were lucky they might be able to tell a younger brother or a girl who lived nearby that the pig was going to be killed, so they could feel wonderment and curiosity in the other and could thus display wisdom and attractions. Also, if the only answer given the children to whom it was not yet permitted to take part in the death of the pig, when they asked what was the meaning of those strident wails they had never heard before, was just, "It's the pig, little one, it's the pig, child," and if the sight of the pig being slain was denied to them, at least they could see the man who was going to kill the pig and many times they gathered enough courage to ask, are you the one who is going to kill the pig? And more often than not he would answer, smiling like somebody who was not going to kill the pig: I am, yes. If the murderer of the pig was a stranger, then it was best to keep a certain distance from him who brought death with a smile, and if some of the children went as far as to talk to him, they would never go alone nor lose sight of the better known and more trusted older people. But there were some children whose pig killers were their own

fathers, and so, on those sunny mornings when the sun rose differently and things would never again be the same, the father was the
most different thing of them all. Being the father, he could not but be
a reason for pride, but it was strange to be in fear of one's own pride,
and this made the children's hearts rush and their eyes follow their
mothers everywhere, because the mothers did not kill pigs. There were
also things to unriddle, since the father spoke, or if it was another
adult who spoke he showed his look of approval so familiar to everyone, about the animals and the affection he held for them, and told of
the suffering of a cow whose calf had got stuck as it tried to be born.
For Aloísio and all his brothers and sisters, the moment was always to
be remembered when their father took all of them to see the red sow
Noca, and said to them this sow Noca was the miracle of nature. And
they all remained looking at the sow Noca suckling her many little
pigs, and some of them never ceased to go back there to admire her
thick blubbers unfolding over the burrowing snouts of all those little
pigs, some more concerned with how the little pigs grew, the others
only contemplating the sow and wishing for her to talk and trying to
guess her thoughts. Aloísio, this day in which he even mistook the light
of the moon that came down through a glass shingle for the light of the
sun and almost had a fever from wanting so much to leave his bed, was
told that the pig to be killed was the sow Noca herself, but did not dare
ask the father why he was going to do that, not so much because he was
afraid the father would be angry, although he would not explain anything either, but because he did not want to appear to be a boy who
did not understand things and did not want people to say then that
they would no longer allow him to see the killing of the pig. He imagined that maybe the reason why the sow Noca had never given an
answer to the things he had said to her every once in a while, even
when they were all by themselves and with guarantees of secrecy, was
that she knew that one day he would betray her and would be watching
her execution in all coldness, learning in that operation the manner in
which he would kill his own pigs in the future. For, since he was a man,
his wife would surely expect him to know how to kill the pigs he raised
or fattened, so she could also have her days for killing the pig, like her

mother before her and the mother of her mother and all the other mothers, this being the way the world is organized. But he spoke nothing of what he felt, and he was also ashamed to ask what time they were going to kill the sow, so he began to shadow his father wherever he went. He then saw that if the father could not now avoid having another presence, killing the pig was not something to occupy him more than the time necessary to do the killing. Because the father had time to go out of the house, already carrying the pig-killing knife on his belt, and to walk to the store to buy cigarettes, and to write in his blue-covered notebook. And the mother, without conferring with the father, gave orders for the sow Noca to be taken to the place of death, and remained arranging vinegars, bowls, lemons and all the seasoning she used to pile up on a corner of the stove, on top of the place where the firewood was kept, a smell of feasting already in the air, and it could even be that relatives would come visiting, with their faces that changed from year to year and their slight strangeness, especially on account of how familiar one had to be with them as a matter of obligation. The housemaids and the neighbor women and the persons who went in and out of the kitchen and the pantry talked more than usual and also much louder. Aloísio became impatient from watching the father write in the blue notebook, even more so because before each line or word he wagged his pen in airy scrolls without writing anything, and he had the sensation the father was going to die, so he went out to see how they caught the sow Noca and took her to the wooden block where they would tie her, and ignoring her cries would turn her into sausages and pork loins and meats. No, he would never forget the day, he did not know how long ago, when his brother Honório, who was now in the seminary and wrote letters the mother would read at night crying and shaking her head, had looked to him so wise and worldly as he told him, as if making a remark on something trivial, that they were going to kill the pig Leleu and would let Honório watch, but would not let Aloísio, and of course Leonor, watch. Now Aloísio could not resist it, and when he saw Leonor leaning against one of the pillars of the porch and remembered she would still be likely to ask what were those cries as they started to kill the sow Noca, he walked forward pretending not to have seen her, stopped, and as though he was doing his sister a great favor, spoke in her ear: Today we are going to kill the sow Noca. And he even felt more pleasure than he had expected, to see that her face paled and she began to cry. At that moment, he thought he had been revenged a little for all the times she had had an advantage over him because the father always wore a different look when he came home and put her in his lap, and he had never been picked up that way and now only the mother would put him in her lap, but very few times. Maybe the father would now be drawn there by her weeping and would scold him, but Aloísio felt an odd confidence as he had never felt before, and anticipating any questions the father might ask, he pointed at his sister with his thumb, and said: She is crying because we are going to kill the sow Noca, can you imagine? Now why did you tell her, the father said, but without showing annoyance, and started to stroke her head. If it was me, Aloísio thought, people would laugh. But he got over that quickly, because he remembered that his sister was a woman and women cried a lot, and besides she was not going to see the death of the sow. Indeed, when he was already near the wooden block, and the tree, once so familiar, gave out a loaded shade full of things not known, and all objects were now sinister, the father propped his right boot on a root to tighten the straps a little more and made a low pitched comment which brought warmth to Aloísio's face, and he wanted very, very much to be a man, he wanted nobody to be ever, ever able to say that he had not been a man even if only for an instant. Women are like that, the father said almost whispering, with the same amused chuckle he would have when he was talking in a low voice to his friends, and Aloísio, his face on fire, nodded and managed to say, speaking with as deep a voice as he could, "That's right, that's right." Then the father finished tying his boot, put his hand on Aloísio's shoulder, and they marched together toward the block, and Aloísio remembered he was also wearing boots and they were new. The sow Noca was tied down and whining, knowing very well what was going to happen. Aloísio decided he would not turn his eyes away nor would he show emotion, but he could not keep himself from feeling an immense fear when, after all the preparations and rites he had never imagined, he saw the father surmount the loins of the great sow and, with a face even more distant than when he talked about life to the mother, raise the knife. The sow began to be killed, and all around Aloísio's eyes there seemed to be a dark wheel and one could only see the middle of this wheel, where the sow Noca lay being killed. In the very beginning, less blood came out than he had expected, but soon everything turned into a red, spattering ball and shouts and imprecations from the men, and brisk motions among troughs, cloths and bowls, and the sow tumbled down with a thump. Aloísio, his breath arrested, was not even able to notice the moment they started demolishing the sow Noca as though they were demolishing a house, and was only aware of feeling sick, and he did not know there existed so many black and gray and white and red and limp and throbbing and slippery things inside a pig and that many of those things gave out a hideous smell and the father's hands were covered with blood, with bits of those things and with that slime up to his elbows. Neither did he know that they would use saws and hatchets, and he tightened his jaw very hard as he looked at the men sawing the sow's hindquarters on top of the block and filling the bowls with all those things. Those there, the father said as they were getting ready to head back to the house, are the bowels, which we are going to clean, which we are going to make sausage skins out of. He nodded yes and hoped the father had not noticed he had closed his eyes and had glanced only furtively at the bowl filled with blue, stenchy snakes. Without touching him because his hands were dirty, the father made a gesture with his chin and they went back to the house, and although Aloísio knew he had behaved in the most correct way, he was ashamed to be feeling sick and could not even remember well what had happened. He saw that his boots had been sprinkled with the blood of the sow Noca, and almost retched. He imagined that as soon as he went in the house he would go to the bathroom, but he did not want to run, so no one would take notice of anything. And then, while time dragged itself on like a snail, they went in the house and stopped in front of the mother, but fortunately the father was in a hurry to wash himself and the mother had to go about her chores in the kitchen, and also fortunately the father preferred to wash at the backyard spigot, instead of in the bathroom. He had never known one could sweat so much, while he scrubbed the stains, real and imaginary, from his vomit spewed all over the bathroom because he had hardly been able to close the door when his cheeks were filled up and before he could bend over the toilet, he exploded as if he were going to turn inside out. But he managed to relieve himself anyway and was patient enough to clean all the mess he had made and to still wash his face twice, one time for the vomit, the other time for the sweat. Looking in the mirror to study the expression he wanted to have as he left to participate in the comments about the sow, he opened the door and came out and was happy to see that neither the father nor the mother was on the porch, where it was perfectly natural for him to stay, looking ahead and enjoying the breeze, after all he had seen his first pig. He was still secretly bothered by what had happened, but was confident that the next time it would not be like this, although he did not think now that he would have the courage to go near the block again. But people grow up, Aloísio thought, trying to imagine whether he would grow a moustache when he grew up, and then, through a crack between the doors that opened onto the porch, he saw that the father was talking contentedly to the mother, rubbing a towel behind his ears. He guessed they were going to talk about him, came close to the door, put his ear against the small opening and listened to the father telling the mother—and he was sure of the way the father was smiling—how Aloísio had behaved fine during the sow's dying. He is a man, the father said with admiration, and Aloísio felt his eyes wet, and pride with sickness again, and pulled back to the porch, not knowing what it was that he had. Maybe this is the reason why when he now sees the family gathered together on sunny holidays or when he wakes up among the noises of his children, and grandchildren and parents and grandparents and all relatives, when he sits in a quiet corner and looks at all this, his chest feels heavy and he has the impression that if someone speaks to him, he will begin to cry without ever again being able to stop. (Translated by the author)

HOW TO MAKE A PIGEON CRY
–M. F. K. Fisher–

Here's a pigeon so finely roasted, it cries, Come, eat me!
Polite Conversation, *Jonathan Swift*

For centuries men have eaten the flesh of other creatures not only to nourish their own bodies but to give more strength to their weary spirits. A bull's heart, for example, might well bring bravery; oysters, it has been whispered, shed a new potency not only in the brain but in certain other less intellectual regions. And pigeons, those gentle flitting creatures, with the soft voices and their miraculous wings in flight, have always meant peace, and refreshment to sad humans.

Perhaps it is an old wives' tale; perhaps it is a part of our appetites more easily explained by *The Golden Bough* than by a cook or doctor: whatever the reason, a roasted pigeon is and long has been the most heartening dish to set before a man bowed down with grief or loneliness. In the same way it can reassure a timid lover, or comfort a woman weak from childbirth.

It is not easy to find pigeons, these days. Most of the ones you know about in the city are working for the government. In the country there are few farmers, any more, that have kept their dove-cotes clean and populous . . . and fewer hired men who will kill the pretty birds properly by smothering them. By far the easiest way to make a pigeon cry "Come, eat me!" is to buy it, all cleaned and trussed, from a merchant.

It is usually expensive, in a mild way. [How can extravagance be mild? And what is mild about a minimal $1.25 per bird? But I still say it is worth it, now and then.] But if you like the idea at all, it is worth saving your meat-money for a few days, and making a party of it; eating a roasted pigeon is one of the few things that can be done all by yourself and in sordid surroundings with complete impunity and a positive reaction of well-being. [And for two, four, or six people who know each other well enough to eat with their fingers, there is no pleasanter supper than hot or cold roasted pigeons, with kasha or wild rice and undressed watercress and good bread . . . and, of course, plenty of good red wine.]

[It seems impossible that there is, apparently, no recipe for Kasha in this book so trustingly dedicated to my fellow philosophers in Operation Wolf. Kasha is a fine thing. In spite of unhappy political as well as gastronomical overtones just now, I must say that Russians are strong people because of it (. . . and cabbage and black bread and sour cream and floods of hothothot tea). It can be bought most easily, at least in Western America, from "health food stores." Package directions should be followed carefully, for unfortunately some of the stuff is pre-cooked now, and turns into a horrid mush if you go on with the old routine of slow steaming. Properly prepared, kasha makes a wonderful aromatic nutty accompaniment to meat or fowl, and alone it is delicious, with an extra pat of butter, and combined with mushrooms it is heavenly, and and and. . . .

KASHA

2 cups kasha (whole or cracked groats)   *butter or fat, about $^3/_5$ T*
1 or 2 fresh eggs   *salt, pepper*
4 or more cups hot water or stock

Put kasha into heavy skillet and mix egg into it until each grain is coated. Stir often over very low fire, until the grains are glazed and nut-like. Add liquid slowly, put fat in center, and cover closely, to cook until fluffy and tender (about $^3/_4$ hour). Season and add more butter if wished. Serve.

I have eaten a great many pigeons here and there, and I know that the best was one I cooked in a cheap Dutch oven on a one-burner gas-plate in a miserable lodging. The wolf was at the door, and no mistake; until I filled the room with the smell of hot butter and red wine, his pungent breath seeped through the keyhole in an almost visible cloud.

Supper took about half an hour to prepare (I could have done it more quickly, but there was no reason for it), and long before I was ready to put the little brown fuming bird on my one Quimper plate, and pour out my second glass of wine, I heard a sad sigh and then the diminishing click of his claws as he retreated down the hall and out into the foggy night. I had routed him, because of the impertinent recklessness of roasting a little pigeon and savoring it intelligently and voluptuously too.

This is the way I cooked that innocent brown bird, and the way, with small variations, I have often treated other ones since then:

ROAST PIGEON

1 pigeon	*red wine (or cider, beer,*
1 lemon	*orange juice, tomato juice,*
2 slices fat bacon	*stock . . .), about a cupful*
(or 2 tablespoons butter or oil)	*water*
parsley	*salt, pepper*

Melt the fat. [If bacon is used, cook it until crisp, and then remove it until time to serve it alongside, over, or even under the little bird.] See that the bird is well plucked, and rub her thoroughly with a cut lemon and the seasoning. Push the parsley into the belly. Braise well in the hot fat.

Add the liquid, put on the lid quickly, and cook slowly for about 20 minutes, basting two or three times. If you are going to eat the bird cold, put into a covered dish so that it will not dry out. [And if hot, make a pretty slice of toast for each bird, butter it well (or spread it with a bit of good pâté de foies for Party!), and place the bird upon it. Swirl about one cup of dry good wine and 2 tablespoonfuls butter in the pan, for 4 birds, and spoon this over each one immediately, and serve.]

The accompaniments to this little bird (I ate it hot) were what was left of the red wine, which was a Moulin-à-Vent at twenty-six cents a quart, a rather dry piece of bread which was perfect for sopping all the juice from the plate, and three long satiny heads of Belgian endive. Celery hearts would have been just as good, I think, or *almost as* good.

Another heartening thing to eat, made from a wild creature, has always been associated with good-fellowship and even a bit of jolly poaching, if not with the reconciliation of man and his fate. Rabbit, or hare, or *lièvre*; it makes a strong and yet delicate dish no matter how it is prepared, if you remember one or two subtle tricks to play upon it first.

Always soak the hare for an hour or so in salty water, which has lemon juice or about a quarter-cup of vinegar in it. Then dry it well before cooking. A small piece of fat pork, either salted or fresh, will make the flavor of the meat much richer if they are cooked together. A tender hare [or domestic rabbit, for that matter] can well be prepared for frying like a chicken, but it is a dry meat and is usually better with a sauce around it. Almost all such recipes begin with soaking and then braising the meat, and letting it simmer slowly in a juice which can be as your wishes dictate. The following has always pleased me:

RABBIT IN CASSEROLE

1 large or 2 smaller rabbits	salt, pepper, speck of clove, etc.
hot water	
salt	1 cup stock or water
lemon juice (or vinegar)	1 cup red wine
3 slices fat bacon	1 handful chopped fresh herbs
4 tablespoons butter	(parsley, sage, etc.)
4 tablespoons olive or other oil	1 cup tomato juice
$\frac{1}{2}$ cup flour	

Cut up rabbit and soak for an hour or more in the hot salty water and lemon juice. Cut the bacon into small pieces and fry in the butter and oil.

Dry the meat, and shake well in a paper bag with the flour and condiments. Fry in the hot fat, turning often until each piece is very brown.

Add the stock, wine and herbs, and cover closely. Cook slowly about one hour or until tender.

Remove the meat to a hot casserole. Add the tomato juice to the skillet and stir thoroughly until the sauce is thick and bubbling. Pour over the rabbit and serve.

This recipe can of course be varied according to what supplies you have and how much time and money you want to spend on its preparation. Another good one which takes longer and is worth it, is a kind of composite of *civet de lievre*, hasenpfeffer, and

JUGGED HARE

1 large or 2 small rabbits	*salt, pepper, cloves, bay leaves*
water	*butter*
vinegar or wine	*oil*
1 onion, sliced	*1 cup sour cream*

Cut up the rabbit and lay in a jar. Cover with equal parts of water and either vinegar or wine; add the onion and spices. Allow this to soak two days, turning the meat at least once.

Remove the meat, and brown thoroughly in a mixture of oil and butter, turning it often. When it is well browned, cover gradually with the pickling sauce, as much as you want. Let it simmer for about half an hour, or until tender. Before serving stir the sour cream into it.

This dish, like any other honorable stew, is best served with noodles or rice or French bread to help with its dark-brown delectable juices, and a salad of green leaves from the garden. [Classic accompaniments are Brussels sprouts, puréed chestnuts, watercress, fried bread spread with tart jelly, variations of *sauce espagnole*, sliced lemons, fried hominy, fresh dill somewhere or other, dumplings, stewed prunes or pears, grilled mushrooms . . . !] If red wine is a part of it, the same honest, rather crude wine is meant to drink along with it (since, *bien entendu*, you would not use a wine anywhere in cooking that was disagreeable to drink by itself). If the sauce has been helped by plain stock, a rather heavy ale is good, since it relates itself well to the rich aromatic flavors of the dish.

It may seem that such birds as partridges are far from the cupboards of good wolf-cookers, but now and then a friend sends you one, or there is a little stock of them at the market begging to be bought.

The following recipe, given to me by a Nivernais farm woman who to her own constant surprise was a famous lecturer on Greek at a French university, can be used for any poultry or small game which may seem dry or a little tough, although it is meant for partridge or pheasant. I have cooked an ancient chicken and an equally experienced rabbit according to its formula.

PARTRIDGE OR PHEASANT WITH SAUERKRAUT

salt and pepper

2 small or 1 large bird (or rabbit)

bacon slices

3 tablespoons butter or good oil

1 $\frac{1}{2}$ pounds sauerkraut

1 cup peeled and sliced apples

1 cup dry white wine (or half

    and half with water or

    vegetable stock)

1 tablespoon flour

Rub birds with cut lemon, and salt and pepper them. Wrap with the bacon and tie securely with twine. Heat the fat and brown the birds.

Wash the drained sauerkraut (unless it is very mild, when just drain it). Place a layer of it with the apple slices in the bottom of a casserole and imbed the birds. Cover with the rest of the kraut and apple, add the liquid, and cover closely. Let simmer very slowly for about 2 hours.

Put the birds on a hot plate, and thicken the kraut with the flour. Make nests in it, and replace the birds in them, ready to serve.

[An even better dish, I feel since I have become the willing victim of an annual donation of frozen pheasant, is the recipe I give herewith. I am sorry to say that I have never handled freshly killed game in this country, but I have coped, for want of a better procedure, with an infinitude of withered, almost sexless, apparently ageless birds in their repulsive peaky feathers and their gaseous envelopes filled with invisible but still potent "dry ice." I have done horrendous things with them, and then admitted my own courage and downed my own successes. (Once I roasted ducks and pheasants in the same big pan . . . it was a marvellous thing, which I have never before confessed to.) This present recipe is an excellent rule for enjoying a bird of questionable dates (birth, death, all that), and as far as I know it would be somewhat better with one of *proper* timing.

NORMANDY PHEASANT

Brown pheasant in butter. Quarter, peel, mince, and slightly toss in hot butter 6 medium-sized apples and 3 small minced onions. Place pheasant on mixture in terrine, sprinkle with about cup fresh cream, cover, and cook in moderate oven about $\frac{1}{2}$ hour.]

Most of the ways for cooking poultry and game with economy seem to end inevitably as one form or another of the primeval stew. There are several reasons, most of which are followed almost intuitively by people who want to eat the best possible food for the least amount of money and time.

Roasting, for instance, except in the case of very small birds like pigeons, takes two hours or so of almost constant attention with a basting spoon, whereas a stew, after the meat is first braised, can be left to its own devices for about the same length of time. (You should make sure that the fire is under control and the casserole reasonably filled with liquid before you leave it.)

A roasted bird or little beast, while one of the most delicious things to eat that man has invented, emerges from the oven with no accompaniment except its own few unconsumed essences, and more often than not it has shrunk some into the bargain. A stew, on the other hand, seems to make a much bigger meal, because other things are usually cooked with it and have absorbed some of its flavor, and at the same time it is making a generous amount of fine odorous sauce which can be eaten with the meat and also with rice or potatoes or the humble and almighty crust of bread.

As for frying poultry, who could deny the delights of young pullets put to this test, if they are properly treated? Indeed, to believe the menus everywhere in America, fried chicken is neck and neck with grilled steak as the dish most people will order when they "eat out."

On the other hand (the wolf's side of the question!), it is an expensive job to fry enough young chicken in good fat for a family, and accompany it with the rich gravy, the mashed potatoes, the buttered peas, the hot biscuits and honey, and finally the pie or ice cream, that since our country first stood on its own legs have meant Company or Sunday Dinner.

A frying chicken, if he escapes being broiled, should weigh about three pounds. If he keeps on growing and in turns escapes being roasted at about five pounds, he is ready (albeit unwilling) "to grace the fricassee pot with aplomb and elegance," Mrs. Mazza says, "still young, still tender, but mature and at his zenith of plumpness." And when you consider the various exciting sauces which can smother his neat sections, once he is browned in honest fat, you wonder at ever believing that the only good way to prepare him was fried in a skillet.

One thing to remember about cooking any fowl, whether wild or domesticated, is that a good scrub with a cut lemon, never water, will make it tenderer and will seal in its flavors. Another thing is that a mixture of butter and oil or fat is the best one for braising it: it seems to make an evener and more delicious brown.

If you have bought or been given a chicken (it is very nice indeed, these days, to have generous friends who live in the country and send you unexpected lagniappes!), cut it up, scrub it with lemon, and season it. Try a little cinnamon and allspice with the omnipresent salt and pepper. After it is brown, put in a generous handful of chopped herbs (parsley, rosemary, basil, thyme, whatever you and your whims can pluck or purchase), and a minced clove of garlic. Add a cup or so of tomato, either fresh or canned, and some dry white wine. Stir the whole thing, cover, and let simmer until tender.

In Italy such a savory dish used to be called *polio in umido*. [One Yankee standby I have never been able to savor with more than a clinical interest is stewed hen with dumplings and gravy. I have probably eaten it at its best, and I am sure I have eaten it at its worst, and I still find it a pale thing.] It varied a little in every district or village—in every kitchen, really—but always it was served with the sauce in a separate dish, to be eaten with the spaghetti or the polenta.

You can see, probably, how good it would be. It is one of those "naturals" which take their own dignified place in any meal, whether it is served in midsummer on a breathless balcony, or in the windy months beside a fire. Whatever its milieu, it is eminently satisfying, and at the same time a great deal easier on your pocketbook than the same amount of chicken Maryland, even though you add wine and mushrooms and perhaps a crazy dash of pickled capers or nasturtium seeds.

You can eat it tomorrow, too . . . and fool the wolf . . . and if it is necessary, comfort yourself by reading this strange quotation from Wesker's *Secrets of Nature*, which was published in 1660:

Take the goose, pull off the feathers, make a fire about her, not too close for smoke to choke her, or burn her too soon, not too far off so she may escape. Put small cups of water with salt and honey . . . also dishes of apple sauce. Baste goose with butter. She will drink water to relieve thirst, eat apples to cleanse and empty her of dung. Keep her head and heart wet with a sponge. When she gets giddy from running and begins to stumble, she is roasted enough. Take her up, set her before the guests: she will cry as you cut off any part and will be almost eaten before she is dead . . . It is mighty pleasant to behold.

WILD MEAT AND THE BULLY BURGERS
–Lois-Ann Yamanaka–

Sheep stew smells up the whole house. Like the mornings when my father starts boiling tripe. But sheep stew stinks worse. Even if rubbed igoudhe doesn't listen. She sucks the stringy strands of goat meat until all the juice is gone. Right out of the drying box.

And smoke pig. Father cooks this well in lots of oil with pepper and shoyu to kill all the germs. He cannot kill the wild taste, but Uncle Ed and Gabriel Moniz sit with him in the garage, drink beers, and eat the smoke pig.

I hear Mr. Moniz tell my father about deer hunting on Moloka'i. That he shot a doe and when he got there, "she was crying, Hubert, I no joke you, brah, crying like one goddamn baby. Nah, like one goddamn wahine, so I had to put her outta her misery. Me, I no can stand for see things suffa, know what I mean, eh? So I tole my bradda Stanley, 'Eh, brah, I gotta put her outta her misery.' So I went up to her head right between the eyes, brah, and wen' shoot um and you know what, Hubert, all the fuckin' brains wen' shoot out and stuck on my glasses, and all blood and brains all over my face except where had my glasses, brah."

Everyone laughs. And drinks beer. And eats smoke pig.

The venison from Mr. Moniz tastes good, though. It's the only wild meat that I enjoy. My father grates ginger and puts in green onion with shoyu and mirin. And lots of roasted sesame seeds. He soaks it overnight, and the next day I help him weave the thin strips of meat onto bamboo sticks and we hibachi it.

Once my father cooked turtle meat and said it was steak. It tasted like fishy chicken. He never tells us when he changes the meat. I can only tell by a faint smell in the kitchen. Yesterday's fishy-chicken smell turned out to be frog legs. And rabbit also tasted like chicken, though he never tells us.

Today my father brings home a black-and-white calf. Father, Gabriel Moniz, and Uncle Ed put together their money to buy this calf for meat. The black-and-white calf, with round brown eyes and crying so loud that Calhoon and me see his fat black tongue. Cal and me pet him. He cries all day and all night for two days.

Calhoon names him Bully, and Father says, "Don't name him. Don't you dare call him that. We going eat um and how you going eat if you name him?" But every day now, Calhoon and me go to play with Bully. Cal with her goat jerky and me with my handful of milkweeds.

"Gimme it, gimme it," says Calhoon as she shoves the jerky into her mouth. She pets Bully first, who begins jumping up and down, up and down with his big black hoofs, and stomps Cal on her toes. She screams, grits her teeth, and punches the rusted car we have Bully tied to. Her toenail turns black in a few days.

Pretty soon, my father starts clearing the honohono grass on the other side of the lychee tree for Bully to eat. Lots of honohono that he cuts with his cane knife. And me, I give him the whole ti leaf. What I like most is the sound of Bully eating and the way a cow smiles. I also like his smell.

Father tells us that Gabriel Moniz will be taking Bully to the pasture behind his house since it's larger with lots of honohono and California grass. Some guava and waiwi on the side and lots of ti leaf. I tell Cal that they'll kill Bully soon. They want to make Bully nice and fat and want us to forget him. She says she'll never forget Bully and runs outside. I see her cut some of Bully's tail hair. She comes inside and wraps thread from the sewing chest around the hair. She puts it in her pocket.

It takes Mr. Moniz, Uncle Ed, Katy's husband Jeffrey, stupid Ernest, Larry, and my father to tie Bully's four legs together and lift him into Uncle Ed's Ford truck. Lots of swearing from everyone. And Bully crying, not like a baby, but like a grown man.

Cal hits the toes of her rubber boots in the dirt harder and harder. All the men shake hands and pat each other hard on the back. *We can't help him.* And they drive away.

My father never lets Calhoon and me see Bully again. Not even to visit or say hi with some milkweeds or ti leaves. "How you going eat the delicious steaks and veal cutlets I going cook for you? I told you no name him." Father keeps saying this over and over to us.

On Friday night, I hear this story. Father, Uncle Ed, and Gabriel Moniz are drinking beer in the garage. Gabriel tells the story.

"So this damn Hubert, he bring his .22 Mag my house and tell me, 'Here, Gabriel, you go shoot Bully.'

"Nah, nah, I stay telling him, you do um, gunfunnit, Hubert. I no like kill the cow.

"'Nah, go, Gabriel,' this bugga telling me, 'I no can kill Bully, I mean, the cow—was my house too long.'

"What you mean too long? I tell him.

"'Here, you shoot um. C'mon,' he tell. 'Thass half yo' cow.' Then this Hubert, he keep pushing the gun at me, so I take um. Then I ask this bugga how I going kill um and he tell me, 'I dunno, Gabriel. Just do um, gunfunnit. No ask me questions. I dunno. Go shoot um right between the eyes. Shit, just kill um. I no care.'

"So me, I walk toward the cow, get grass hanging out his mouth still yet, and next thing I turn around, Hubert, he stay running behind the house. Gunfunnit this bugga, whassamatta you, Hubert, I stay yelling. I betchu wen' cova your ears and close your eyes, eh, you bas-ted you. Me, I neva like shoot um but I wen' close my eyes and blass um right between the eyes."

Calhoon closes the window. She falls on our bed and pulls out the Bully hair from under her pillow. She sweeps it over her lips.

———

Father made hamburger for us tonight. With real hamburger buns and Orelda crinkle-cut fries baking in the oven. And a plate of tomatoes, lettuce, and Maui onions sliced real thin. A bowlful of pitless olives. And the mayo, relish, ketchup, and mustard all on the table.

Father stands over the frying pan with hot oil jumping up and onto the stovetop. He folds a paper towel and puts it on a plate. With the spatula he presses the burger patties down as if to make them well done, then places them on the plate. The oil spreads out brownish red on the paper towel.

There is a faint smell in the kitchen.

Calhoon fixes up her hamburger all the way Big Mac. Me, I don't fancy mine up too much. I put lots of olives on my plate. Father watches this and says cheerfully, "C'mon, Lovey, eat up." Father even says we can have dinner on the coffee table and watch TV.

The first bite tastes strange. Not sheep or goat. To me like hono-hono grass. To Cal like guavas and waiwi. She puts her hamburger down. "This is a Bully burger, isn't it, Daddy?" She swallows hard. My father looks at her for a long time, then puts his hamburger down too. I see Father's first bite—a large lump that slides slow and fat down his throat.

Tonight, nobody eats. Nobody cleans the kitchen. The faint smell in there stays. Father will boil some saimin later on and fry two eggs and Vienna sausage. He'll put it in big saimin bowls for Calhoon and me and give us strawberry Nehi. We don't have to drink our milk tonight. We eat later on without speaking in front of the TV. Father, Calhoon, and me.

AM I BLUE?
—Alice Walker—

For about three years my companion and I rented a small house in the country that stood on the edge of a large meadow that appeared to run from the end of our deck straight into the mountains. The mountains, however, were quite far away, and between us and them there was, in fact, a town. It was one of the many pleasant aspects of the house that you never really were aware of this.

It was a house of many windows, low, wide, nearly floor to ceiling in the living room, which faced the meadow, and it was from one of

these that I first saw our closest neighbor, a large white horse, crop-
ping grass, flipping its mane, and ambling about—not over the entire
meadow, which stretched well out of sight of the house, but over the
five or so fenced-in acres that were next to the twenty-odd that we had
rented. I soon learned that the horse, whose name was Blue, belonged
to a man who lived in another town, but was boarded by our neighbors
next door. Occasionally, one of the children, usually a stocky teen-ager,
but sometimes a much younger girl or boy, could be seen riding Blue.
They would appear in the meadow, climb up on his back, ride furiously for ten or fifteen minutes, then get off, slap Blue on the flanks,
and not be seen again for a month or more.

There were many apple trees in our yard, and one by the fence
that Blue could almost reach. We were soon in the habit of feeding
him apples, which he relished, especially because by the middle of
summer the meadow grasses—so green and succulent since January—
had dried out from lack of rain, and Blue stumbled about munching the dried stalks half-heartedly. Sometimes he would stand very
still just by the apple tree, and when one of us came out he would
whinny, snort loudly, or stamp the ground. This meant, of course: I
want an apple.

It was quite wonderful to pick a few apples, or collect those that
had fallen to the ground overnight, and patiently hold them, one by
one, up to his large, toothy mouth. I remained as thrilled as a child
by his flexible dark lips, huge, cubelike teeth that crunched the apples,
core and all, with such finality, and his high, broad-breasted *enormity*;
beside which, I felt small indeed. When I was a child, I used to ride
horses, and was especially friendly with one named Nan until the day I
was riding and my brother deliberately spooked her and I was thrown,
head first, against the trunk of a tree. When I came to, I was in bed
and my mother was bending worriedly over me; we silently agreed that
perhaps horseback riding was not the safest sport for me. Since then I
have walked, and prefer walking to horseback riding—but I had forgotten the depth of feeling one could see in horses' eyes.

I was therefore unprepared for the expression in Blue's. Blue was
lonely. Blue was horribly lonely and bored. I was not shocked that

this should be the case; five acres to tramp by yourself, endlessly, even in the most beautiful of meadows—and his was—cannot provide many interesting events, and once rainy season turned to dry that was about it. No, I was shocked that I had forgotten that human animals and nonhuman animals can communicate quite well; if we are brought up around animals as children we take this for granted. By the time we are adults we no longer remember. However, the animals have not changed. They are in fact *completed* creations (at least they seem to be, so much more than we) who are not likely *to* change; it is their nature to express themselves. What else are they going to express? And they do. And, generally speaking, they are ignored.

After giving Blue the apples, I would wander back to the house, aware that he was observing me. Were more apples not forthcoming then? Was that to be his sole entertainment for the day? My partner's small son had decided he wanted to learn how to piece a quilt; we worked in silence on our respective squares as I thought . . .

Well, about slavery: about white children, who were raised by black people, who knew their first all-accepting love from black women, and then, when they were twelve or so, were told they must "forget" the deep levels of communication between themselves and "mammy" that they knew. Later they would be able to relate quite calmly, "My old mammy was sold to another good family." "My old mammy was — —." Fill in the blank. Many more years later a white woman would say: "I can't understand these Negroes, these blacks. What do they want? They're so different from us."

And about the Indians, considered to be "like animals" by the "settlers" (a very benign euphemism for what they actually were), who did not understand their description as a compliment.

And about the thousands of American men who marry Japanese, Korean, Filipina, and other non-English-speaking women and of how happy they report they are, "*blissfully*," until their brides learn to speak English, at which point the marriages tend to fall apart. What then did the men see, when they looked into the eyes of the women they married, before they could speak English? Apparently only their own reflections.

I thought of society's impatience with the young. "Why are they playing the music so loud?" Perhaps the children have listened to much of the music of oppressed people their parents danced to before they were born, with its passionate but soft cries for acceptance and love, and they have wondered why their parents failed to hear.

I do not know how long Blue had inhabited his five beautiful, boring acres before we moved into our house; a year after we had arrived—and had also traveled to other valleys, other cities, other worlds—he was still there.

But then, in our second year at the house, something happened in Blue's life. One morning, looking out the window at the fog that lay like a ribbon over the meadow, I saw another horse, a brown one, at the other end of Blue's field. Blue appeared to be afraid of it, and for several days made no attempt to go near. We went away for a week. When we returned, Blue had decided to make friends and the two horses ambled or galloped along together, and Blue did not come nearly as often to the fence underneath the apple tree.

When he did, bringing his new friend with him, there was a different look in his eyes. A look of independence, of self-possession, of inalienable *horseness*. His friend eventually became pregnant. For months and months there was, it seemed to me, a mutual feeling between me and the horses of justice, of peace. I fed apples to them both. The look in Blue's eyes was one of unabashed "this is *itness*."

It did not, however, last forever. One day, after a visit to the city, I went out to give Blue some apples. He stood waiting, or so I thought, though not beneath the tree. When I shook the tree and jumped back from the shower of apples, he made no move. I carried some over to him. He managed to half-crunch one. The rest he let fall to the ground. I dreaded looking into his eyes—because I had of course noticed that Brown, his partner, had gone—but I did look. If I had been born into slavery, and my partner had been sold or killed, my eyes would have looked like that. The children next door explained that Blue's partner had been "put with him" (the same expression that old people used, I had noticed, when speaking of an ancestor during slavery who had been impregnated by her owner) so that they could mate and she conceive. Since that was accomplished, she had been taken back by her owner, who lived somewhere else.

Will she be back? I asked.

They didn't know.

Blue was like a crazed person. Blue *was*, to me, a crazed person. He galloped furiously, as if he were being ridden, around and around his five beautiful acres. He whinnied until he couldn't. He tore at the ground with his hooves. He butted himself against his single shade tree. He looked always and always toward the road down which his partner had gone. And then, occasionally, when he came up for apples, or I took apples to him, he looked at me. It was a look so piercing, so full of grief, a look so *human*, I almost laughed (I felt too sad to cry) to think there are people who do not know that animals suffer. People like me who have forgotten, and daily forget, all that animals try to tell us. "Everything you do to us will happen to you; we are your teachers, as you are ours. We are one lesson" is essentially it, I think. There are those who never once have even considered animals' rights: those who have been taught that animals actually want to be used and abused by us, as small children "love" to be frightened, or women "love" to be mutilated and raped. . . . They are the great-grandchildren of those who honestly thought, because someone taught them this: "Women can't think," and "niggers can't faint." But most disturbing of all, in Blue's large brown eyes was a new look, more painful than the look of despair: the look of disgust with human beings, with life; the look of hatred. And it was odd what the look of hatred did. It gave him, for the first time, the look of a beast. And what that meant was that he had put up a barrier within to protect himself from further violence; all the apples in the world wouldn't change that fact.

And so Blue remained, a beautiful part of our landscape, very peaceful to look at from the window, white against the grass. Once a friend came to visit and said, looking out on the soothing view: "And it *would* have to be a *white* horse; the very image of freedom." And I thought, yes, the animals are forced to become for us merely "images" of what they once so beautifully expressed. And we are used to drinking milk from containers showing "contented" cows, whose real lives we want to hear nothing about, eating eggs and drumsticks from "happy" hens, and munching hamburgers advertised by bulls of integrity who seem to command their fate.

As we talked of freedom and justice one day for all, we sat down to steaks. I am eating misery, I thought, as I took the first bite. And spit it out.

VII

EPILOGUE

||||||||||||||||||||||||||||

THE LIMITS OF TROOGHAFT
–Desmond Stewart–

The Troogs took one century to master the planet, then another three to restock it with men, its once dominant but now conquered species. Being hierarchical in temper, the Troogs segregated *homo insipiens* into four castes between which there was no traffic except that of bloodshed. The four castes derived from the Troog experience of human beings.

The planet's new masters had an intermittent sense of the absurd; Troog laughter could shake a forest. Young Troogs first captured some surviving children, then tamed them as "housemen," though to their new pets the draughty Troog structures seemed far from house-like. Pet-keeping spread. Whole zoos of children were reared on a bean diet. For housemen, Troogs preferred children with brown or yellow skins, finding them neater and cleaner than others; this preference soon settled into an arbitrary custom. Themselves hermaphrodite, the Troogs were fascinated by the spectacle of marital couplings. Once their pets reached adolescence, they were put in cages whose nesting boxes had glass walls. Troogs would gaze in by the hour. Captivity—and this was

189

an important discovery—did not inhibit the little creatures from breeding, nor, as was feared, did the sense of being watched turn the nursing females to deeds of violence. Cannibalism was rare. Breeders, by selecting partners, could soon produce strains with certain comical features, such as cone-shaped breasts or cushion-shaped rumps.

The practice of keeping pets was fought by senior Troogs; the conservative disapproved of innovations while the fastidious found it objectionable when bean-fed humans passed malodorous wind. After the innovation became too general to suppress, the Troog elders hedged the practice with laws. No pet should be kept alive if it fell sick, and since bronchitis was endemic, pets had short lives. The young Troogs recognised the wisdom behind this rule for they too disliked the sound of coughing. But in some cases they tried to save an invalid favourite from the lethal chamber, or would surrender it only after assurances that the sick were happier dead.

Adaptability had enabled the Troogs to survive their travels through time and space; it helped them to a catholic approach to the food provided by the planet, different as this was from their previous nourishment. Within two generations they had become compulsive carnivores. The realisation, derived from pet-keeping, that captive men could breed, led to the establishment of batteries of capons, the second and largest human caste. Capons were naturally preferred when young, since their bones were supple; at this time they fetched, as "eat-alls," the highest price for the lowest weight. Those kept alive after childhood were lodged in small cages maintained at a steady 22 degrees; the cage floors were composed of rolling bars through which the filth fell into a sluice. Capons were not permitted to see the sky or smell unfiltered air. Experience proved that a warm pink glow kept them docile and conduced to weight-gain. Females were in general preferred to males and the eradication of the tongue (sold as a separate delicacy) quietened the batteries.

The third category—the ferocious hound-men—were treated even by the Troogs with a certain caution; the barracks in which they were kennelled were built as far as possible from the batteries lest the black predators escape, break in and massacre hundreds. Bred for speed, obedience and ruthlessness, they were underfed. Unleashed they sped like greyhounds. Their unreliable tempers doomed the few surreptitious efforts to employ them as pets. One night they kept their quarters keening in rhythmic sound; next day, they slumped in yellow-eyed sulks, stirring only to lunge at each other or at their keepers' tentacles. None were kept alive after the age of thirty. Those injured in the chase were slaughtered on the spot and minced for the mess bowl.

Paradoxically, the swift hound-men depended for survival on the quarry they despised and hunted: the fourth human caste, the caste most hedged with laws.

The persistence, long into the first Troog period, of lone nomadic rebels, men and women who resisted from remote valleys and caves, had perplexed the planet's rulers. Then they made an advantage out of the setback. The wits and endurance of the defeated showed that the Troogs had suppressed a menace of some mettle. This was a compliment and Troogs, like the gods of fable, found praise enjoyable. They decided to preserve a caste of the uncorralled. This fourth caste, known as quarry-men or game, were protected within limits and seasons. It was forbidden, for example, to hunt pre-adolescents or pregnant females. All members of the caste enjoyed a respite during eight months of each year. Only at the five-yearly Nova Feast—the joyous commemoration of the greatest escape in Troog history—were all rules abandoned: then the demand for protein became overpowering.

Quarry-men excited more interest in their masters than the three other castes put together. On one level, gluttonous Troogs found their flesh more appetising than that of capons. On another, academically minded Troogs studied their behavior-patterns. Moralising Troogs extolled their courage against hopeless odds to a Troog generation inclined to be complacent about its power. The ruins which spiked the planet were testimony to the rudimentary but numerous civilisations which, over ten millennia, men had produced, from the time when they first cultivated grains and domesticated animals till their final achievement of an environment without vegetation (except under glass) and with only synthetic protein. Men, it was true, had never reached the stage where they could rely on the telepathy that served the Troogs. But this was no reason to despise them. Originally Troogs, too, had conversed through sound hitting a tympanum; they had retained a hieroglyphic system deep into their journey through time; indeed, their final abandonment of what men called writing (and the Troogs "incising") had been an indirect tribute to men: telepathic waves were harder to decipher than symbols. It moved antiquarian Troogs to see that some men still frequented the ruined repositories of written knowledge; and though men never repaired these ancient libraries, this did not argue that they had lost the constructional talents of forbears who had built skyscrapers and pyramids. It showed shrewd sense. To repair old buildings or build new ones would attract the hound-men. Safety lay in dispersal. Libraries were a place of danger for a quarry-man, known to the contemptuous hound-men as a "book-roach." The courageous passion for the little volumes in which great men had compressed their wisdom was admired by Troogs. In their death throes quarry-men often clutched these talismans.

––––

It was through a library that, in the fifth Troog century, the first attempt was made to communicate between the species, the conquerors and the conquered.

Curiosity was a characteristic shared by both species. Quarry-men still debated what the Troogs were and where they had come from. The first generation had known them as Extra-Terrestrials, when Terra, man's planet, was still the normative centre. Just as the natives of central America had welcomed the Spaniards as gods till the stake gave the notion of the godlike a satanic quality, millions of the superstitious had identified the Troogs with angels. But Doomsday was simply Troog's Day. The planet continued spinning, the sun gave out its heat and the empty oceans rolled against their shores. Living on an earth no longer theirs, quarry-men gazed at the glittering laser beams and reflected light which made the Troog-Halls and speculated about their tenants. A tradition declared that the first space vehicles had glowed with strange pictures. The Troogs, it was correctly deduced, had originally conversed by means analogous to language but had discarded speech in order to remain opaque, untappable. This encouraged some would-be rebels. They saw in precaution signs of caution and in caution proof of fallibility. A counter-attack might one day be possible, through science or magic. Some cynics pretended to find the Troogs a blessing. They quoted a long-dead writer who had believed it was better for a man to die on his feet when not too old. This was now the common human lot. Few quarry-men lived past thirty and the diseases of the past, such as cardiac failure and carcinoma, were all but unknown. But most men dreamed simply of a longer and easier existence.

––––

The first human to be approached by a Troog was a short, stocky youth who had survived his 'teens thanks to strong legs, a good wind and the discovery of a cellar underneath one of the world's largest libraries. Because of his enthusiasm for a poet of that name, this book-roach was known to his group as "Blake." He had also studied other idealists such as the Egyptian Akhenaten and the Russian Tolstoy. These inspired him to speculate along the most hazardous paths, in the direction, for example, of the precipice-question: might not the Troogs have something akin to human consciousness, or even conscience? If so, might man perhaps address his conqueror? Against the backspace of an insentient universe one consciousness should greet another. His friends, his woman, laughed at the notion. They had seen what the Troogs had done to their species. Some men were bred to have protuberant eyes or elongated necks; others were kept in kennels on insufficient rations, and then, at the time of the Nova Feast or in the year's open season, unleashed through urban ruins or surrounding savannah to howl after their quarry—those related by blood and experience to Blake and his fellows. "I shall never trust a Troog," said his woman's brother, "even if he gives me a gold safe-conduct."

One Troog, as much an exception among his species as Blake among his, read this hopeful brain. It was still the closed season and some four months before the quinquennial Nova Feast. Quarry-men still relaxed in safety; the hounds sang or sulked; the Troogs had yet to prepare the lights and sounds for their tumultuous celebrations. Each morning Blake climbed to the Library. It was a long, rubbish-encumbered place with aisles still occupied by books, once arranged according to subject, but now higgledy-piggledy in dust and dereliction, thrown down by earthquake or scattered in the hunt. Each aisle had its attendant bust—Plato, Shakespeare, Darwin, Marx—testifying to a regretted time when men, divided by nationality, class or colour, suffered only from their fellows.

In the corner watched by Shakespeare, Blake had his reading place. He had restored the shelves to some order; he had dusted the table. This May morning a Troog's fading odour made him tremble. A new object stood on his table: a large rusty typewriter of the most ancient model. In it was a sheet of paper.

Blake bent to read.

Are you ready to communicate question.

Blake typed the single word: *yes.*

He did not linger but retreated in mental confusion to the unintellectual huddle round babies and potatoes which was his cellar. He half feared that he had begun to go mad, or that some acquaintance was playing him a trick. But few of his group read and no man could duplicate the distinctive Troog smell.

———

The days that followed constituted a continual seance between "his" Troog and himself. Blake contributed little to the dialogue. His Troog seemed anxious for a listener but little interested in what that listener thought. Blake was an earphone, an admiring confessor. Try as he feebly did, he got no response when he tried to evoke his woman, his children.

"Trooghaft, you are right," wrote the unseen communicator, attested each time by his no longer frightening scent, "was noble once." Blake had made no such suggestion. "The quality of being a Troog was unfrictional as space and as tolerant as time. It has become—almost human."

Then next morning: "To copy the habits of lower creatures is to sink below them. What is natural to carnivores is unnatural to us. We never ate flesh before the Nova; nor on our journey. We adopted the practice from reading the minds of lower creatures, then copying them. Our corruption shows in new diseases; earlier than in the past, older Troogs decompose. It shows in our characters. We quarrel like our quarry. Our forms are not apt for ingesting so much protein. Protein is what alcohol was to humans. It maddens; it corrupts. Protein, not earth's climate, is paling our. . . ."

Here there was a day's gap before the typewriter produced, next morning, the word *complexion*. And after it, *metaphor*. Blake had learnt that the old Troog hieroglyphs were followed by determinants, symbols showing, for example, whether the concept *rule* meant tyranny or order. Complexion could only be used metaphorically of faceless and largely gaseous creatures.

To one direct question Blake obtained a direct answer: "How," he had typed, "did you first turn against the idea of eating us?"

"My first insight flashed at our last Nova Feast. Like everyone, I had been programmed to revel. Stench of flesh filled every Troog-Hall. Amid the spurt of music, the ancient greetings with which we flare still, the coruscations, I passed a meat-shop where lights pirouetted. I looked. I saw. Hanging from iron hooks—each pierced a foot-palm—were twenty she-capons, what you call women. Each neck was surrounded by a ruffle to hide the knife-cut; a tomato shut each anus. I suddenly shuddered. Nearby, on a slab of marble, smiled a row of jellied heads. Someone had dressed their sugar-hair in the manner of your Roman empresses: 'Flavian Heads.' A mass of piled up, tong-curled hair in front, behind a bun encoiled by a marzipan fillet. I lowered myself and saw as though for the first time great blocks of neutral-looking matter: 'Paté of Burst Liver.' The owner of the shop was glad to explain. They hold the woman down, then stuff nutriment through a V-shaped funnel. The merchant was pleased by my close attention. He displayed his Sucking Capons and Little Loves, as they call the reproductive organs which half of you split creatures wear outside your bodies."

"Was this," I asked in sudden repugnance, "Trooghaft?"

Encouraged by evidence of soul, Blake brought to the Troog's notice, from the miscellaneous volumes on the shelves, quotations from his favourite writers and narrative accounts of such actions as the death of Socrates, the crucifixion of Jesus and the murder of Che

Guevara. Now in the mornings he found books and encyclopaedias open on his table as well as typed pages. Sometimes Blake fancied that there was more than one Troog smell; so perhaps his Troog was converting others.

———

Each evening Blake told Janine, his partner, of his exploits. She was at first sceptical, then half-persuaded. This year she was not pregnant and therefore could be hunted. For love of her children, the dangers of the Nova season weighed on her spirits. Only her daughter was Blake's; her son had been sired by Blake's friend, a fast-runner who had sprained his ankle and fallen easy victim to the hounds two years before. As the Nova Feast approached, the majority of the quarry-men in the city began to leave for the mountains. Not that valleys and caves were secure; but the mountains were vast and the valleys remote one from another. The hound-men preferred to hunt in the cities; concentrations of people made their game easier.

Blake refused to join them. Out of loyalty Janine stayed with him.

"I shall build," the Troog had written, "a bridge between Trooghaft and Humanity. The universe calls me to revive true Trooghaft. My Troog-Hall shall become a sanctuary, not a shed of butchers."

Blake asked: "Are you powerful? Can you make other Troogs follow your example?"

The Troog answered: "I can at least do as your Akhenaten did."

Blake flushed at the mention of his hero. Then added: "But Akhenaten's experiment lasted briefly. Men relapsed. May not Troogs do likewise?" He longed for reassurance that his Troog was more than a moral dilettante.

Instead of an answer came a statement:

"We can never be equals with *homo insipiens*. But we can accept our two species as unequal productions of one universe. Men are small, but that does not mean they cannot suffer. Not one tongueless woman moves, upside-down, towards the throat-knife, without trembling. I have seen this. I felt pity, *metaphor*. Our young Troogs argue that fear gives flesh a quivering tenderness. I reject such arguments. Why should a complex, if lowly, life—birth, youth, growth to awareness—be sacrificed for one mealtime's pleasure?"

———

Although Blake recognised that his Troog was soliloquising, the arguments pleased him. Convinced of their sincerity, Blake decided to trust his Troog and remain where he was, not hide or run as on previous occasions. There was a sewer leading from his refuge whose remembered stench was horrible. He would stay in the cellar. On the first day of the Nova Feast he climbed as usual to his corner of the library. But today there was no paper in the typewriter. Instead, books and encyclopaedias had been pulled from the shelves and left open; they had nothing to do with poetry or the philosophers and the stench was not that of his Troog. Sudden unease seized him. Janine was alone with the children, her brother having left to join the others in the mountains. He returned to his cellar and, as his fear already predicted, found the children alone, wailing in one corner. The elder, the boy, told the doleful tale. Two hound-men had broken in and their mother had fled down the disused sewer.

Blake searched the sewer. It was empty. His one hope, as he too hid there, lay in his Troog's intervention. But neither the next day nor the day after, when he stole to the library, watching every shadow lest it turn to a hound-man, was there any message. This silence was atoned for on the third morning.

"If we still had a written language, I should publish a volume of confessions." The message was remote, almost unrelated to Blake's anguish.

He read, "A few fat-fumes blow away a resolution. It was thus, the evening of the Nova Feast's beginning. Three Troog friends, *metaphor*, came to my Hall where no flesh was burning, where instead I was pondering these puny creatures to whom we cause such suffering. 'You cannot exile yourself from your group; Trooghaft is what Troogs do together.' I resisted such blandishments. The lights and sounds of the Nova were enough. I felt no craving for protein. Their laughter at this caused the laser beams to buckle and the lights to quiver. There entered four black hound-men dragging a quarry-female, filthy from the chase, her hands bound behind her. I was impassive. Housemen staggered under a great cauldron; they fetched logs. They placed the cauldron on a tripod and filled it with water; the logs were under it."

Blake shook as he read. This was the moment for his Troog to incarnate pity and save his woman.

"They now unbound and stripped the female, then set her in the water. It was cold and covered her skin with pimples.

"Again laughter, again the trembling lights and the buckling lasers.

"We, too, have been reading, brother. We have studied one of their ways of cooking. *Place the lobster*—their name for a long extinct sea-thing—*in warm water. Bring the water gently to the boil. The lobster will be lulled to sleep, not knowing it is to be killed. Most experts account this the humane way of treating lobster.*

"The logs under the cauldron gave a pleasant aroma as they started to splutter. The female was not lulled. She tried to clamber out: perhaps a reflex action. The hound-men placed an iron mesh over the cauldron."

Blake saw what he could not bear to see, heard the unhearable. The Troog's confession was humble.

"The scent was so persuasive. 'Try this piece,' they flashed, 'it is so tender. It will harden your scruples.' I hesitated. Outside came the noise of young Troogs whirling in the joy of satiety. A Nova Feast comes only once in five years. I dipped my hand, *metaphor*"—(even now the Troog pedantry was present)—"in the cauldron. If one must eat protein, it is better to do so in a civilised fashion. And as for the humanity, *metaphor*, of eating protein—I should write Trooghaft—if we ate no capons, who would bother to feed them? If we hunted no quarry, who would make the game-laws or keep the hound-men? At least now they live, as we do, for a season. And while they live, they are healthy. I must stop. My stomach, *metaphor*, sits heavy as a mountain."

As Blake turned in horror from the ancient typewriter, up from his line of retreat, keening their happiest music, their white teeth flashing, loped three lithe and ruthless hound-men. All around was the squid-like odour of their master.

THE WRITERS
||||||||||||||||||||||||||||

CLEVELAND AMORY (1917–1998) was born in Nahant, Massachusetts. While attending Harvard University he was the editor of the
Harvard Crimson. Upon graduating, he became the youngest editor in
the history of the *Saturday Evening Post.* He served during World War
II in military intelligence; after the war he wrote three classic social
critiques: *The Proper Bostonians* (1947), *The Last Resorts* (1952), and *Who
Killed Society?* (1960). He would later become a social commentator for
the Today Show and chief critic at TV Guide.

Many of his books were influenced by Amory's fondness for animals, particularly his cat named Polar Bear. In addition to cofounding
the Humane Society of the United States, and founding both the Fund
for Animals and the Black Beauty Ranch, he wrote three best-selling
books about Polar Bear, now available as *The Compleat Cat.*

Amory died in 1998, and true to his passionate care for Polar Bear,
he was buried alongside his feline companion at Black Beauty Ranch.

M. PABST BATTIN (1940–) is distinguished professor of philosophy
and adjunct professor of internal medicine, division of medical ethics,
at the University of Utah. She is a graduate of Bryn Mawr College, and

holds an M.F.A. in fiction-writing and a Ph.D. in philosophy from the University of California at Irvine. The author of prize-winning short stories, she has authored, coauthored, edited, or coedited some twenty books, among them *Ethical Issues in Suicide* (1982); a collection on age-rationing of medical care, *Should Medical Care be Rationed by Age?* (1987); a volume of case-puzzles in aesthetics, *Puzzles About Art* (1989); a study of ethical issues in organized religion, *Ethics in the Sanctuary* (1990); and a collection of her essays on end-of-life issues, *The Least Worst Death* (1994).

In 1997 she received the University of Utah's Distinguished Research Award, followed in 2000, by the Rosenblatt Prize, the University of Utah's mostprestigious award.

LEIGH BUCHANAN BIENEN is a senior lecturer at Northwestern University School of Law and a criminal defense attorney whose areas of expertise include capital punishment, sex crimes, and rape reform legislation. She has taught law at the Woodrow Wilson School of Princeton University, at the University of Pennsylvania School of Law and the University of California (Berkeley) School of Law.

A graduate of Cornell University, the University of Iowa Writers' Workshop, and the Rutgers–Newark School of Law, she has worked as a journalist and an editor and published fiction and essays in *TriQuarterly*, *The Ontario Review*, *Transition*, and *The O.Henry Prize Stories*. "My Life as a West African Gray Parrot" was first published in the *Ontario Review* and later became part of Bienen's collection of short stories, *The Left-Handed Marriage* (2001). A short play of hers was included in *Winters' Tales 1994*, McCarter Theatre's New Play Festival.

A. E. COPPARD (1878–1957) was born in the town of Folkestone on the southern coast of England. Coppard came from humble beginnings and had little formal education. However, after moving to Oxford he became an influential member of the New Elizabethans, a literary group whose meetings were sometimes attended by W. B. Yeats. To his disappointment, the first story he submitted for publication was rejected, not because of its merits but because of its length—12,000 words. Today, to commemorate his challenge to received opinion, the Coppard Prize is awarded annually to the winner of the International Long Story Contest.

Coppard was a prolific writer, publishing collections of short stories, including *Adam & Eve & Pinch Me* (1921) and *Lucy in Her Pink Coat* (1954); poems, *Hips and Haws* (1922) and *Cherry Ripe Poems* (1935); and an autobiography, *It's Me, O Lord!* (1957).

STEPHEN (TOWNLEY) CRANE (1871–1900), an American novelist and short-story writer, is now acclaimed as a pioneer of the Realist tradition. Crane left school in 1891 to take a job as a reporter. His first novel, *Maggie: A Girl of the Streets* (1893), was self-published and attracted few readers. However, his second novel, *The Red Badge of Courage* (1895), about the Civil War and written without any personal battle experience, won international acclaim. In addition to his fiction, Crane published two volumes of poetry, *The Black Riders and Other Lines* (1895) and *War Is Kind* (1899). After that book's publication, he would contract tuberculosis and die in Germany at the age of 28.

At the time of his death, Crane was a well-known and much-discussed author; then, for a few decades, he was all but forgotten. In 1990 the Stephen Crane Society, founded by Crane scholar Paul Sorrentino, is devoted to research and discussion of the author's life and work.

CHARLES EASTMAN (1858–1939), a Native American writer, physician, and reformer, was named Ohiyesa in Dakota. His mother died at his birth. Except for a temporary separation during the Dakota Uprising, he lived with his father, who emphasized the importance of education, sending his son to Dartmouth College and Boston University Medical School.

In addition to starting a private medical practice, Eastman became actively involved in establishing Indian groups of the YMCA and helped found the Boy Scouts of America. He served in national politics as a lobbyist for the Dakota people, and was appointed by President Theodore Roosevelt to revise the allotment method of dividing tribal lands. In 1902 Eastman published an autobiography, *Indian Boyhood*; eleven more books would follow. "The Gray Chieftain" is one of the stories in Eastman's collection *Red Hunters and the Animal People* (1904).

ORIANA FALLACI (1929–2006) was born in Florence, Italy. She earned her fame as a pioneering journalist, who interviewed powerful and influential public figures, including the Dalai Lama, Henry Kissinger, Yassir Arafat, and Ayatollah Khomeini. Despite her youth, she joined the resistance movement and, along with her father, opposed the politics and policies of Fascist leader Benito Mussolini. In addition to her influential interviews, she worked as a war correspondent in Vietnam during the Indo-Pakistani War, in the Middle East, and in South America.

In the 1970s, American surgeon Dr. Robert White conducted a series of experiments that involved transplanting the head of one monkey to the body of another monkey. Animal rights advocates found White's work grotesque and inhumane. Wanting to find the truth, Fallaci interviewed White about his research; part of her interview is reproduced here.

MARY FRANCES KENNEDY (M. F. K.) FISHER (1908–1992) is known as one of the foundational writers in the culinary world. After growing up in small communities with her family, she attended the University of California, where she met her first husband, and spent three years at the University of Dijon, where she fell in love with food. Her years in Dijon are recounted in her later book *Long Ago in France* (1991).

Fisher wrote and published over thirty culinary works and memoirs, including *Serve It Forth* (1937), *Consider the Oyster* (1941), *The Gastronomical Me* (1943), *Here Let Us Feast, A Book of Banquets* (1946), and *An Alphabet for Gourmets* (1949). "How to Make a Pigeon Cry" was originally published in *How to Cook a Wolf* (1942).

ERNEST HEMINGWAY (1899–1961) is perhaps best known for his novels written against the backdrop of international war; the contribution to this collection, however, highlights his interest in big game hunting. Born to a physician father and puritanical mother, Hemingway was raised in the countryside and introduced to game sports by his father.

Much of Hemingway's popular writing was influenced by his time spent in Europe during the world wars. He eventually became part of a group of expatriate authors, including Gertrude Stein, who significantly influenced his writing. After traveling throughout Europe, he returned to North America and published his first major novel, *The Sun Also Rises* (1924). He wrote simply, without flourish, often—especially in his short stories, including the collection *Men without Women* (1927)—with restrained understatement. He received the Nobel Prize for Literature in 1954.

WILLIAM KOTZWINKLE (1938–) was born in Scranton, Pennsylvania. He has published more than thirty novels including *The Midnight Examiner* (1989), *The Game of Thirty* (1994), *The Million-Dollar Bear* (1995), *The Bear Went Over the Mountain* (1996), and *The Amphora Project* (2005), in addition to several collections of short stories. He is especially well known for his popular serial children's story, *Walter the Farting Dog* (2001). He novelized *E.T. The Extra-Terrestrial* (1982) in collaboration with Melissa Mathison, the original screenplay writer.

Doctor Rat (1976) is one of his best-known books and is probably the most biting satire of animal experimentation ever published. It won the World Fantasy Award for Best Novel, and also the National Magazine Award for fiction.

ANDREW LINZEY (1952–) is widely regarded as the preeminent theologian on the status of animals, and his name is virtually synonymous with "animal theology," a discipline that he can claim to have single-handedly invented. Born in Oxford, England, he has been a member of the faculty of theology in the University of Oxford for seventeen years and is director of the Oxford Centre for Animal Ethics (http://www.oxfordanimalethics.com/).

Linzey's work has attracted fierce controversy from religious communities that have found his animal-inclusive theology threatening to traditional theological insights. But gradually his work has gained a wide hearing, as churches have become sensitized to ecological concerns. In 2001 he was awarded a D.D. (Doctor of Divinity) degree by the archbishop of Canterbury in recognition of his "unique and massive pioneering work at a scholarly level in the area of the theology of creation with particular reference to the rights and welfare of God's sentient creatures." This was the first time the award, the highest that the archbishop can bestow on a theologian, was given for theological work on animals.

Author or editor of more than twenty books in moral theology, Linzey will be chiefly remembered for his pioneering works on animals: *Animal Rights: A Christian Assessment* (1976), *Christianity and the Rights of Animals* (1987), *Animal Theology* (1994), *Animal Rites* (1999), and *Why Animal Suffering Matters* (2009). His work has been translated into Italian, French, Spanish, German, Chinese, Taiwanese, Croatian, and Japanese. His many other honorary positions include honorary professor at the University of Winchester, special professor at Saint Xavier University, Chicago, and the first professor of Animal Ethics at the Graduate Theological Foundation, Indiana.

BOBBIE ANN MASON (1940–) is an American novelist, short story writer, essayist, and literary critic. She was born and raised on her family's dairy farm in rural Kentucky. From a young age, she had a passion for literature, attracted to two series in particular: the Bobbsey Twins and the Nancy Drew mysteries. Her love for these books would later motivate her to write scholarly feminist works about young women's literature.

After graduating from the University of Kentucky with a major in journalism, Mason began writing about pop culture stars while earning her Ph.D. in literature at the University of Connecticut. She published her first story, "Offerings," in *The New Yorker* in 1980. Since then she has published four collections of short stories, including *Shiloh and Other Stories* (1982) and *Nancy Culpepper* (2006); and four novels, *An Atomic Romance* (2005) the most recent.

ROBERT MCALMON (1896-1956), expatriate U.S. author, whose books, published mainly in France, made him a spokesperson for the postwar nihilistic pessimists of the "lost generation"—was born in Kansas and raised in South Dakota. He initially attended the University of Minnesota, but left after he enlisted in World War I. When the war ended, he enrolled in the University of Southern California but moved to New York before graduating. Once in New York, he joined forces with William Carlos Williams to cofound *Contact*, a literary magazine. In 1921 he married the British author Winifred Bryher and the two moved to Paris, where McAlmon added his voice to the chorus of American expatriates expressing disillusionment with American society and values.

McAlmon was a prolific writer, publishing several novels, including *Explorations* (1921), *The Portrait of a Generation* (1926), *North America, Continent of Conjecture* (1929), and *Not Alone Lost* (1937), in addition to volumes of poetry and an autobiography.

GEORGE ORWELL (1903-1950) was born Eric Arthur Blair in India. However, after his first birthday, he moved with his mother to England, and grew up in Henley-on-Thames. Orwell attended St. Cyprian's school in Sussex, where he began what was to be a prolific and influential writing career with his poem "Awake! Young Men of England." Orwell left St. Cyprian's to attend Eton College on a scholarship; while there, he was taught French by Aldous Huxley.

He joined the Indian Civil Service in Burma and grew fond of the Burmese and distrustful and critical of the British imperial presence. This transformation motivated him to become a writer, and many of his works are heavily saturated with social criticism, including his most popular books, *Animal Farm* (1945) and *1984* (1949). Orwell's "Shooting an Elephant" is one of the most widely anthologized stories in British literature.

TOM REGAN (1938-) has been described by *Utne Reader* as "the philosophical leader of the animal rights movement." Among his major works are *The Case for Animal Rights* (1983), *The Struggle for Animal Rights*

(1988), *Defending Animal Rights* (2001), *Animal Rights, Human Wrongs: An Introduction to Moral Philosophy* (2003), and *Empty Cages: Facing the Challenge of Animal Rights* (2004).

During his more than thirty years of teaching at North Carolina State University, Regan received numerous awards for excellence in undergraduate and graduate teaching, was named University Alumni Distinguished Professor, published hundreds of professional papers and more than twenty books, won major international awards for film writing and direction, and presented hundreds of lectures throughout the United States and abroad. Upon his retirement in 2001, he received the Alexander Quarles Holladay Medal, the highest honor North Carolina State University can bestow on one of its faculty.

JOÃO UBALDO RIBEIRO (1941–) is a Brazilian author born on the island of Itaparica, in the state of Bahia. He has worked as a law professor, scriptwriter, and journalist, but it is largely owing to his fiction—short stories, novels, children's literature—that he is among the most celebrated figures in his country. Throughout his youth he developed a passion for literature, reading works by Shakespeare, Joyce, Faulkner, Swift, Cervantes, and Homer, as well as Brazilian authors.

Four of his novels, including *An Invincible Memory* (1989) and *The Lizard's Smile* (1994), have been translated into English. Since 1994 Ribeiro has been a member of the Brazilian Academy of Letters, whose forty members are known as "the immortals." In 2008 he received the Camões Prize, the highest honor for a Portuguese-language writer.

WILLIAM SAROYAN (1908–1981) was an Armenian-American novelist, playwright, and short-story writer, born in Fresno, California. His father died before Saroyan turned three, and reflections on death and dying inform many of his works. He wrote more than thirty books, including *Chance Meetings* (1978), *Obituaries* (1979), *Births* (1983), *My Name Is Saroyan* (1983), *An Armenian Trilogy* (1986), *Madness in the Family* (1988), and *Boys and Girls Together* (1995), as well as more than twenty plays.

Saroyan served in the U.S. Army during World War II and narrowly avoided court martial when some influential people interpreted his novel *The Adventures of Wesley Jackson* (1946) as advocating pacifism. He refused a Pulitzer Prize for his play *The Time of Your Life* (1939). In 1944 he won an Academy Award for "The Human Comedy" (Best Writing, Original Story).

ISAAC BASHEVIS SINGER (1902–1991) won the 1978 Nobel Prize for Literature. He was born in Leoncin, Poland. At age five, his family moved to Warsaw, where his father was a rabbi. It was there that he began his writing career, working as a journalist. He moved to America in 1935 to escape the growing Nazi threat in Germany. He initially took a job as a journalist and columnist at a Yiddish newspaper in New York.

He would publish eighteen novels and fourteen children's books but is best remembered for his short stories, including "The Slaughterer," which appeared in *The Collected Stories of Issac Bashevis Singer* (1982). In this story, Singer describes the agony that a man experiences performing his job as a ritual slaughterer while struggling to maintain his sense of compassion for animals. Singer famously claimed that he became a vegetarian not for his health, but for the health of animals.

DESMOND (STIRLING) STEWART (1924–1981) described himself as "educated in England, re-educated in Iraq." A distinguished Arabist, he was a prolific writer, poet, and historian. He wrote extensively on the Middle East—where he lived most of his life dating from 1948—and was the author of more than twenty books, including the novel *The Vampire of Mons* (1976); two biographies, *Theodor Herzl: Artist and Politician* (1974) and *T. E. Lawrence* (1977); and a series of books on Arabian history and culture, including *The Arab World* (1962), *The Alhambra: A History of Islamic Spain* (1974), and *Early Islam* (1978).

His "Limits of Trooghaft," originally published in *Encounter* in February 1972, has been widely praised as a key imaginative work in defense of animals.

IVAN TURGENEV (1818–1883) was born to a wealthy, though troubled, Russian family. His father died when Turgenev turned 16, leaving him and his brother to be raised by his heiress mother. Turgenev expressed an interest in literature from a young age. His early writing showed enough promise to receive a favorable judgment from Vissarion Belinsky, the foremost Russian literary critic of the time.

Turgenev completed his first substantial work, *Sketches from a Hunter's Album*, in 1852. These stories are based on his observations of nature and peasant life made on hunting trips in the forests surrounding his mother's estate. The book helped change public opinion in favor of abolishing serfdom in Russia.

Turgenev went on to write many short stories, plays, and novels, including the novel for which he is most famous, *Fathers and Sons* (1862).

LAURENS VAN DER POST (1906–1996) was born in South Africa to parents of Dutch and German descent. Throughout his life, he believed in his shared humanity with black fellow countrymen and called for a nonsegregated South Africa.

In 1931 he traveled to England and befriended members of the Bloomsbury Group, including J. M. Keynes, E. M. Forster, and Leonard and Virginia Woolf, who published his first novel, *In Province* (1934), portraying the injustice of a divided South Africa. He would later rise to social prominence, becoming a personal friend of Prince Charles and the godfather of Prince William.

His "Hunting at Sea," from *On Being Someone Other* (1982), as with his earlier *The Heart of the Hunter* (1961), conveys an ambivalent attitude toward hunting.

ALICE WALKER (1944–) is an American writer of poetry, fiction, and essays as well as a progressive activist, best known for her Pulitzer Prize-winning novel, *The Color Purple* (1982), which also earned the National Book Award. Although she was one of eight children born to black parents who suffered the effects of Jim Crow laws, her mother insisted on the importance of her children's education, her daughter, Alice, starting public school a full year before the usual age.

Walker in time attended Spelman College in Atlanta and Sarah Lawrence College in New York. While at Spelman, she met Dr. Martin Luther King Jr., who inspired her to join the civil rights movement. She became a lifelong activist advocating for racial and gender equality, an end to violence, and in support of animal rights.

Walker completed a collection of poetry, *Once* (1968), while still attending Sarah Lawrence College, and published her first novel, *The Third Life of Grange Copeland* (1970), two years later.

Among her many awards: the O. Henry Award for her short story "Kindred Spirits" (1986) and the Rosenthal Award from the National Institute of Arts & Letters (1973).

LOIS-ANN YAMANAKA (1961–) is a Japanese-American poet and novelist from Hawaii. Like her parents, she pursued a career in education, teaching English and language arts. Written in the Pidgin dialect of Hawaii, her first book, *Saturday Night at the Pahala Theatre* (1993), was published to critical acclaim, receiving both the Pushcart Prize for poetry and an award for fiction given by the Association for Asian American Studies. This was followed by *Wild Meat and the Bully Burgers* (1996), *Blu's Hanging* (1997), *Heads by Harry* (1998), and *The Heart's Language* (2005), among other works. She has been named one of the "25 Most Influential Asians in America" by *A Magazine*. Speaking of her writing, Yamanaka has said, "My work involves bringing to the page the utter complexity, ferocious beauty and sometimes absurdity of our ethnic relationships here in the islands."

ACKNOWLEDGMENTS

IIIIIIIIIIIIIIIIIIIIIIIIIII

The following indicates the original source (where known) of the selections. The editors and publishers gratefully acknowledge copyright permission where indicated.

1. Stephen Crane, "The Snake," was first published in *The Pocket Magazine*, vol. 2, August 1896. It appeared again in 1956 in the *Bulletin of the New York Public Library* (vol. 60), and was included in Thomas A. Gullason (ed.), *The Complete Short Stories and Sketches of Stephen Crane* (New York: Doubleday, 1963).

2. William Saroyan, "Snake," from *The Daring Young Man on the Flying Trapeze, and Other Stories*, © copyright 1934 William Saroyan, reprinted with permission of the Trustees of Leland Stanford Junior University.

3. A. E. Coppard, "Arabesque—The Mouse" (1921). © Copyright the Estate of A. E. Coppard, and reprinted with permission of David Higham Associates Ltd.

4. George Orwell, "Shooting an Elephant" from *Shooting An Elephant and Other Essays* by George Orwell (copyright © George Orwell, 1936) by permission of Bill Hamilton as the Literary Executor of the Estate of the Late Sonia Brownell Orwell and Secker and Warburg Ltd, and © copyright 1950 and renewed 1978 by Sonia Pitt-Rivers, reprinted by permission of Houghton Mifflin Harcourt Company.

5. Robert McAlmon, "The Jack Rabbit Drive," was originally published in *Transition,* February 1929, and included in *McAlmon and the Lost Generation*, edited by Robert E. Knoll, University of Nebraska Press.

6. Cleveland Amory, "Pilling the Cat" from *The Cat Who Came for Christmas*. Copyright © 1987 by Cleveland Amory (Text); 1987 copyright © by Edith Allard (Illustrations). Used by permission of Little, Brown, and Company and by permission of Marian Probst, Trustee of The Cleveland Amory Trust.

7. Bobbie Ann Mason, "Lying Doggo" from *Shiloh and Other Stories*, Harper & Row, 1982; and © copyright, Bobbie Ann Mason, 1982, and reprinted by permission of International Creative Management, Inc.

8. Leigh Buchanan Bienen, "My Life as a West African Gray Parrot," first published in *The Ontario Review* (1981). © Copyright Leigh Buchanan Bienen, 1981, reprinted with permission of the author.

9. Ernest Hemingway, "The Pleasures of Hunting," extract from *Green Hills of Africa*, Charles Scribner's Sons, Ltd, 1935. Reprinted with the permission of Scribner, a Division of Simon & Schuster, Inc., from *Green Hills of Africa* by Ernest Hemingway. Copyright © 1935 by Charles Scribners Sons. Copyright renewed © 1963 by Mary Hemingway. And printed by permission of the Random House Group.

10. Ivan Turgenev, "Sketches from a Hunter's Album," extract from *Sketches from a Hunter's Album* by Ivan Turgenev,

translated by Richard Freeborn (Penguin Classics, 1967) © copyright Richard Freeborn, 1967.

11. Laurens van der Post, "Hunting at Sea," extract from *Yet Being Someone Other*, published by Chatto & Windus. Reprinted by permission of The Random House Group Ltd.

12. Charles Eastman, "The Gray Chieftain" from *Red Hunters and the Animal People* by Charles A. Eastman, originally published by Harper & Brothers, 1904.

13. Oriana Fallaci, "The Dead Body and the Living Brain," extract from an article of the same title originally published in *Look*, 26, 1967, pp. 99-105. © Copyright 2009 The Estate of Oriana Fallaci, and reproduced with their permission.

14. William Kotzwinkle, "Doctor Rat," extract from *Doctor Rat* by William Kotzwinkle. Copyright © 1977 by William Kotzwinkle, and reproduced with the author's permission.

15. Margaret Pabst Battin, "Terminal Procedure," from *The Best American Short Stories*, edited by Martha Foley, Houghton Mifflin, 1976. © Copyright Margaret Pabst Battin 1976, and reproduced by permission of the author.

16. Isaac Bashevis Singer, "The Slaughterer," from *The Collected Stories of Isaac Bashevis Singer*, published by Macmillan (Farrar, Straus & Giroux Paperbacks), August 1983, and reprinted with permission of Farrar, Straus & Giroux.

17. João Ubaldo Ribeiro, "It Was a Different Day when They Killed the Pig," from *A Hammock Beneath the Mangoes*, edited by Thomas Colchie, Dutton 1991. © Copyright, João Ubaldo Ribeiro 1991, reproduced with kind permission of the author and the Colchiel Literary Agency.

18. M. F. K. Fisher, "How to Make a Pigeon Cry," from *How To Cook A Wolf*. Included in *The Art of Eating*. Published by Wiley Publishing Inc. © Copyright 1942, 1954, 2004 by M. F. K. Fisher. Reprinted with permission of Lescher &

"Two of the world's most important scholars of the human-animal relationship have crafted an original and compelling anthology. It will be of great value to students, teachers, and anyone else who wants to think more clearly, feel more deeply, and—hopefully—act with more moral integrity."

–*Roger S. Gottlieb, Professor of Philosophy at Worcester Polytechnic Institute and author of* Engaging Voices: Tales of Morality and Meaning in an Age of Global Warming

"Carefully selected pieces of literature from a wide range of authors offer both an introduction to and a grounding for further work in the area of animals and literature. This is a beautifully constructed, timely collection."

–*Laura Hobgood-Oster, Professor of Religion and Environmental Studies at Southwestern University and author of* The Friends We Keep: Unleashing Christianity's Compassion for Animals